HUMBUG

Praise for Amanda Radley

Under Her Influence

"Light, sweet, and remarkably chaste, this sapphic love story will make as enjoyable a vacation pick as it is an armchair getaway."—*Publishers Weekly*

"My heart is just…filled with love and warmth! Finally, I have found an author who does not rely on sex to make a book interesting!! I'm probably going to go on an Amanda Radley read-a-thon."—*Periwinkle Pens*

"*Under Her Influence* by Amanda Radley is a sweet love story and leaves the reader feeling happy and contented. And that's exactly what I want from a romance these days. Ms Radley keeps angst to a minimum and lets her readers enjoy the blossoming of love between her characters."—*Kitty Kat's Book Review Blog*

Detour to Love

"If you're on the lookout for well-written sapphic romance with stellar characters, wonderful pairings, and outstanding plots, I wholeheartedly recommend any of Amanda's books!!"—*EloiseReads*

Flight SQA016

"I'm so glad I picked this book up because I think I've found my new favourite series!…The love brewing between these two is beautifully written and I was onboard from the beginning. I had some laugh out loud moments because this is British rom-com at its best. The secondary characters really added to the novel and the rollercoaster ride that is this book. The writing is tight and pace is perfect."—*Les Rêveur*

Lost at Sea

"A.E. Radley knows how to write great characters. And it's not just the main characters she puts so much effort into. I loved them, but I was astounded at how well drawn the minor characters were…The writing was beautiful—descriptive, real and very funny at times." —*Lesbian Review*

"This book was pure excitement. The character development was probably my favourite overall aspect of the book…A.E. Radley really knows how to keep her readers engaged, and she writes age-gap romance books beautifully. In fact, she probably writes some of my favourite age-gap romance tropes to date. A very intriguing book that I really enjoyed. More Captain West, please!"—*Les Rêveur*

"Absolutely amazing, easy to read, perfect romance with mystery and drama story. There were so many wonderful elements that gave twists and turns to this adventure on the sea. I absolutely loved this story and can't rave about it enough."—*LesbiReviewed*

Going Up

"I can always count on this superb author when it comes to creating unforgettable and endearing characters that I can totally relate to and fall in love with. A.E. Radley has given me beautiful descriptions of Parbrook and the quirky individuals who work at Addington's." —*Lesbian Review*

"It was an A.E. Radley story, so I naturally, I loved it! Selina is A.E. Radley's iciest Ice Queen yet! She was so cold and closed off, but as the story progresses and we get a good understanding of her, you realise that just as with any other Ice Queen—she can be thawed. I loved how they interacted, with a wit and banter that only A.E. Radley can really deliver for characters like these."—*LesbiReviewed*

"This story is a refreshing light in the lesfic world. Or should I say in the romance lesfic world? Why do you ask me? Well, while there is a lot of crushy feeling between wlw characters and all, but, honestly that's the sub-plot and I've adored that fact. *Going Up* is a lesson in life."-—*Kam's Queerfic Pantry*

"The author takes an improbable twosome and writes such a splendid romance that you actually think it is possible…this is a great romance and a lovely read."—*Best Lesfic Reviews*

Mergers and Acquisitions

"This book is fun, witty, and adorable. I had no idea which way this book was going to take me, and I loved it. Each character is interesting and loveable in their own right. You don't want to miss this one—heck, if you have read any of A.E. Radley's books you know it's quality stuff."—*Romantic Reader Blog*

"Radley writes with a deceptively simple style, meaning the narrative flows naturally and quickly, yet takes readers effortlessly over rocky terrain. The pacing is unrushed and unforced, yet always leaves readers wanting to rush ahead to see what happens next."—*Lesbian Review*

The Startling Inaccuracy of the First Impression

"We absolutely loved the way the relationship between the two ladies developed. There is nothing hurried about the relationship that develops perfectly organically. This is a lovely, easy to read romance."—*Best Lesfic Reviews*

Huntress

"The writing style was fun and enjoyable. The story really gathered steam to the point of me shirking responsibilities to finish it. The humor in the story was very well done."—*Lesbian Review*

"A.E. Radley always writes fantastic books. *Huntress* is a little different than most of her books, but just as wonderful. The humor was fantastic, the story was absolutely adorable, and the writing was superb. This is truly one of those books where the characters really stick with you long after the book has ended. I wish I'd read it sooner. 5 Stars." —*Les Rêveur*

Bring Holly Home

"*Bring Holly Home* is a fantastic novel and probably one of my favourite books by A.E. Radley…Such a brilliant story and one I know I will read time and time again. This book has two ingredients that I love in novels, Ice Queens melting and age-gap romance. It's definitely a slow burn but one I'd gladly enjoy rereading again."—*Les Rêveur*

Keep Holly Close

"It was great to go back into the world of the Remember Me series. The first book in the series, *Bring Holly Home*, is one of my favourite A.E. Radley books. I love Holly and Victoria; they tick all the boxes for me when it comes to my favourite tropes. Plus, Victoria's kids are adorable, especially little Alexia. She melts my heart."—*Les Rêveur*

"So much drama…loved it!!! I already loved Holly and Victoria from the first book in the series, *Bring Holly Home*, so it was brilliant to be back with them. Victoria hasn't changed and I adore her as much as before. She was utterly brilliant at every moment of this follow-up story and she even managed to surprise me from time to time. The Remember Me series is so beautiful and one of my all time favourites. 5 of 5 stars."—*LesbiReviewed*

Climbing the Ladder

"What a great introduction to what will undoubtedly be another fantastic series from A.E. Radley. After I finished it I just kept thinking that this book is amazing and it's just the start…enough said!"—*Les Rêveur*

"Radley has a talent for giving us memorable characters to love, women you wish you knew, and locations you wish you could experience firsthand."—*Late Night Lesbian Reads*

Second Chances

"This is an absolute delight to read. Likeable characters, well-written, easy flow and sweet romance. Definitely recommended."—*Best Lesfic Reviews*

"I always know when I get a new A.E. Radley book I'm in for a treat. They make me feel so good after reading them that most of the time I'm just plain sad that they have finished…The chemistry between Alice and Hannah is lovely and sweet…All in all, *Second Chances* has landed on my favourites shelf. Honestly, this book is worth every second of your time. 5 Stars."—*Les Rêveur*

The Road Ahead

"I really enjoyed this age-gap, opposites attract road trip romance. This is a romance where the characters actually acknowledge their differences and joy of joy, listen to each other. I love it when a book makes me feel all the feels and root for both women to find their HEA. Hilarious one minute, heart-tugging the next. A pleasure to read." —*Late Night Lesbian Reads*

Fitting In

"Writing convincing love stories with non-typical characters is tricky. Radley more than measures up to the challenge with this truly heart-warming romance."—*Best Lesfic Reviews*

By the Author

Romances

Mergers & Acquisitions

Climbing the Ladder

A Swedish Christmas Fairy Tale

Second Chances

Going Up

Lost at Sea

The Startling Inaccuracy of the First Impression

Fitting In

Detour to Love

Under Her Influence

Flight SQA016

Protecting the Lady

Humbug

The Remember Me Series

Bring Holly Home

Keep Holly Close

The Around the World Series

The Road Ahead

The Big Uneasy

Mystery Novels

Huntress

Death Before Dessert

Visit us at www.boldstrokesbooks.com

HUMBUG

by

Amanda Radley

2021

HUMBUG

© 2021 By Amanda Radley. All Rights Reserved.

ISBN 13: 978-1-63555-965-1

This Trade Paperback Original Is Published By
Bold Strokes Books, Inc.
P.O. Box 249
Valley Falls, NY 12185

First Edition: December 2021

THIS IS A WORK OF FICTION. NAMES, CHARACTERS, PLACES, AND INCIDENTS ARE THE PRODUCT OF THE AUTHOR'S IMAGINATION OR ARE USED FICTITIOUSLY. ANY RESEMBLANCE TO ACTUAL PERSONS, LIVING OR DEAD, BUSINESS ESTABLISHMENTS, EVENTS, OR LOCALES IS ENTIRELY COINCIDENTAL.

THIS BOOK, OR PARTS THEREOF, MAY NOT BE REPRODUCED IN ANY FORM WITHOUT PERMISSION.

Credits
Editor: Ruth Sternglantz
Production Design: Stacia Seaman
Cover Design by Amanda Radley

Acknowledgments

Thank you to the wonderful team at Bold Strokes for helping to get this book out there!

Apologies to my wife, Emma, for suffering through me playing Christmas music in the summer while writing this book.

For the readers.

CHAPTER ONE

Ellie Pearce could barely contain her excitement as she spiritedly stomped her boots on the large temporary mat in reception.

It had snowed.

It wasn't a lot of snow, but enough to provide a small blanket that crunched underfoot. It was already turning into a dark sludge in many places as the thousands of Canary Wharf commuters made their way to work in their high-rise London offices.

On her way from the Underground station, Ellie had managed to find some pure white snow. She'd paused her music and gingerly pressed her foot into the soft powder and enjoyed the sound. The sound of pure Christmas.

Ellie wasn't sure why Britain associated snow with Christmas, considering how very rare a white Christmas was. But snow was somehow synonymous with the festive day. A typical Christmas vision consisted of turkey dinners, silly paper hats, trees brightly decorated in the living room, and snow outside the window.

It was only the start of November, and it was unseasonably cold in London. While everyone else was complaining, Ellie was thrilled. She loved a cold winter. It made everything feel more Christmassy, and it brought with it the tantalising prospect of a white Christmas.

"It's freezing!" a familiar voice complained.

Ellie turned around and beamed at Will Hampton, her best friend and work colleague.

"I know—it's great," she told him excitedly. "I hope it doesn't warm up before Christmas."

Will shook his foot over the mat to encourage the icy build-up to let go of his shoe. He looked miserable. "I hope it does warm up. I know you love it, but it's too cold for me. Cold and dark. No thank you. This weather always makes me want to jet off to the sun. It's just a shame that I don't have any money. Or time. Or anyone to go with."

Ellie shook her head at him. "You just have the wrong mindset, Will. You've been told that cold is bad, but cold can be good. The weather reports are conditioning people to think that cold weather is horrible, but it doesn't have to be that way. Cold means warm drinks and soft scarves. It means seeing your breath in the air and sometimes, if we're really lucky, playing in the snow."

Will gave her a long hard look. "No," he said simply after a few moments' consideration. "I'm with the weather reports. Cold is horrible."

Ellie laughed. "Okay, okay. I'll be the happy one, and you be the grumpy one. That's fine."

He took his hands out of his pockets, rubbed them together, and then blew on them. "Shall we get to our desks? It's freezing standing here." He indicated the large revolving glass door that kept bringing in the cold chill of winter air every time someone new arrived for work.

Ellie took one last look at the beautiful white scene outside before sighing and walking towards the spiral staircase at the end of the large reception space. She and Will passed a group of people gathered by the elevators, all complaining about the extremely cold weather and hoping that it would pass quickly.

The elevator dinged to indicate its arrival, and she jumped at the sound. Not for the first time, Ellie thanked her lucky stars that she was able to walk to her desk. Caldwell & Atkinson occupied almost all of the twenty-two-story building, starting from the second floor and going to the top of the skyscraper. The succession of floors operated as an unofficial ladder of success, minions on the second floor and the executives and meeting rooms on the twenty-second.

Ellie was a minion and very happy to be one.

The ground floor of the building was taken up by Caldwell &

Atkinson's reception as well as restaurants and cafes that served the surrounding buildings. A grand spiral staircase led from reception to the second floor, where Ellie, Will, and a number of other overlooked employees quietly went about their work, largely forgotten by the rest of the building.

A year ago, when Ellie had twisted her ankle, she'd been forced to use the dreaded elevator four times. One time, the terrifying contraption hadn't registered her tentative tap of the second-floor button and had whisked her all the way to the top of the building. As she'd gone higher and higher, her heart rate had spiked and her breathing had shallowed to an almost non-existent shudder.

The doors had finally opened at the very top floor, but there was no one there. Ellie had quickly stabbed the button to take her back down to ground level again. After an eternity, the doors had closed and the elevator had started its descent. The experience had taken no more than two minutes, and yet Ellie remained convinced that it had taken ten years off her life.

Since then, Ellie had decided never to take the elevator again. Her fear of heights was just too great to take the risk. At least with the stairs, she wouldn't suddenly find herself at the top of an impossibly high building and wondering how such a structure didn't just fall over in a strong wind.

Will reached into his pocket, took out his staff card, and held it against the magnetic reader by the side of the door. The light flashed green, and Will opened the door for Ellie, gesturing for her to enter before him.

"Do you still need the figures for the last quarter for construction?" Will asked as they walked across the office.

"No, I managed to speak with Kathy, and she got them for me, but thank you anyway."

"No problem. I'm still working on the report from 2010 accounting redundancies, and I'll get that to you tomorrow, probably."

"That would be great, thanks so much," Ellie replied.

Will ran the archives, both digital and paper-based. Regulations meant that the recruitment firm had to keep records of many things for a set number of years. Which meant that he often received strange requests from people, asking if he could find a phone number from four years ago or an invoice from eight months ago.

Ellie didn't know how he did it. He was literally in charge of millions of documents and could pull together data and reports without a second thought.

They approached their desks, shrugged out of their wet coats, and hung them on the coat rack. Ellie put her bag under her desk and switched on her computer.

"Coffee?" Will asked. He rubbed his hands together to get some feeling back into them.

"You know, you wouldn't be so cold if you wore gloves," Ellie told him.

"Can't find them." He shrugged.

Ellie rolled her eyes. Every year was the same thing—Will had to go out and buy new winterwear. And every spring he put it away somewhere, never to be seen again. The next time it got cold the cycle continued.

"Coffee?" he asked again.

"Oh yes, please."

With Will gone, Ellie set about her morning rituals. She opened her Advent calendar and popped a piece of chocolate in her mouth. It was only November, but Ellie loved the run-up to Christmas so much, that she had long ago started a tradition of treating herself to an advent calendar in both November and December.

She ticked off another day on her monthly calendar and lifted up the page to see December. It wasn't far away. Just fifty-three days until Christmas. And fifty-one until she was officially off work for the Christmas break and able to travel down to Torquay to see her parents.

She looked out of the window and sighed—the snow had turned to rain. It wasn't surprising, but it was disappointing. She wondered if she'd see snow again before Christmas.

Logically, she knew it was very unlikely. In fact, being a statistician, she knew that the chance of seeing a white Christmas in London was nine per cent and falling each year. Down in Torquay, on the south coast of England, it was even less. How she wished her parents had bought a hotel in the Highlands of Scotland rather than down south. Not that a white Christmas was guaranteed up there, but it was closer to a forty per cent chance.

"Stop daydreaming about snow," Will commanded as he placed a cup of coffee down on her Santa coaster.

"I'm not," she denied.

He stared at her.

"Okay, just a little," Ellie admitted. "But do you know the odds of snow in November? Especially with the change in climate we've been seeing lately?"

"No, but I suspect you're going to tell me." He chuckled and sat at his desk.

"Six point two per cent," Ellie said. She reached forward and turned on the battery-operated fairy lights that surrounded her monitor.

"Wow," Will said, definitely not at all wowed. He turned on his computer, slumped in his chair, and sipped at his coffee.

Ellie ignored him and logged on to her system. Her custom background sprang to life—a winter scene complete with reindeer and a present-laden sleigh. To say that Ellie was obsessed with Christmas would be a gross understatement.

The Christmas knick-knacks that covered Ellie's workspace were there all year round. The decor was certainly ramped up in November and reached something of a fever pitch in December. But Ellie's love of all things festive was not confined to winter. She'd loved the season since she was a kid and was unashamed in her enjoyment of it.

She reasoned that if Will could have a collection of action figures on his desk, then she could have year-round tinsel.

Her phone beeped, and she took it out of her bag. She opened the text message from Matt, one of her housemates, and sighed. It was a reminder that they were running out of milk and a suggestion that she pick some up on her way home. She wished she'd never taken responsibility for the groceries.

Her email program came to life, and a series of emails pinged as they arrived. As she suspected, the marketing manager was very keen for her statistical paper on the construction industry. She put her phone down and rubbed at her forehead. The paper would be a tough one.

The construction industry was not doing well at all, but Ellie had been tasked with massaging the data to come up with a paper that suggested otherwise. The idea was to present the construction industry as buoyant in order to encourage companies to feel confident enough to hire more staff.

She desperately wished she could do what she was trained to do—show the data. Instead, she was constantly asked to use the data to prop up a narrative that didn't exist. It was a backwards approach to statistics, but Ellie didn't have much choice. It was a competitive industry, and beggars couldn't be choosers. Which was why she was a statistician working in a recruitment company rather than a university or a science company where she actually belonged.

She sipped her coffee and wondered just how she would manage to make the very clear data look like it was saying exactly the opposite to what it was saying. Movement from across the office caught her eye, and she looked up from her screen. Her eyes widened and her heart nearly stopped beating.

Rosalind Caldwell swept onto the floor. Ellie looked around, catching the panicked eyes of her co-workers. Some couldn't hide their shock and stared at Rosalind, while some quickly bowed their heads to avoid her steely gaze as it whipped around the office.

Everyone was wondering the same thing: What was the CEO doing on the second floor?

Ellie put her coffee down with a shaky hand, pulled her chair a little closer to her desk, and tried to look like she was fully focused on work. In Ellie's three years at Caldwell & Atkinson, she had never once laid eyes on Rosalind Caldwell in person. She'd seen photos of her or caught a glimpse of her in the distance but nothing more. Now Rosalind was here and marching across the floor like a woman on a mission. She was equal parts impressive and intimidating to Ellie. She carried herself with the grace of someone comfortable in the knowledge that they had single-handedly built up a successful business empire. She scanned a room with steely eyes and kept any emotion hidden behind a mask of indifference.

Ellie felt rather than saw Rosalind stop by her desk.

She swallowed and looked up.

"Christmas Girl," Rosalind greeted her, "congratulations, you've been promoted. Pack all of this up, and come to the twenty-second floor. Straight away."

Before Ellie could say a word, Rosalind had turned on her heel and was leaving as quickly as she'd arrived.

Ellie stared after her, confused as to what had just happened. She turned to look at Will who was gaping at her in equal shock.

"What just happened?" Ellie asked, wondering if she'd dreamt the entire thing. She hoped she had.

"You've been promoted, apparently. I don't think I've ever seen her down here on this floor." Will shook his head as if to clear the cobwebs and confirm his eyes were not deceiving him. "Goodness. She's intimidating, isn't she."

"I don't want to be promoted," Ellie said. "And I certainly don't want to go up there. I did hear her right, didn't I? She said to come up to the twenty-second floor?"

"She did. And I don't think you get much choice in the matter. She is the boss," Will pointed out.

"How dare she come down here and tell me I've been promoted and then…then leave like that?"

"Most people would be happy to be promoted," Will said. "Maybe it will be more money?"

Ellie glanced towards the window. She wasn't on ground level, but she could see people, and they didn't look like ants. It had taken her a few weeks to get used to being on the second floor. Her preference would have been the ground floor, but there was little call for statisticians on reception.

After six months of working on the second floor, she'd been able to stand by the window and not feel as though she was going to pass out. That had been a big day for Ellie. The thought of there even being a twenty-second floor caused her knees to wobble a little.

"Well, I'm not one of those people. I like my job here. I like my desk. I like being no higher than this off the ground. This is fine."

Will leaned a little closer so no one could overhear their conversation. "I don't think you have much choice, Ellie. You better get up there. If you can?"

Ellie swallowed. She didn't know if she could. Her ongoing battle with heights was far from over, but she had managed to learn new coping mechanisms through blog posts and podcasts. Now was the chance to put them to the test.

Chapter Two

Rosalind Caldwell burst out of the elevator before the doors had fully opened. She stalked down the corridor towards her office, pausing to straighten a framed photograph as she passed.

At the end of the corridor, she swiped her access card to enter the office and nearly took the doors off their hinges in her hurry. As she walked towards her office, her gaze rested upon Vanessa's desk.

Vanessa's old desk, she corrected herself.

She bristled at the memory of her former personal assistant's overly dramatic behaviour. Arriving in the office to find a letter of resignation wedged into her keyboard was not the morning she had planned for.

"Ros?" Eric Atkinson—her best friend, financial director, and business partner—poked his head out of his office and looked at her quizzically.

"Not a word," she told him.

He quickly scurried back into his office. Eric was a wiz with numbers, a shoulder to cry on, an unrivalled business mind, but not a brave man. The reason they got on so well and had managed to work together in harmony for years was chiefly down to Eric's ability to give Rosalind space when she needed it.

And right now, she really needed it.

She stormed into her office and flopped into her chair. She spun around and looked out at the view of the bustling business district of London.

The Thames snaked its way around the Canary Wharf estate and slipped into small waterways and docks throughout the area. Skyscrapers had popped up all over the place, often with glorious views of the water and the yachts and other pleasure boats that occupied that part of the river. She'd recently moved into an apartment with a view and enjoyed the convenience of being close to the office as well as the calming views of the boats bobbing on the water.

Rosalind took some deep breaths while she stared at the view and willed it to calm her. It didn't, and a moment later she turned her chair back to face her desk.

"Who does she think she is?" she asked the empty office, picking up Vanessa's letter of resignation and reading through it again.

It had clearly been placed on her desk after she had left work the evening before. After they'd had a furious row about the tea tray. It wasn't the first time that Rosalind had been forced to discuss the importance of the intricacies of the tea tray with Vanessa.

Over the months, Vanessa had become more and more lax about following the rules that Rosalind was so very precious about. She had built up a company with the client at the very heart of everything they did. Recruitment was a competitive and cut-throat business, and the only way to be successful was to treat every client as if they were the only client. It was essential to know that client inside out and to offer a bespoke experience each time they met.

Part of that was the tea tray. Rosalind kept detailed notes of all her clients, as did every consultant who worked for her. The notes included tea and coffee preferences, allergies, and biscuit observations.

And while she knew it would probably sound like overkill to the average person, Rosalind had long ago started noting which biscuits clients enjoyed with their tea or coffee—shortbread, chocolate, plain digestives, or filled with fruit. The next time the client came to the office, the tea tray was made up for them. It was a tiny detail but an essential one.

Vanessa had started to slip up. She'd given plain chocolate

digestives to Greg Ashton from Adams Estates. Greg didn't like dark chocolate, and the tiny frown on his face when the tea tray had been deposited in front of him ate at Rosalind throughout the meeting.

When the meeting was done, she'd had a long and loud discussion with Vanessa about the importance of the tea tray. The air had become charged, and a flash of something shone in Vanessa's eyes.

The resignation letter was the reply that Vanessa had been reluctant to give in person. Rosalind had called her and requested that she come back, but Vanessa was committed to her actions and told Rosalind to go to hell. She'd also said something else that had sent a chill down her spine. Something that was currently spinning around Rosalind's head and causing her level of internal panic to ratchet up with every passing minute.

Rosalind realised that someone was watching her and looked up to see the little mouse from the second floor standing in the doorway. She looked petrified, with wide eyes and a sheen of sweat on her forehead.

Ordinarily, Rosalind would have opened the database of candidates looking for work and picked a PA from there. She did run a recruitment company, after all. But a pit of worry was building within her at what Vanessa might have done. She needed someone quickly, and she needed someone who might be able to unpick the mayhem that Rosalind suspected Vanessa had caused before she left, a parting gift that could have terrible consequences.

"Did I not tell you to pack your desk?" Rosalind asked, noting that the girl was empty-handed.

"I…I don't want a promotion."

"Fine, then you're fired." Rosalind shrugged. She put on her glasses and pulled her laptop closer. The girl remained in the doorway. Rosalind looked up at her. "You can go."

The woman before her blinked a few times in shock. "You can't do that. There are rules!"

"There are. But by the time you manage to take me to tribunal, you'll be sick of the taste of cheap noodles and utterly desperate."

She took off her reading glasses and pinned her with her most withering look. She didn't ordinarily bend the rules in this way, but she was desperate and needed the girl to accept the job so that she could clean up Vanessa's mess. "The fact of the matter is, you have a new job, if you want it. If so, pack up your things and set yourself up out there." She pointed at Vanessa's old desk. "If not, then you can go home. Unemployed."

"What's the job?"

"Well, it's my PA's desk. So I presume the job would be my PA," Rosalind said. "Or maybe I've been misinformed? Our illustrious Human Resources department told me that you were competent. Is that not the case?"

"I…" The young woman paused, her mouth opening and closing but no words forthcoming.

"Am going to go downstairs to pack my desk up and report up here immediately afterwards, thus securing myself employment over the Christmas period? What a very good idea." Rosalind grinned.

The woman nodded and stumbled away. A few seconds later, Eric took her place in the doorway.

"Didn't I say not a word?" Rosalind asked him.

Eric ignored the cold tone and stepped inside her office. "What's going on?"

Rosalind sighed. He had chosen a fine time to grow a backbone. "Vanessa has handed in her notice."

Eric regarded her suspiciously. "Surely that's not all. You've lost assistants before."

"Why thank you for pointing that out, Eric." She put her glasses back on and returned her attention to the laptop in front of her. Yes, she'd had a few assistants, but that was only because she placed them in very good jobs with clients, thus securing each of them a good career path, herself a commission payment, and the client an excellent employee. Everyone was happy.

She was known to be very particular and, at times, demanding. But she always rewarded good work with excellent career advancement opportunities, either within Caldwell & Atkinson or with one of their clients.

Vanessa was one of the first people to throw that in Rosalind's face and walk away.

"Ros?" he asked again, clearly not about to leave without getting answers.

Rosalind rolled her eyes. "If you must know, I suspect that Vanessa might have...thrown a little spanner in the works before she left."

"What kind of spanner?"

"She told me to enjoy the Christmas party just after she told me to go to hell," Rosalind admitted. She squeezed some hand sanitiser onto her hands and rubbed them together vigorously. "I wonder if she might have sabotaged the arrangements somehow."

Eric's eyebrows rose, and Rosalind held up a hand to forestall any further comments.

"Before you hyperventilate, I am dealing with it. I spoke to Amy in HR and told her I needed a new assistant very quickly, and it had to be someone who could continue with the arrangements for the Christmas party. She suggested that one from the second floor, you know, the one who permanently celebrates the season judging by the state of her desk."

"Who?" Eric asked.

"The one on the second floor. You must have seen her desk when you've dropped something into the post room late at night. All that tinsel, Santa, and lights—it looks like an explosion at a Christmas shop. If *she* can't organise a Christmas party, then who can?"

"Does she have any experience organising events?" Eric asked, nervously fidgeting with his wristwatch.

"How should I know? What I do know is this, she now has the appropriate motivation. You'll be surprised what someone can do when they have motivation."

Eric gave her one final look before deciding he didn't have anything further to say and leaving. Rosalind removed her glasses and pinched the bridge of her nose. She didn't like what she had said to the young woman. Threatening someone's employment status wasn't the kind of person Rosalind Caldwell usually was.

But desperation had struck, and Rosalind knew she needed the woman to take the offered job. The Christmas party was a few weeks away, and Vanessa had been in charge of all arrangements. Rosalind knew nothing about it, didn't know how to organise an event, and had a company to run.

If it was any other event, she might have reacted differently. But this was *the* Christmas party—the Caldwell & Atkinson Christmas party—that people talked about for months before and after the event. The party had become so important in the recruitment sector that other companies had given up on hosting their own in order to not even attempt to compete with the renowned celebration.

She needed someone who could pick up the reins and make sure the damn thing happened. Amy in HR seemed to think that the Christmas-obsessed woman on the second floor was the best person in the company to do it. Rosalind just hoped she was right.

CHAPTER THREE

Ellie stumbled out of the elevator and held on to the wall for a few seconds until she got her equilibrium back. She once again cursed her hatred of heights. Why couldn't she just be normal? Other people didn't feel sick, dizzy, and petrified when they were on a higher floor, so why did she?

"Hey, everything okay?" Will approached, having obviously been hanging around the hallway and waiting for her return.

"I've been demoted," Ellie explained. "I'm Rosalind's PA. Me! It's insane. She threatened to fire me if I didn't take the job. I just don't get it."

"Wow." Will shook his head sadly. "Well, I'll miss you."

"I'm not going." She folded her arms determinedly. "I won't do it."

"She's the boss—you kinda have to, Ellie."

Ellie bit her lip for a moment as she tried to think of a way out of her predicament. "Then I'll...be bad at the new job. I'll be so bad at it that she'll get sick of me and send me back to my old job."

Will look unconvinced.

"What?" Ellie asked.

"I don't think that would work. She'll just sack you if you're not good at the job," he said. "This isn't like when you were a kid, and you could just pretend to be bad at washing the dishes and your mum wouldn't ask you to do it again. This is the real world. And it's Rosalind. She'd just fire you, not send you back down here, surely?"

Ellie rubbed at her forehead and willed her scrambled mind to think straight. There had to be a way out of the mess. She didn't want to work for the boss, didn't want to be a PA, and didn't want to work on the top floor. Fear was rising within her, and she couldn't see a way out.

"Thing is," Will said gently before pausing, suggesting he was building up to say something he knew she wouldn't like, "and I say this with love and respect, Ellie, but the company doesn't really need you."

After the terror-inducing trip to the top floor, Ellie didn't have the energy to cast him the evil look he clearly deserved. Also, she knew it was true. The simple fact was that recruitment consultancies did not need statisticians. It had been a strange fluke that she had gotten a role at Caldwell & Atkinson at all. A temporary job in the marketing department had led her then-boss to notice her flair for numbers and statistics.

After a while, a new role was created for her. It was apparently somewhat useful for the marketing team to have a numbers guru. It had been well established that official-looking reports and information graphics did better than standard advertisements, and Ellie had the ability to sift through data and pull out numbers that helped with whatever marketing campaign they were working on at that time.

Ellie's role wasn't critical to the business. If she left, nothing would happen. Most people probably wouldn't even notice. She had wondered a few times throughout the years how long her luck would hold and when the company might get rid of her during a round of cost cuts. Her previous manager had protected her from the chop for a while, but he'd left the company, and now Ellie was alone in the game of office politics.

So far, she had skated by through keeping her head down and working hard on the tasks she was given. But in her heart she had always known her role was untenable in the long run.

"I don't know how to be a PA," Ellie grumbled.

"Sure you do," Will said. "Rosalind will give you jobs, and you'll do them. It will be easy. Better than what you're doing now.

Don't you always say that you're fed up with having to lie in those marketing reports, spending all that time trying to find the one figure that proves the opposite to what is actually happening? You won't have to do that any more."

Ellie let out a sigh. She wasn't yet fully willing to accept her fate but knew it was going to happen no matter how she felt.

"And this is Rosalind Caldwell," Will reminded her. "If anyone can get you the perfect statistician job of your dreams, then it's her, right?"

Ellie met his gaze with excitement as a realisation awakened within her.

"I mean, she's one of the top recruitment consultants in the country. Show her how brilliant you are, and then she'll help you get any job you like. A word from Rosalind…"

Ellie felt a smile tug gently at her cheeks. Getting a job where she could actually use her extensive skills would be like a dream come true. She was already in a dead-end job, so what difference would it make to be a PA for a few months, especially if at the end of it she had a chance of getting a proper job.

Reality hit and she sucked in a deep nervous breath. "It's up there," she muttered, indicating the ceiling with her head.

"You can do it. You said yourself—you sometimes get used to heights as long as you don't think about it too much or look out of a window. A lowly PA isn't going to have a window view," he said. "And you've been working on those breathing exercises, right?"

Ellie slowly nodded.

"Then try it. What's the worst that can happen?"

"An embarrassing panic attack," Ellie told him. She'd experienced many throughout the years, but Will had never seen one. Ellie prayed he never would. It was utterly humiliating to lose all control of your body and mind. Having that happen in front of a friend was mortifying.

Wherever possible, she kept her fear of heights a secret. She had only confided in Will after countless invites to join him on the London Eye, the large Ferris wheel that teetered over the River Thames. Eventually she'd had to admit why she kept saying no or risk ruining their burgeoning friendship. Will knew more than most, but he'd never seen the result of Ellie pushing herself too far.

She blew out a long breath. "It's not like I have much of a choice, is it?"

He shook his head. "'Fraid not."

"Help me pack up my desk?"

Will smiled sadly. "Sure. I'm going to miss you. It will be weird to not have you around here any more."

"I'll miss you, too." Ellie threw her arms around his neck and hugged him tightly. "We'll still meet up for lunch, right?"

"Absolutely. And I'll still email you all the best memes," Will promised.

"You better." She pulled away and nodded towards her desk. Ellie wasn't sure how she was going to manage it, but somehow she was going to work on the twenty-second floor, be a perfect assistant, and convince Rosalind to help her find the job of her dreams.

"Rather you than me. She's scary," Will said. He placed an empty cardboard box on her desk.

"She's not—she just pretends to be," Ellie said.

Sure, Rosalind projected the image of a cold-hearted boss who must be obeyed. But Ellie had worked at the company long enough to know that the generous holiday package, maternity and paternity schemes, and donations to charities had to come from the top. Caldwell & Atkinson wouldn't be such a nice company to work for with great benefits if Rosalind Caldwell and Eric Atkinson weren't thoroughly decent people.

It was an act—Ellie was sure of it. She had some experience in pretending to be something she wasn't, and she thought she could detect a kindred spirit in Rosalind.

Not that she would push that assumption. Ellie had been known to be wrong, and Rosalind was still the boss. While Ellie suspected the ice queen visage was all an act, she was in little doubt that Rosalind would sack her if she needed to. No one got to the top of their profession by being too kind. There had to be a balance, and Ellie would need to learn it.

Fast.

CHAPTER FOUR

Rosalind gathered up her leather folio and her glasses and exited her office. She was pleased to see her new PA arriving with her belongings as she passed the desk.

"Welcome to the twenty-second floor," she said. "I'll need you to organise lunch for my twelve o'clock with Jason Cooper. Also, get me the marketing budget forecast before my meeting with them this afternoon. Oh, and check on all the arrangements for the Christmas party—should be right in your area of interest."

Rosalind watched as not one but two chocolate Advent calendars were taken out of the archive box and placed on the desk. Inside the box she could see various Christmas decorations that had been haphazardly packed to be brought upstairs. If only they would just be around for the season, but Rosalind had been informed that Christmas Girl was so called because of her fixation with this time of year. Apparently, her desk remained a full-on Santa's grotto all year round. Rosalind would have to get used to it. She wasn't about to go through the upheaval of training up two PAs in a short period of time.

Unless any of the decorations played a tune—then Christmas Girl would be out.

"Yes, Miss Caldwell," the girl mumbled.

"Rosalind. We're not formal up here," she said.

The girl didn't reply, smile, or acknowledge anything as she unpacked her box of tinsel and fairy lights. Rosalind decided to not push the matter just yet. She'd give her a few hours to settle into her new role, especially considering the shock she was about to receive when she discovered whatever it was Vanessa had done to the Christmas party arrangements.

She made her way towards the main conference room. She was a little early, but it would give her time to read through the previous meeting minutes to prepare. Eric was already in the room, pouring tea from the correctly set up tea tray. Thankfully Eric's PA, Irene, was always on the ball.

"Tea?" he offered.

"Please." She slumped into the chair at the head of the table.

"You shouldn't have been so harsh on Vanessa," he told her. "She wasn't *that* bad."

"She was becoming careless." She opened her folio and started to leaf through the pieces of paper within.

"Isn't that a little strong?" Eric asked.

"I don't think so. She wilfully ignored my requests whenever they didn't suit her. The tea tray was the straw that broke the camel's back, but there were other instances of her bending whatever rules she desired. I can't have that kind of person working for me. Not after what happened with Ava."

"I think you worry a little too much sometimes," Eric said in his gentlest tone.

"I think I worry exactly the correct amount, all considered, thank you very much." Her fingers grasped a sheet of paper a little tighter than she intended, and it started to crumple around the edges.

Eric placed a teacup and saucer in front of her. "Dare I ask about the Christmas party?"

"It's in hand."

He took a seat to the side of her and stirred his tea. "I don't want to add extra stress, but you know how important the party is. Our reputation relies on this event going smoothly."

She looked up at him and saw the worry in his eyes. He was right—she didn't need the extra stress. But she recognised that he was concerned and doing exactly what he needed to as her business partner, telling her the truth even if she didn't want to hear it. Having someone who pulled your head out of the sand was essential. Even if she didn't necessarily like it.

"I know, Eric," she said. "Trust me—I'm working on it. In fact, Christmas Girl is working on it."

Eric put the spoon down on the saucer and slowly nodded. "Very well, I won't nag you about it. And she has a name, you know."

"I know," Rosalind lied. Things had happened so quickly that she hadn't had time to do any research into her new assistant at all. Not even to find out her name.

"You'll let me know about the Christmas party?" he asked.

"As soon as I know, I'll let you know."

That wasn't technically true. Eric worried over the little details, probably enough to put himself into an early grave if allowed. Rosalind took the brunt of any business wobbles, so he didn't have to. If she needed to tell him everything was fine when it wasn't, then that was precisely what she would do.

Chapter Five

Ellie opened her reporter's notepad and jotted down the three things Rosalind had requested she do. She supposed she'd better get used to such action in her new role. She slammed the pen down and stared off into the distance. She was a personal assistant, quite suddenly and unexpectedly, and it irked her more than she thought it would.

She sighed. She'd left university with an impressive set of credentials, and here she was, six years later, as a personal assistant and not even working in a company where her skills were required or regarded.

Sadly, she couldn't blame her circumstances entirely on Rosalind Caldwell. Yes, Rosalind had essentially changed her job description that very morning, but prior to that it had all been on Ellie's head.

Six months of travel to celebrate the end of university, six months of looking for the perfect job while living at home, and then panic at the realisation that an entire year had gone by, and she was unemployed. Over the next few months, Ellie's requirements for a job had slipped lower and lower. The salary went first, from a reasonable level that she thought could sustain her to anything she could get. Then location—the job didn't have to be in Devon. In fact, she'd consider anywhere in the country. Then the status of the company she was looking at. Before long she was scrambling for any job at all.

A temporary marketing position one summer at a recruitment agency in London had seemed like a good idea. It would ensure money was coming in while she continued her search for employment, and she'd be based in London, which was surely where all the good jobs were.

Now, some years later, Ellie found herself working for the same company and living in the same houseshare with four men who resembled overgrown toddlers. She hadn't realised how much time had passed her by, how much time she'd wasted. And now her career truly felt as though it was going backwards. Not simply because she was a personal assistant—she knew many would consider it a prestigious job. It just wasn't what Ellie wanted to do. And being forced into the role or face unemployment two months before Christmas was the bitter lemon icing on the cake of disappointment.

She shook her head to clear the cobwebs and tried to focus on her work, or she would be out of a job. She didn't get the impression that Rosalind gave many second chances.

She looked at her notes and picked up the telephone. At least the second item was easy enough. She had connections in the marketing department, and they'd be able to help her with what she wanted.

A short call later, and she was promised that the appropriate documents would be emailed to her within the next few minutes. Ellie sat a little taller at her desk. This PA business wasn't as hard as she thought.

The next item on the list was lunch for a meeting with Jason Cooper. Ellie frowned. That one sounded a little tougher. Was she supposed to guess what Jason wanted for lunch? Or maybe there was a lunch platter that they frequently ordered from a local cafe?

She looked around the floor to see if there was anyone she could ask, but it was empty. It seemed there were only two offices, Rosalind's and Eric's. Eric's PA, a lovely older lady called Irene, had welcomed Ellie to the fold before heading out to run some errands.

Ellie looked at the desk pedestal unit and opened some of the drawers. The previous desk dweller had left a lot behind. Ellie wondered what had happened and how Rosalind had come to find herself suddenly without an assistant. She pushed the thought to one side before she became overwhelmed with images of Rosalind making some poor assistant walk the plank for getting her coffee order wrong. She was sure she wasn't like that, but the unfamiliar situation had made her mind wander.

She flicked through the paperwork and notebooks before taking them all out of the drawer and placing them on her desk. There seemed to be a well of information hidden away in folders and books. She quickly located travel expense forms, order forms, past diaries, staff contact details, and a whole folder dedicated to clients.

Ellie eagerly looked through the documentation and found a list of meals preapproved for a variety of upcoming breakfast, lunch, and dinner meetings that Rosalind was holding. She held on to the paper as if she had found the Holy Grail and grabbed the telephone to call the restaurant.

Whoever had previously had her role was a genius and incredibly well organised. Everything was written down and meticulously filed. If Ellie ever met them, she'd definitely shake their hand.

Lunch sorted, she looked at the final item on her list. A sensation of pride surged through her at the thought that she might actually be able to complete the list of things Rosalind had given her before she even returned from her meeting.

The fact that the final item on the list was the Christmas party just made things even sweeter. Ellie loved the Caldwell & Atkinson yearly celebration—it was by far the highlight of her calendar.

It was a party for all—staff, clients, candidates, and suppliers. Ellie fondly remembered every one of the parties she had attended. Each had been in a different location, expertly decorated and supplied with the best food and an open bar. While some people used the opportunity to drink as much as possible, Ellie simply enjoyed the Christmas feel the party gave. While she celebrated Christmas spirit all year round, the work Christmas party was the real start to the peak of all things festive for Ellie.

With a gleeful giggle, she picked up the folder labelled *Christmas Party*. The theme of the event was often kept a secret until just four weeks before the date, and Ellie felt like a child sneaking a look at the wrapped presents under the tree.

She opened the folder and gasped and then giggled—this year's party had a Nutcracker theme. She quickly considered her wardrobe and what she would be able to repurpose. On the next page she saw the venue details, a beautiful conference room in one of the Royal Colleges.

"This is going to be amazing," Ellie whispered to herself.

Before getting carried away with the rest of the details, she picked up the phone to call the venue. Rosalind had asked her to check on all of the details, and it would obviously be a good idea to introduce herself as the new organiser. It was, after all, one of the few benefits of this new—unwanted—job.

When the call was answered, she asked to be put through to the events team.

"Events, how may I help you?" A man's voice cut through Ellie's daydreaming of outfits and speciality cocktails.

"Oh, hello, I'm calling from Caldwell & Atkinson—"

"Contracts are final, I'm afraid," he said briskly.

"Um. Sorry?" Ellie frowned.

"The contract was signed, and it clearly says that the deposit is non-refundable."

"I don't want the deposit back," Ellie explained. "I'm calling to check our reservation."

"What?"

"Our reservation, I'm calling to check it. And to introduce myself. I'm Ellie Pearce, the new organiser."

"Well, first off, you'll be organising a new venue." He chuckled.

Fear pricked at Ellie. "What do you mean?"

"Vanessa called last night to cancel. Told me you'd found a new venue."

Ellie looked at the paperwork in front of her. Vanessa had been her predecessor. The former well-organised genius had cancelled the venue for some reason. If Ellie ever met her, she'd kill her.

"Well, she was lying. We still want the booking," Ellie said.

"No can do. We have a waiting list. The moment the cancellation was made, the venue was offered elsewhere."

"What? No! We need that space!" Ellie stood up and grasped the phone tightly to her ear.

"Sorry, what's done is done."

Ellie thought he didn't sound very sorry at all. "Please, there must be something you can do."

"Well, I could book you in for next year," he offered.

"That's no use to me now. I'm more worried about this year."

"Look, Ellie, was it? I'm sorry, but it's been cancelled. There's not a lot I can do. And I can't refund the deposit either, before you ask. It's done."

"Where am I supposed to get a new venue now?" Ellie asked, almost to herself.

He laughed. "For this year? In London? At this late date? Good luck."

He hung up the call. Ellie started to feel a little faint and collapsed into her chair. They had no venue. It was November, and they had no venue.

After a full minute had passed, she put the phone receiver back. She stared down at the information in front of her. Vanessa had cancelled the venue, but why? She looked around the desk in shock. There were no personal effects, but the space still had the air of someone who'd left quickly. Paperwork had been carelessly swept to one side, the email folder was full to bursting, nothing had been left for a handover to the next person. It was becoming clearer and clearer that Vanessa had left quite suddenly. And if she'd cancelled the venue, it must have been out of spite.

Ellie swayed a little in her chair as a wave of panic hit her. If Vanessa had cancelled the event space, what else might she have done? She leafed through the event folder and looked at the bookings that had been made and wondered if any of them still existed.

Probably not.

The Christmas party had been cancelled with just six weeks to go. And now it was her problem.

❖

Rosalind exited the conference room and headed back towards her office, hoping that the rest of the day would see some improvement over what she had experienced so far. The sight of her new assistant looking positively ashen while wringing her hands didn't fill her with much confidence.

"Miss—um, Rosalind?"

Rosalind paused by her desk and regarded her with a look that she knew demanded brevity. "Out with it."

"We have a problem."

"Do we?" Rosalind asked, even though she was fairly sure she already knew the answer.

"I called the venue to check arrangements, like you asked, but it had been cancelled. And they couldn't uncancel it. Then I called the caterer, the musicians, the waiters. Everything has been cancelled. Everything."

"I see." Rosalind looked around the desk, which looked like a bomb had gone off. A confusing mix of legal contracts and tinsel. "It's a good thing that you're Christmas Girl, isn't it? I'm sure you'll manage to fix it."

Rosalind used the momentary pause in conversation to make her escape. She continued on her way to her office and slammed the door behind her.

"Damn."

She knew Vanessa could have a spiteful streak, but she would never have suspected she'd be capable of doing something quite so drastic. She sat down and turned her chair to look out at the view.

Long ago, she and Eric had agreed that an enormous, expensive party bought a large amount of goodwill throughout the year. It had become something of an expectation that each year outdid the last. The bill got bigger, but so did the reward.

For a few hours every December, Rosalind showed her appreciation to staff and clients alike. Without fail, new contracts were discussed and, shortly afterwards, agreed upon. It wasn't a simple party, and it had nothing to do with Christmas. It was an excuse to get many people together in a fun and casual environment and show off their generosity with endless trays of canapés and champagne.

Now that was all at risk.

All because Vanessa had finally snapped. They'd never gotten on that well, but Rosalind had no idea that things were that bad.

She sucked in a deep breath and slowly blew it out again. She didn't know the first thing about events management, but she did know organising a party this close to Christmas was absolutely impossible. Throwing money at the problem wasn't going to make it go away.

She needed to give the new girl a chance. Maybe her love of the season would see her through. Maybe there was such a thing as a Christmas miracle, for those who believed.

Rosalind didn't believe. Never had. Christmas was just an event on the calendar that required much planning and created a mountain of unavoidable stress. It irritated her that people would hoist the very notion of Christmas atop some glittery plinth for all to worship.

Forced merriment had never been Rosalind's thing. She didn't like birthdays, baby showers, or family gatherings for that very reason. All required a mask of politeness, but none was as bad Christmas. The festive season topped them all. Everyone had to be having the most fun they'd ever had, at all times. Christmas had to be both traditional and yet better than the previous year. No one could have a bad day at Christmas, even though Christmas was one of the more trying times of the year. And, for reasons that Rosalind could not comprehend, everyone seemed just fine with that. It seemed that everyone loved Christmas, and anyone who didn't was stared at like some oddity.

She turned her chair back to face her desk and applied some hand sanitiser. She'd give Christmas Girl a few days to sink or swim. She only hoped she swam, because if she didn't, Rosalind didn't know what she'd do.

Her current strategy of an authoritative glare and a demand to fix things wouldn't hold for long. Eventually, reality would take over, and the party would either happen or it wouldn't.

CHAPTER SIX

Ellie hung up the call and glanced at her watch. She couldn't believe it was ten to five. The day had gone by in a flash, something she wasn't used to at all.

She'd had no idea how easy-going her workdays had been before. Her phone rang maybe once or twice a day, her inbox was always neat and organised, she chatted with Will and other people around her desk, and she generally took her time with the small amount of work she had to do.

Less than one full day of being Rosalind's PA had shown her what a real hectic workday was like. Since unpacking her box of belongings, she hadn't stopped working. Phone calls, planning meetings, organising Rosalind's diary, welcoming clients, preparing tea trays and lunch menus, opening mail, replying to emails, and so much more that she'd already forgotten half of it. She'd had to cancel her lunch with Will and grab a sandwich to eat at her desk instead.

On the bright side, she'd never known a day in the office to fly by so quickly. She'd usually count down the minutes until an acceptable time to go to lunch, but today she'd had lunch at two o'clock. The end of the day often approached at a slow crawl, but today it had suddenly arrived with no warning.

Ellie had just about managed to keep on top of everything but felt exhausted. She didn't feel she had any right to complain about how busy she had been as she'd watched in awe while Rosalind zipped around the office like a hummingbird.

Of course, she'd always known that CEOs were busy people who achieved a lot, but seeing just how much Rosalind crammed into a day had been an eye-opening experience. It was just a few hours into her new job, and she had a greater understanding of why Caldwell & Atkinson was such a successful company. Rosalind ran from meeting to meeting and call to call, brokering large deals, negotiating with suppliers, meeting new recruits, and chairing staff meetings.

Eric Atkinson had an equally packed schedule but completed his tasks at a slower and calmer rate. Ellie could see how Rosalind's and Eric's differences made them the ideal business partners. They were almost complete opposites, but between them, they were the perfect well-oiled machine.

While Ellie was pleased that the end of the day was finally approaching, she wasn't pleased that she had gotten no further at all with the Christmas party. She'd slipped in a few phone calls in between her other tasks and had discovered, unsurprisingly, that Vanessa had managed to cancel everything. Ellie had begged and pleaded with a couple of suppliers and managed to get them back on board. But she was still without a venue, a caterer, and music. Her head throbbed just thinking about it.

She needed to speak to Rosalind, which meant going into her boss's office—terrifying on two counts. First, Rosalind hadn't exactly demonstrated herself to be all that approachable. Second, the large corner office had floor-to-ceiling windows, showing just how high up they were. For those who enjoyed looking down upon the smaller office blocks of Canary Wharf and over into the distance at the City of London it was probably a delight. For Ellie it was a nightmare just waiting to happen. Just the thought of getting near to those horrifying panes of glass sent Ellie's pulse skyrocketing.

Ellie had spent the day very studiously ignoring the fact that she was extremely high above the ground. She'd avoided the nearest photocopier because it was thoughtlessly located right next to a window. Instead, she chose to go downstairs to use a copier in the accounts department, which was sensibly located in a windowless room in the middle of the office.

Ellie turned around. Rosalind's office door was open, and she wasn't on the phone. It was the perfect opportunity to go in and talk to her. Ellie's gaze flicked from her boss to the windows behind her. The tops of smaller high-rises were visible, and Ellie quickly looked away. Panic was rising up inside her, and she reminded herself of her breathing strategy.

Slowly in, and slowly out.

After a few moments, she felt ready to go speak to Rosalind. She stood up, smoothed down her trousers, and adjusted her cardigan. She then sucked in a deep and calming breath before she approached Rosalind's office and knocked on the frame of the open door.

"Come in," Rosalind said without looking up.

Ellie took a few steps in but stopped in the middle of the room. She didn't want to get any closer to the large windows than she absolutely needed to.

"Um. It's about the Christmas party," Ellie said.

"All sorted?" Rosalind asked, continuing to write and not give Ellie her attention.

"Not exactly."

Rosalind stopped writing, looked up, and removed her glasses. "You're not going to tell me you can't cope with this new position, are you? No, wait. Don't tell me—you thought assistants just chewed gum, did their nails, and answered the occasional phone call?"

"No, of course not," Ellie said, though it was a pretty accurate depiction of what she'd thought prior to that day. She'd never been a personal assistant before, and television had informed her that it was a fairly easy ride. Damn television.

"So why are you here? Do you want me to assign the task to someone else? Are you admitting defeat after"—Rosalind checked her watch—"under eight hours?"

"Uh, well—"

"I'm happy to let you step aside," Rosalind said. "But it will be from the job as a whole. It can't have escaped your knowledge that we don't need a statistician. To be perfectly honest, I'm shocked you've managed to survive as long as you have. You've survived by keeping your head down and not by excelling. You've not stayed here because you are invaluable—you've stayed because you are invisible. That ended this morning, and I'm sure it seems unfair to you, but it's business. In fact, it's life. If you can't take control of this situation, then step aside, and I'll be more than happy to find someone who can."

Ellie clenched her jaw. She hated that Rosalind was right, hated even more that the nail in the coffin of her previous, oh-so comfortable job had been so firmly hammered into place. Her choice was clear—be Rosalind's PA or be unemployed. Ellie itched to throw the job in Rosalind's face and walk out. Thankfully, she was sensible enough to keep that desire caged within her. She didn't need to be job hunting a few weeks before Christmas. She had bills to pay and precious little savings to rely on.

"I can do it," Ellie said, even though she didn't quite believe it herself.

Rosalind smiled and put her glasses back on. "Excellent, I thought you might say that." She returned to what she was writing.

As she lowered her head, Ellie caught a glimpse of the petrifying view. She sucked in a quick breath before hurrying from the office. She practically fell into her chair and gripped the desktop like a lifeline.

"Damn, damn, damn," she muttered.

Chapter Seven

Prior to her unexpected demotion, Ellie could guarantee getting home at exactly one minute past six, every single day. She frequently—and unashamedly—packed her bag, turned off her computer, and sat with her coat on at ten minutes to five o'clock. The moment the big hand hit the top of the clock, she would jump to her feet and make a beeline for the Tube station. Two Tubes and a bus later and she'd arrive at her houseshare in Clapham.

It irked her that she was approaching thirty and still lived in a single room, sharing a house with four men who had the collective emotional age of a deflated football. The boys, as she referred to them, were nice enough. But they were also like children—messy, loud, and immature.

As much as it frustrated her to live with them three years on from when she had supposedly temporarily become the fifth person in the shared accommodation, she attributed it to a slow jobs market, a costly housing market, and simply the way life in London was.

She unlocked the front door and shouldered it open. It had never been the same since Charlie and Neil were playing rugby in the hallway and crashed into it. They'd been promising to call the landlord to get it fixed for the last four months. Ellie had given up all hope of that ever actually happening, the same as the cracked window in the bathroom, the missing glass plate from the microwave, and the handle to the living room door.

She took off her winter wear and hung it on the coat rack, taking the stack of coats from the floor and hanging them up as well.

The clock on the wall told her it was eight o'clock, and she blinked a few times, not quite believing it.

After Rosalind's speech, Ellie had made the effort to stay late and organise her desk and familiarise herself with the filing system. She wanted Rosalind to see her working longer than her hours to prove that she was serious about her job. In the end, she had left just ten minutes after Rosalind went home, briefly wondering if the woman ever left the office.

She tiredly stumbled into the kitchen and switched on the light. She blinked and stared at the devastation on every surface. Used crockery, cutlery, and pots and pans lined the worktops. The sink was still full from the breakfast things that morning.

It was clear that the boys had become bored of waiting for her to get home and cook for them and had taken matters into their own hands, with destructive results.

Two years ago, Ellie had made the mistake of pointing out how much money they wasted on food when they cooked separately. She'd made the argument that combining their funds and buying for one big meal instead of five smaller ones would be much more economical.

Since then, she'd been in charge of the shopping and the cooking. The boys did the washing up around half the time as if that was a fair arrangement. Ellie hadn't bothered to argue the point and had instead slipped into her new role as lead shopper and chef with nothing more than the occasional mutter under her breath.

She opened the fridge and sighed at the mess. A quick look through the cupboards and drawers uncovered one clean spoon. She washed and dried a bowl and filled it with cereal and milk. It wasn't much of a dinner, but it was all she could be bothered to prepare considering the late hour.

"If they think I'm cleaning this, they have another think coming," she mumbled, turning the light off on the mess.

She took her bowl of cereal upstairs and knocked on Theo's door.

"Yeah?" he called out.

"It's Ellie, got a minute?"

The door opened, and Theo gestured for her to come in. "I was getting worried about you. Hot date?"

Ellie laughed. "As if."

He pulled his desk chair out and gestured for her to sit down, taking a seat on the edge of the bed. Theo was the most mature of the boys and held down an important job in marketing. If anyone might have some useful advice for her, then it was him.

"What's up?"

"I've been promoted demoted." She sat down and ate a mouthful of cereal.

"What's promoted demoted?"

"It's where the boss of the entire company makes you her PA because she realises that a recruitment company doesn't need a statistician," Ellie explained.

Theo shook his head in shock. "What? She just…made you her PA?"

"Yep. I now work on the twenty-second floor." She took another bite of food.

Theo's eyes widened. "That's pretty high up, you okay?"

"Yeah, it's that or be fired, apparently." Ellie sighed. "But that's not the really big problem. I always knew I was an anomaly at work, and it was just a matter of time before they found that out. And I can figure out how to be a PA—there's notes everywhere, and a really lovely lady called Irene is helping me. As long as I'm not near a window, I can forget how high up I am."

"So what's the really big problem?"

"My predecessor cancelled everything to do with the Christmas party, and it's my job to fix it."

"That is a really big problem," Theo agreed. "Why did she cancel it?"

"I don't know, probably had a run-in with Rosalind and wanted to teach her a lesson." Ellie chewed another mouthful thoughtfully. Irene hadn't got a clue why Vanessa had left, and Rosalind wasn't about to explain anything. Not to mention that solving the mystery wouldn't bring Ellie any closer to fixing the Christmas party.

"Is your new boss a bit of a bitch, then?"

Ellie stirred the cereal around her bowl. Her knee-jerk reaction was to say that she was, but she knew that wasn't fair. She was angry at Rosalind for demoting her, angry at the speech she'd given, angry at the impossible task, but Rosalind hadn't been as awful as Ellie had worried she might be. In fact, Ellie admired Rosalind in some ways. Even if she hated to admit that fact.

It was hard not to be impressed by someone who had built all she had and continued to work with such dedication. Rosalind's work ethic was stunning, and she never expected others to do something she wouldn't do herself. She wasn't the boss Ellie had expected. She was driven, as Ellie had expected, but there were no long, boozy lunches. No power trips, no ego. Ellie had to respect that.

"She seems okay," Ellie said eventually. "It's only been a day. But the problem is, how do I organise a Christmas party in less than fifty days?"

Theo ran his hand through his short curls. "Whoa. Well, sorry to say but I don't think you can, Ellie. These things are usually organised over a year in advance."

Ellie sagged in the seat. She hadn't expected Theo to be able to help, but he had also been her only hope, the only person she knew who might know anything about events planning.

"I can speak to some people at work and see what they say," Theo offered. "They might have some ideas."

"I'd really appreciate that. Otherwise, I'll be throwing a party in the office with some lemonade from Tesco."

Theo laughed. "Having heard you talk about the Caldwell & Atkinson Christmas parties in the past, I think that's going to get you fired if you do that."

Ellie nodded sadly. The parties were out of this world fantastic, and now she was left with nothing but a framework idea from Vanessa and hardly a single useful supplier to help her put it together. She'd phoned a couple of events planners during the day, and they'd all laughed at her when she asked for help, except one who seemed very keen to help, until she realised Ellie meant *this* year and not *next*. And then she'd also laughed.

"No offense, but you look exhausted," he said.

"I am. It's been a really long, really hard day. I don't think I've done a proper day's work in a couple of years. I'd gotten really comfy downstairs, out of everyone's way," Ellie admitted.

"Get some sleep. You'll figure it out. You're the smartest person I know."

"If I don't figure it out, I'll be the smartest unemployed person you know."

"Don't give up yet," Theo told her. "I'll drop you a message tomorrow if any of my contacts have any advice."

"Thanks, Theo." Ellie stood up and trudged out of his room and back downstairs. The sound of Neil and Charlie playing on a games console echoed through the upstairs landing. Matt was probably out playing football with his friends from work. It felt weird that while her workday had been completely turned upside down, home was just as it always was.

She walked into the kitchen and looked around at the mess. She doubted anyone would clean anything up, which would mean there would be no bowls or spoons for breakfast the following morning.

With a resigned sigh, she started to clean the kitchen. She hated herself for doing it, but she hated the thought of doing it in the morning even more.

Chapter Eight

Ellie gripped the handrail in the elevator so tightly that she wondered if she'd bend the metal. If she was going to work on the twenty-second floor for the foreseeable future, then she needed to get used to it fast. Her terror of heights had been with her since she was a child, but she was lucky in that some of the coping mechanisms she'd developed over the years did help.

She'd deliberately gotten into the office early, so she wouldn't have to share the elevator up with anyone. She hadn't been able to sleep much, anyway. At half-past five, she'd given up entirely and decided to go into the office to confront her party problems head-on.

Not that she had a plan for working on the giant Christmas party yet. All she knew was that it was her problem, and she needed to solve it fast.

The elevator doors opened, and Ellie escaped into the hallway as quickly as she could. She knew in her mind that the elevator was safe, but the thought of flying high into the sky with nothing but a few inches of metal beneath her feet made her feel positively sick.

The office was empty. Rosalind, Eric, and Irene were nowhere in sight, and Ellie sighed in relief. It would be nice to have a few moments to calm down and compose herself before the rush started.

She sat down and booted up her computer. While she waited, she opened her Advent calendar and popped a square of chocolate into her mouth.

The silence was a little eerie. She was used to the post room staff getting in before her and arriving to a lively office. Now that she was alone, the only sounds she could hear were the distant whir of the photocopier and the creaking of the building.

Ellie had discovered yesterday that the building creaked. Irene said it was a common occurrence and completely normal. She'd also mentioned that you could feel the building sway ever so slightly in heavy winds, which was, quite frankly, the last thing Ellie needed in her life.

The groaning of a building seemingly struggling to remain stationary had disappeared into the background of the office hubbub during the previous day, but was much clearer on that quiet morning.

"Shut up," she told the building.

She got her phone out of her bag and put in her headphones. While Rosalind wasn't around, she could listen to some music and drown out the sound of the office crumbling around her.

Her playlist of carols sung by the famous King's College Choir filled her ears, and she let out a relieved sigh. Ellie listened to Christmas music all year round. There was enough variety that she didn't get bored, from cheesy pop, to carols, to instrumental. Her friends thought she was mad, but that didn't bother her. If she wanted to enjoy something, she would.

She reached into her bag and got her notepad and pen out. When she sat back up, she was surprised to see a blur of a person hurrying into Rosalind's office, a person who was far too short to be Rosalind, who towered nearly a head above Ellie.

Ellie did a double take and then stood up. "Excuse me!"

She took out her headphones and rushed into Rosalind's office.

A young girl, a teenager, in a school uniform was rummaging around the sofa cushions.

"Um…excuse me?" Ellie repeated.

The girl lifted one of the large back cushions and handed it to Ellie. For some reason, Ellie took it and stood there, assisting in the wilful destruction of Rosalind's office.

"I'm looking for something," the girl said, picking up two other cushions and throwing them to the floor.

"I can see that. You can't be in here," Ellie said.

The girl looked up, and Ellie was suddenly hit by a wave of recognition. She was the spitting image of her boss. This had to be Rosalind's daughter.

"Unless your mum…?" Ellie asked hesitantly.

"I'm Ava. Your boss is my mum." Ava smiled warmly before turning back to continue her demolition. "You're new."

"I am," she agreed. "I'm Ellie. What have you lost?"

"My school pass," Ava replied, crawling on the floor to look under the sofa. "I've been off school for a few days, and I've lost it. I'm sure the last place I had it was in here."

Rosalind walked into the office and eyed Ellie standing there with a large sofa cushion in her hands. Ellie wanted the floor to open up and swallow her.

"Have you found it, sweetness?" Rosalind asked her daughter, ignoring Ellie for the moment.

"Not yet." Ava stood up and started to pull the sofa away from the wall.

Rosalind put her handbag and laptop bag on her desk and levelled a glare at Ellie. "Have you run out of work? Are you reduced to rotating the cushions on my sofa? I don't think interior design is your strength."

Ellie hurriedly put the cushion back. "I'll…um…"

One further glower from Rosalind told her that it was time to leave. She dropped the cushion to the sofa and ducked out of the office as quickly as she could.

❖

Rosalind walked around her desk and closed the door behind her assistant. She wasn't too sure about the new hire yet and wasn't happy about her getting too close to Ava. Not until she had a better idea of her.

She turned to look at her daughter and sighed. Ava was now moving books around in her bookcase, hunting for the missing school security pass.

"Do you really think it jumped up to the middle shelf and wedged itself behind a book on management techniques?" Rosalind asked as she picked up sofa cushions and put them back.

"Maybe," Ava said, desperation clearly setting in.

It was the third pass Ava had lost since the term had started in September. Rosalind didn't mind the cost of applying for a new one each time, but she did mind the tardiness and the suggestion that Ava was disorganised, and that by extension, she was, too.

She ran her hand along the back of the sofa to double-check before looking around the floor area. She knew it was pointless. If it had been left lying around last week, the cleaner would have found it and placed it on her desk. Despite Ava's assurances, it clearly wasn't in the office.

"I'll email the school," Rosalind said. "They'll have a new pass for you by the time you get there."

Ava sagged in disappointment. "Sorry, Mum."

"It's fine. I'm getting used to it. Although I might suggest they tattoo a barcode on your forehead this time." Rosalind sat at her desk and pulled her MacBook out of her bag.

"Can I walk today?" Ava asked.

"Certainly not."

Ava flopped into the visitor chair in front of Rosalind's desk.

Rosalind silently pointed to the hand sanitizer pump. She heard a heartfelt sigh before Ava sat forward and cleaned her hands.

"It's so wasteful for Thomas to drive me there," Ava complained. "It takes less time to walk, too. I only need to go over three footbridges. Thomas needs to take the tunnel."

"Well, then it's a good thing Thomas isn't scared of the dark." Rosalind opened an email and started to write to the school security office.

Ava sighed. "I can't believe you won't let me walk. It would take less than fifteen minutes."

"And I can't believe you think that I'd allow a twelve-year-old to walk to school in the centre of London on her own," Rosalind replied. She looked up. "Unless you want me to get a nanny for you again. Then you can walk, accompanied, of course."

Ava's eyes widened and she shook her head. "Nope. No, thank you."

Rosalind smiled and returned to her email. She was glad that Ava had wanted to ditch her nanny when she turned eleven. Thankfully, her daughter was as independent minded as she was.

With no nanny, they could move out of the house in Surrey and take up an apartment in West India Quay, just minutes from the office. It suited them both perfectly—in the middle of a busy business district, but still with all the amenities a mother and daughter could want. Great schools, plenty of friends who lived locally, fantastic restaurants and cafes. Best of all, Rosalind could get into the office early and leave late and still spend a lot of her time with Ava.

"I'm very mature for my age, you know," Ava added. "You've said so yourself."

"I have," Rosalind agreed. "And I stand by that statement. But it's not you that I'm worried about, sweetness. It's other people. I'm sorry, Ava. I know this seems grossly unfair, but you are just too young to be walking to school on your own. Thomas will take you. That's my final word on the matter."

Ava didn't argue. They'd had the discussion a few times, and Rosalind knew they'd have it a few more before Ava's age and Rosalind's resistance finally met somewhere down the line, and she ultimately gave in.

She sent the email. "There. Go to the security office, and they should have a pass ready for you when you arrive. You better hurry, or you'll be late as well."

"I wouldn't be if I walked," Ava said, standing up and rounding the desk to give her mother a kiss on the cheek.

"Go," Rosalind said. "And give my new PA a wide berth."

Ava rolled her eyes.

"I haven't approved her yet," Rosalind said.

"You worry too much," Ava told her.

"I worry just enough," Rosalind said.

CHAPTER NINE

An email arrived from Theo, and Ellie quickly put down her sandwich to read it. She'd been waiting to hear from him all morning. Somehow, she'd managed to convince herself that he would be able to provide the answer. As she read the email, she began to realise that wasn't going to be the case at all.

Theo was very apologetic, but none of his contacts could think of anything that would help her situation. One suggested she look for new employment now rather than wait to be fired.

Ellie closed the email and sighed. She'd wasted the entire morning waiting to see what Theo would come up with, hoping for a silver bullet. Now her bleak situation looked even worse, and she had no plan B to fall back upon.

She suddenly felt as if she was being watched. She knew it couldn't be Rosalind—she'd gone out over an hour ago and wouldn't be back for a while. She slowly turned around in her chair and saw Eric Atkinson pretending to read a newspaper while peeking over the top at Ellie.

"Hello," he greeted in a very soft voice. "I just wanted to welcome you."

Ellie smiled at him. "Thank you."

Eric Atkinson seemed like a very nice man, quiet and thoughtful and not at all what Ellie had expected from the co-owner of the company. She'd always assumed male executives were brash and egocentric, driving fancy cars and staring suggestively at women. Eric was none of those things. Ellie had only seen him in passing so far but had already made up her mind that he was a thoroughly lovely person.

He took a hesitant step forward. “Would you like some advice?”

His voice had become even softer, and Ellie realised he was trying to avoid Rosalind. “She’s not in,” Ellie told him, thumbing the empty office behind her.

“Oh. Good.” He stepped a little closer, peeking into the office for himself just to be certain.

Ellie thought it adorable how Eric seemed to be afraid of his supposed friend. She’d noticed that the co-owners had more of a sibling relationship rather than just business partners. While Eric was the older of the two, Rosalind most definitely acted like the dictating older sister.

“I’d love some advice,” Ellie added to remind him of the reason for his approach.

He looked around to check they were alone. “Do you have any hand gel?”

“Yep.” Ellie picked up her bag and dug through its contents.

“No, no, not for me,” Eric explained quickly. “Just, maybe, make it visible. In case that kind of thing is important to some people.” He turned to leave, then paused and looked over his shoulder. “Maybe make sure it’s good quality hand gel, too.”

Cryptic information distributed, he rushed back to his office. Ellie looked down at the small bottle of hand gel she had. It was in novelty packaging that resembled a Christmas elf. She removed the elf’s hat and squirted a small amount of gel into her hand and looked at the bottle thoughtfully.

Before she had too much time to consider it, she noticed Will walking across the floor. He had a piece of paper in his hand and was attempting to look like he was simply delivering something.

Ellie knew better. Will never delivered anything to anyone. Will would do anything to not get up from his chair if he had the choice. And there were only four people on the top floor, and Ellie knew for certain that Will had never delivered a single thing to any of them. To save him from his embarrassing attempt at being casual, she leapt up and rushed over to him.

"Hi," he said with a grin, looking around the space nervously. "I've never been up here. Is she here?"

"No, but she might come back. What are you doing here?" Ellie asked.

"I wanted to check you were okay. You cancelled lunch yesterday and didn't reply to my email this morning."

"You sent that twenty minutes ago," Ellie pointed out.

Will nodded. "Yeah, I know. And I heard nothing back from you."

Ellie realised then that twenty minutes on the second floor was completely different to the same period of time in the sky palace where the bosses lived. While just last week she would have replied to an email within twenty seconds of its arrival, now she had only barely noticed an email arriving before the phone rang or a delivery arrived.

Knowing that Eric was around, she grabbed Will's arm and dragged him away from the office space and towards the corridor by the elevators. The only place she could take him to talk in private was the women's bathrooms. Neither Irene nor Rosalind was in the office, so that meant Ellie was the only woman left on the floor.

Will seemed surprised about being dragged into the bathroom but didn't fight it. He stood nervously in the corner and tried to avoid eye contact with everything except Ellie. She wasn't sure what he expected to see in there.

"How are you doing?" he asked.

"It's a nightmare," Ellie told him. She started to pace. "Vanessa, the woman who had the job before me, cancelled the Christmas party."

"What?" Will's eyes widened. "But we're meant to be getting an announcement about it soon. Everyone's looking forward to it."

Ellie levelled a glare at him. "You think *I* don't know that? This is my favourite time of year, remember? I literally hold a party of my own on Christmas Party Announcement Day."

Will nodded. "I remember the little quiches you brought in last year. Spinach and mozzarella."

"Ricotta," Ellie corrected. She shook her head. "That's not

important right now. The important thing is that Rosalind thinks that I'm going to be able to organise the whole thing. I've never organised an event in my life. And the day of the announcement is getting closer and closer, and I can feel the collective held breath of the entire building, and I have nothing to say. Nothing, except, there won't be a party because Vanessa cancelled it."

"There can't *not* be a party," Will said, clearly still shocked at the very idea of such a thing.

"Rosalind's made that clear," Ellie acknowledged, sagging against the sink. "And now Eric is talking to me about hand gel, and I don't know what he means. And Rosalind keeps calling me Christmas Girl."

"Everyone calls you Christmas Girl," Will reminded her.

"I know, but I feel like she's using it to force me into organising a party. As if my Christmas Girl credentials will be revoked if I can't do this. And I *can't* do this." Ellie felt the tears that had been threatening to fall well up in her eyes.

"Hey, you can do this. You can do anything," Will told her gently.

"I can't, Will. I don't know how to organise a massive corporate event like this."

Will folded his arms and looked at her. "Do you remember when we first met?"

Ellie nodded. She'd been a snobby arrival to the company, thinking she was only going to be there temporarily and would soon move on to the job of her dreams. As time went on, she realised she wasn't going anywhere. Will had been friendly and funny, and within a few short days they had struck up a friendship that had held strong ever since.

There had been a little tension at one point when Ellie realised that Will had started to feel a little more than just friendship towards her, but they'd quickly resolved that, eventually becoming the best of friends.

"I'd asked you what a statistician was, and you gave me this really long and really boring reply. And it basically boiled down to someone who collected, analysed, and presented data."

"It's a bit more complicated than that—"

"But that is kinda the root of it?" Will pressed.

"Yes, I guess it is."

"You make sense of a lot of data, right?" Will continued.

"I try to," Ellie agreed.

"This is the same thing. You have a party, well, you *had* a party, and now you don't. You need to start over. So you need to collect the data and look at your options. You do this every day, Ellie. You can do this."

Ellie rolled her eyes. "It's not the same."

"It is," Will insisted. "You need a venue, right?"

"Right."

"So, what's a venue? Analyse it."

Ellie wanted to argue but didn't have the strength. She sighed and considered the question. "Well, a venue is a space where something happens."

"Okay. And how many venues are there in London?" Will asked.

Ellie thought about it for a moment. "There must be thousands. I don't know."

"Guess," Will pressed.

"Well, there are conference rooms, large spaces. I suppose most offices have a large room. And then all the grand buildings have event space—museums, colleges, that kind of thing," Ellie said. "And then there are venues that aren't necessarily venues. Like the arenas used for the Olympics, they've been repurposed. And ice-skating rinks are used for theatre in the summer. And patches of grass that are used for ice-skating rinks in the winter."

Will started to grin. "See? If you break it down into the component pieces and think about it, you know more than you think you do about this. It's like with the reports marketing got you to do. You need to think outside of the box."

"Identifying venues and booking them for a Christmas party are different things," Ellie said.

"I know, but this is where your logic will come in. You'll be able to think of spaces that aren't necessarily venue spaces. Like the skating rink that becomes a theatre, is there a space that we can use? Something that other people might not have thought of? Or can we throw a different kind of party somehow?"

"Or location," Ellie mused. "I don't know, Will. It's just so much to consider."

"Ellie, you see outside the box—you see potential in things. And you love Christmas."

"I do. After all, Rosalind calls me Christmas Girl all the time," Ellie grouched.

"She probably doesn't know your name," Will said.

Realisation struck Ellie. That was maybe true. She squinted. Rosalind couldn't even be bothered to find out her name. Was that how little faith she had in her? Did she not think that Ellie would be around long enough for her to bother? Part of her wondered if Rosalind was right. Maybe Ellie wouldn't see the week out.

"I have to get back to work," she said, realising that she'd been gone for a while and hadn't set her phone to voice mail.

"Yeah, sure. Can we meet up for lunch, or after work one night? So that we can catch up? I miss you," Will said.

"I miss you, too. And sure we can." Ellie opened the bathroom door, and they both exited the female bathroom. "I'll call you, and we'll arrange something."

Will stopped dead in his tracks and stared straight ahead. Ellie followed his gaze and felt a cold chill run up her spine.

Rosalind had stepped out of the elevator and was walking down the corridor, looking at them both with an unreadable expression. It was only then that Ellie realised how terrible it looked to be coming out of the women's bathroom with a man in tow.

"That kind of thing belongs on your own clock, Christmas Girl," Rosalind said as she passed.

Ellie swallowed, not knowing what to say. By the time her brain had caught up with the situation, Rosalind was gone.

"Great," Ellie muttered.

"Does she think we…?" Will asked.

"Yep." Ellie shook her head in despair. Her boss thinking she'd had a quickie in the bathroom was the last thing she needed. She needed Rosalind to consider her a professional. She needed the job, needed the security of the income, needed Rosalind's favours to get her into a statistician job. And now what did Rosalind think of her? Nothing good, that was for certain. She could feel the walls of panic rapidly building within her. She attempted to catch her breath but found she couldn't.

"Ellie?" Will asked.

"I'm sorry, Will," Ellie managed to splutter before making a run for the stairwell and freedom.

Chapter Ten

Ellie had never been so embarrassed in her life. Her boss thought she'd been making out, or worse, with a man in the women's bathrooms on the top floor just a day after she had been supposedly promoted. The mortification was so bad that she had simply run away. The thought of staying for another moment, the idea of Rosalind returning and confronting her, was all too much.

Will knew better than to follow her when she'd made a dash for the stairwell. Now she was out of the building and hurrying through the streets of the city, hoping to somehow escape her humiliation.

The snow had stopped, but the on and off rain hadn't. Ellie winced at the fine, cold mist that was coming down like tiny nails due to the harsh winds. She wished she'd had the forethought to grab her coat, but all she had wanted to do was get away, right then and there. The thought of going back to her desk had made her feel sick. Fight or flight had definitely provided her with only one realistic option: flight.

Flight straight down the stairs and out into the chilly, wet November afternoon.

She pulled her cardigan sleeves down to cover her shaking hands and continued her aimless walk.

"Damn, damn, damn," she muttered.

How would she ever face Rosalind again? Was she supposed to go in there and deny what it so clearly looked like? Was Rosalind already preparing to fire her? She couldn't even imagine making eye contact with Rosalind, never mind trying to explain what had happened.

On top of all that, Rosalind had called her Christmas Girl again. Ellie wondered if that's all she was to the people of Caldwell & Atkinson, just a young woman who liked Christmas so much she decorated her desk year-round.

Did they even know she had a degree in mathematics and another in economics? Did they know that she'd completed a two-year stint at the Royal Statistical Society to become properly accredited?

Her schooling seemed to mean nothing lately, and she had been reduced to someone who really liked Christmas, probably someone who was ridiculed behind her back for that very fact.

Other people could have their football calendars visible on their desks and spend countless thousands on season tickets to matches, and they were simple football fans. Some people took a six-month sabbatical to globe-trot and spiritually find themselves in Tibet. Many of her fellow employees were obsessive about baking and would spend every night and every weekend making all kinds of delicious treats that served no purpose other than to make friends and family eat more cake than was probably healthy.

But none of those people were ever reduced to their interests alone. They weren't Football Fan, Globetrotter, and Cake Baker. They were people.

Yet Ellie was Christmas Girl.

Just because she'd seen a magic in the season that she never wanted to end, the stories of kind gift giving that went back hundreds of years, the traditions that spread around the globe, each unique and special in their own way. Ellie loved it all. She'd met some of her closest friends through activities she took part in at Christmas, from carol singing to ice skating to volunteering at shelters.

Who wouldn't enjoy wrapping up in warm clothes and enjoying bright lights twinkling against a dark sky? Who couldn't smile at the special scents and tastes of the season as coffee shops rediscovered the magic of nutmeg and cinnamon? There were so many different wonderful things about Christmas and the variety of ways people chose to celebrate the season. It wasn't just about presents under a tree and a big fat roasted bird. It was the sense of kind-heartedness and hope that lingered in the cold winter air.

People walked with a little spring in their step, be it from the knowledge of a few days off work, looking forward to seeing family, or because they had just purchased the perfect gift for a loved one.

Christmas had a magic that touched so many people, a magic that Ellie didn't want to cage to just a couple of weeks in December. She wanted to feel that way all year.

She stopped dead as she realised that she'd been losing that feeling lately. She still surrounded herself with decorations and listened to seasonal music, but the feeling had started to fade away. For someone who lived Christmas all year in order to feel that special way, it was a shock to realise that she wasn't on her chosen path any more.

And she was starting to realise why. She was becoming fed up with her life—unsatisfied at work, unhappy at home, and desperately lonely.

Ellie gripped the handrail that separated the walkway from the river and looked into the murky depths of the Thames below her. She'd never known how you could be surrounded by so many people and still feel a deep sense of loneliness, not until she'd come to London. Millions of people lived in the busy city, and she'd never felt more isolated.

Probably her own fault, if she was honest. She'd connected to people in her Christmas groups, but outside of that she never really socialised. She spent her time at work or at home and made little effort to meet up with others unless she was asked directly. Which meant her romantic life had been dead on arrival when she came to London and had remained that way.

Years had passed. Years in a job she didn't enjoy, waiting for the hammer to fall. And years in a house where she was essentially an unpaid maid to four overgrown children. She wasn't happy. She'd been drifting for ages, and she hadn't even realised how unhappy she was.

A strong gust of wind blew, and she shivered. Looking around, she realised she'd walked a lot further than she would have liked. In front of her were large apartment buildings housing local residents, and behind her were skyscrapers containing tens of thousands of employees.

Canary Wharf was a strange place. A former busy port located on the bizarrely named Isle of Dogs, it had been a hectic hub of activity over one hundred years ago, before a decline in shipping had led to the port being closed in the 1980s. Subsequent development had quickly turned Canary Wharf into London's second financial hub, a sea of shiny high-rise buildings and skyscrapers, all crammed onto the small pieces of land in between the various docks, quays, and basins, and surrounded on three sides by the Thames.

Ellie adored how old and new mixed so seamlessly. Cutting-edge design rubbed shoulders with original metal cranes that had once heaved cargo from ships. Old red brick warehouses were now luxury apartments, and the race to build more and more continued all the time.

She looked across the water at the dockside restaurants and their Christmas decorations. The fairy lights twinkled in the water below, a feat, considering just how muddy the Thames was. She watched a young girl skipping with her father, both carrying bags of gifts. The girl, no older than six, wore a princess dress, and her father had a woollen sweater with Santa's face knitted onto it. They were the perfect picture of the season, and Ellie smiled.

She shivered again and sighed as the rain started to increase.

She turned from the riverside and made her way towards a nearby tree for shelter. Watching the rain fall, she realised she had to make changes. If she wasn't happy, then it was up to her to do whatever she could to change her life. Only she had the power to do that, and she was more powerful than she sometimes allowed herself to think.

Her father had always called her bloody-minded, while her mother said she was strong-willed. But Ellie felt as if she had lost some of that fire recently after so many knock-backs. Studying for years to become something and then finding you couldn't get a job was hard. Thinking you were so overly qualified for every job you saw advertised that you'd be snapped up only to be turned down was a bitter pill to swallow. And staying in a job that gave her no enjoyment had sucked the life force out of her.

She chuckled bitterly to herself. She ought to thank Rosalind for turfing her out of her comfortable life and waking her up again. Rosalind probably didn't know Ellie's name, and Ellie couldn't blame her. It wasn't as if Ellie had ever done anything to make herself stand out and be memorable.

She'd spent her working day slumped in her chair, hoping to remain invisible, which now seemed like a ludicrous thing to do, considering she worked for a top recruitment agency and they would surely be able to help her get to where she wanted to be in life.

"What have you been doing?" she murmured to herself as she watched the rain rushing towards a nearby drain.

She'd lost her fight, but that didn't mean it was gone forever. She was strong-willed, she was bloody-minded, and she was Christmas Girl. Will and Theo were right—she had the brainpower to dream up a solution to the party issue. And when she did, Rosalind would know her name, and Ellie might just be able to leverage her gratitude to help her get on the right career path.

She could do this. It would just require some creative thinking. A smile crept across her face as she realised that she was in the process of creating her very own Christmas miracle.

Chapter Eleven

Rosalind noted that her assistant didn't return to her desk after the incident in the hallway. The phone had not been sent through to voice mail, which led Rosalind to assume that she had left her desk unexpectedly. After fifteen minutes had passed, and four phone calls had interrupted her, Rosalind stalked out of her office and put her PA's line through to the voice mail service.

"She was heading out when I came in," Irene spoke up. "Didn't have a coat so I doubt she'll be out for very long in this weather."

Rosalind looked around the desk and saw that all her assistant's belongings were still there. It didn't look like she had walked out, but Rosalind knew that many people did just that. Working in recruitment for the last decade, she knew all too well the startling number of people who walked away from their positions without a single word to their employer.

"We'll see," she said to Irene before returning to her office.

Whether or not she would return remained to be seen. However, worrying about it wouldn't change anything, and so Rosalind knew she would have to wait and see what happened. Either she would send someone for her belongings, come and get them herself, or return to work as if nothing had happened.

Rosalind didn't know which. She was still trying to figure Christmas Girl out. Rosalind took great pride in being able to work people out in a short period of time—it was one of the requirements of working in recruitment. This new assistant had been trickier than most. She was apprehensive, yet efficient in her work. Rosalind couldn't yet tell what lurked beneath the shy exterior, but she was intrigued.

In fact, that mystery had occupied much of her mind, and she found herself distractedly wondering what made Christmas Girl tick.

Her phone rumbled gently from its holder on the desk. She picked it up and smiled at the text from Ava informing her that she was alive and well. Of course, she would be ridiculed later for overreacting and requesting that Ava keep her updated throughout the day, but Rosalind couldn't help but be worried about her only daughter's first day back at school after being off sick.

Thankfully, Ava was understanding of her mother's overprotective nature, though not enough to agree to the private home tutor that Rosalind had suggested on more than one occasion. Ava had put her foot down emphatically at that idea. Rosalind couldn't blame her. She would have been the same at her age if her situation had been the same. But as a mother, she couldn't help but worry.

No matter how worried she became, she had to remind herself that keeping Ava caged wasn't practical, and more importantly, it wasn't fair.

She typed a quick response, thanking Ava for checking in, wishing her well for the last lessons of the day, and asking she check in once more when she got home. She was aware that it was more ammunition for Ava to mock her with later, but Rosalind didn't care. She'd happily be mocked for her overprotective nature if it meant Ava kept her updated.

She pulled her MacBook close and started replying to emails and finishing up a few reports she had been working on for a board meeting the following week.

After quite some time, she looked up and noticed her PA had finally returned. She looked soaked through to the skin but walked with a purposeful and determined step that had been absent before. Rosalind watched through the glass partition as Christmas Girl sat down and got back to work as if nothing had happened.

Rosalind glanced at her watch. Ninety minutes had passed since the hallway incident. She sucked in her cheek and regarded her assistant's back as she decided what to do. After a few moments she decided that no action was best for now. Time would tell.

❖

The rest of Rosalind's afternoon passed as any other would. Phone calls, meetings, emails. The only difference was an unspoken agreement in the air that she wasn't going to communicate with her assistant, not because she was punishing her, but because there was an unwavering determination radiating from her as she flipped through Vanessa's party planning information and made a flurry of phone calls. Rosalind was intrigued as to where the change in dynamic had come from. Yesterday, her assistant was quiet and meek, and today she was working with a sense of urgency Rosalind had rarely seen in an assistant before.

She knew Christmas Girl—she really did need to get her name—would talk to her when she needed to, and so Rosalind got on with her day and waited to see what would happen. There would be no point in interrupting the flow of energy before there was something to actually talk about.

It was half-past five when a tentative knock sounded on her open office door. Rosalind looked up from her desk diary. It seemed the time had finally come.

"Come in," she said to her frazzled-looking assistant. Her hair had never really recovered from the rain she had clearly spent half the afternoon walking through. Rosalind couldn't help but think it looked cute, especially with the determined look that accompanied it.

She entered and stood in the middle of the room, a fair distance from Rosalind's desk, just as she had done the day before.

"Nothing happened in the bathroom. We were just talking," she explained.

Rosalind lowered her pen and removed her glasses. She attempted to keep a straight face as she nodded.

"We weren't...doing anything, if that's what you were thinking," she carried on.

"Very well," Rosalind replied. She hadn't honestly thought that the timid little thing would really be getting frisky with the archive clerk in the executive bathroom, but it had been amusing to see the sheer panic on their faces. "Anything else?"

"We can't have the venue we had booked. It's just impossible."

"The invitations went out in October," Rosalind replied. "It would be costly and embarrassing to have to reprint so close to the day."

"Then it's going to have to be costly and embarrassing, or all your guests will end up going to someone else's party, which would probably be more embarrassing."

Rosalind raised an eyebrow and leaned into her high-backed chair. She hadn't expected such fight from the retiring little mouse. It seemed she was discovering another side to her new assistant.

"I've found another venue, which is nothing short of a miracle, by the way, considering the last-minute change."

"I don't want a new venue—I want the one I approved." Rosalind dug her heels in. She knew it was probably impossible, but if any amount of pressure would make it happen, then she was willing to exert that pressure. Reprinting the invitations and having to explain the change to the stakeholders was not something she was relishing.

"You don't have much choice. It's this or nothing."

It took all Rosalind had to hide her smirk. It had been a while since someone was brave enough to stand toe to toe with her.

"But you're Christmas Girl, can't you just sprinkle some fairy dust and make it happen?" Rosalind asked, just to test the waters to see what would happen. Despite the serious conversation, it was fun to verbally joust with this one.

Rosalind saw her clench her jaw and awaited news of how brave her new assistant could be when pressed.

"Do you even know my name?" she demanded.

As if sent from heaven itself, Ava chose that moment to stroll into her mother's office. "Hey Mum, oh, hi Ellie." Ava tossed her schoolbag onto the sofa.

"Of course I do, Ellie," Rosalind replied with an enormous grin. She really couldn't have planned it any better.

Ellie rolled her eyes and turned away from Rosalind to focus her attention on her daughter. "Hey Ava, did you find your pass?"

Ava shook her head, reached into the pocket of her school blazer, and produced a fresh card. "No, I needed to get another new one. The security manager is getting to know me—it's embarrassing."

"I have something that might help with that, one second." Ellie left the office, leaving Ava and Rosalind to share an equally confused look.

A moment later, Ellie returned with something in her hand. Rosalind's mouth ran dry with nerves. She was about to intervene when she noticed that whatever Ellie held was wrapped up in clear plastic packaging that she'd ripped and held open for Ava to take whatever was inside. She swallowed down the panic, realising that contamination was unlikely.

Ava took the item and grinned. "Oh, cool, how did you know?"

"I saw a *Moana* sticker on your mum's laptop bag and assumed it was probably yours and not hers," Ellie admitted.

"What is it, sweetness?" Rosalind asked, eager to be brought back into the loop.

Ava held up a lanyard. The strap was adorned with all the characters from Ava's favourite Disney movie, *Moana*. Ava clipped her pass into the plastic holder and put the lanyard around her neck.

"Cool, I'm never taking it off." Ava looked down at the lanyard with glee.

"Well, then, you won't lose your pass again," Ellie said with a chuckle.

"What do you say?" Rosalind prompted.

"Thanks, Ellie." Ava turned to face her mother, and Rosalind saw the face of someone who was about to ask for something. "Mum…"

"Yes?"

"Can I go downstairs to Hive with friends until you're finished with work?"

Rosalind sucked in a breath and reminded herself that she had approved Hive as one of the coffee shops she was happy for Ava to go to. It was in the building, which meant the security guards in reception knew her and would keep an eye on her. They had a good cleanliness record, and Ava had begged and pleaded for it to be added to the approved list, so she wouldn't have to spend time hanging around the office waiting for her mother to finish work.

"With?" Rosalind asked.

"Adam, Katie, and Edith."

Rosalind tapped her finger on the edge of the armrest a few times as she considered it. When she was Ava's age, she often went and did things without even telling her parents, never mind asking for permission. And Ava had humoured her for her overprotectiveness and kept her informed of her progress throughout the day.

"Very well, but keep an eye on the time. You know the mobile signal is patchy down there at times, and I don't want to have to come and get you. Meet me in reception at six thirty sharp."

Ava jumped with glee and grabbed her bag.

"Do *not* be late," Rosalind told her again.

"I won't. Thanks, Mum, you're the best," Ava called over her shoulder as she left.

Rosalind smiled and shook her head.

"Sorry if I overstepped," Ellie said, "about the lanyard. I just thought it would be useful. I was forever losing my pass at university, and once I physically tied it around my neck, it wasn't a problem any more. And I made sure the packaging was clean. I assume there's a reason there's hand sanitiser everywhere."

Rosalind glanced at the pump of industrial-strength sanitiser that sat on her desk. She rarely felt comfortable talking to people, especially strangers, about Ava's condition. It gave the situation a realness that she attempted to avoid on a day-to-day basis.

"Her immune system is compromised, her white blood cells..." Rosalind was not ready to have the conversation.

"Okay, I'll make sure to keep everything clean, and I'll keep away if I have a cold or anything," Ellie said.

Rosalind felt a rush of gratitude. Trying to explain the situation with her daughter was so often exhausting. People just couldn't seem to grasp why they had to clean everything before Ava touched it, and sometimes things got missed. An act as simple as handing over a bottle of water could end with Ava being hospitalised. But the average person didn't have to worry about such things, which meant Rosalind felt she had to worry on their behalf.

That was the straw that had broken the camel's back with Vanessa. Rosalind just couldn't shake the feeling that Ava's last bout of illness and Vanessa's vague reassurance that the book she'd bought for her had been introduced to an antibacterial wipe were connected.

"The new venue is New Providence Wharf," Ellie said, moving on swiftly as if detecting her boss didn't want to talk of Ava's health a moment longer than necessary.

Rosalind furrowed her brow and tried to place it. "I know that name."

"It's in between the Blackwall Tunnel and Blackwall station," Ellie explained.

"Oh, the new development of apartments," Rosalind asked, "shaped in a crescent?"

"That's the one."

"I didn't know they had an events space."

"They don't."

Rosalind stared at Ellie, waiting for an explanation. Ellie sucked in a deep breath.

"We're using the roof," Ellie said.

"The roof?"

"Yes. They have a really large rooftop garden. It's very pretty, spread over the whole roof so it's huge, easily accessible by four direct elevators, and it's available."

"You want us to have a Christmas party, in December, on a roof…ten floors—"

"Eighteen."

"*Eighteen* floors above the ground and adjacent to the river?" Rosalind questioned.

"Yes."

"Are you mad?"

"No. I'm going to make it work. Yes, some of the party will be outside, but I'll make it work. Actually, most of it will be outside, but there will be inside elements. I can't explain right now. You'll see. Don't worry—I can do this."

Rosalind couldn't help but stare at Ellie and wonder if she had lost the plot. No one in their right mind would consider having a party outside in London in the winter, not even in October, never mind December. Not only that, but Ellie was also suggesting having it on a roof, of all places. Rosalind just couldn't picture how it would work.

"It will be the best party Caldwell & Atkinson have ever hosted. It will be safe, it will be comfortable, it will be memorable," Ellie said with conviction.

"And why should I trust you to deliver all of that?" Rosalind asked.

"Because I'm Christmas Girl," Ellie said simply, turning on her heel to leave the office. She paused in the doorway. "And you have no other options," she added before continuing to her desk.

Chapter Twelve

Ellie left the pub with a deep sense of satisfaction. It had taken some convincing, but the head chef had agreed to provide the food for the Caldwell & Atkinson Christmas party. It had been a week and a half since she'd taken on her new role, and a week since she'd made the decision to do everything in her power to make the Christmas party not only happen, but be the absolute best it could be.

Never did she imagine that would involve calling up every single bar, pub, and restaurant in the Canary Wharf district and asking if they would even consider the idea of catering an external event.

While Ellie thought it a logical progression for a venue with a kitchen to make extra food, none of the phone calls she had made had been met with any enthusiasm, even when she waved Rosalind's ridiculously large chequebook at them. Anyone who would consider such an endeavour had been booked up long ago.

Finally, Ellie had stumbled upon a reputable gastropub just ten minutes away from the office. She hadn't noticed it at first as it was relatively new and hadn't come up on any of her online searches. It was only when she offered to get Rosalind's lunch earlier in the week and was directed to a Turkish cafe near West India Quay did she see the pub and decide to pop in.

Two phone calls, three emails, and a meeting later and she finally had a caterer for her party. Food and location were the two top things that Ellie had been panicked about, and now she had them both booked in. It didn't sound great to say she was booking a party onto a roof and having it catered by a recently opened pub, but Ellie put that thought to one side.

Especially the roof bit. This was the first Caldwell & Atkinson Christmas party that she knew she wouldn't be able to attend, and she was organising it.

It had been either a moment of madness or a leap of brilliance, she wasn't entirely sure which yet. After her long walk in the rain, she'd returned to her desk and started to make a long list of every space that could technically host a group of people but wasn't considered a venue. It was just her terrible luck that of all the ridiculous places she came up with, the roof of the New Providence Wharf building was the one that was available.

The building manager had asked her to clarify several times that she meant to have the event in December and had warned her of the cold winds that often came in from the river. Once Ellie had explained her plans for a variety of gazebo-type structures and asked if they could be secured, he seemed to understand what she was planning. An hour later, he confirmed the booking and the ability to fix large, temporary structures to parts of the roof.

Now Ellie just needed to pray for good weather. While she would have some cover, it wouldn't be enough to shelter the entire guest list during a downpour of rain. For the first time in her life, she was praying that the weather would be bright and clear in the run-up to Christmas.

There wasn't any point worrying about the weather now. She'd do all she could and cross her fingers on the day. Right now, she was just relieved to have the food and drink ticked off her list.

She walked through the shopping centre to return to the office but paused when she saw a familiar face. Ava sat at a window seat of a dessert shop, staring forlornly into an ice cream sundae.

Ellie bit her lip and looked from Ava to the route back to the office. While Ellie knew that some PAs' roles blended work and home, Rosalind had never done so. Ellie didn't get Rosalind's dry cleaning, she rarely got her lunch, and she didn't even know where she lived. Ellie saw Ava now and then and said hello, but beyond that, she hardly knew the girl.

She glanced at her watch and saw it was after school hours and wondered if Rosalind even knew that Ava was in the shopping centre. Unlikely, she thought. It wouldn't be right to leave the miserable-looking pre-teen on her own, she decided. She sucked in a deep breath and entered the shop.

"Hey," she said.

Ava lit up upon seeing Ellie. "Hey, what are you doing here?" Her face fell in panic. "Is Mum here?"

Ellie shook her head and pulled up a seat at the bar next to Ava. "Nope. She's in the office. I was on my way back from a meeting. The real question is, what are *you* doing here?"

"I sometimes come here to get a snack before I go home for my piano lesson on Wednesdays," Ava explained.

"Does your mother know?" Ellie asked. "Or is it our little secret?"

Ava smiled a little. "Can it be our little secret?"

Ellie nodded. "Absolutely. Just, you know, be careful."

"I'm always careful." Ava sat up a little straighter. "People think I'm a little kid, but I'm not."

"I don't think you're a little kid," Ellie replied. She gestured to the waitress who was passing and ordered a coffee. "But you do need to be careful. This is a very busy place, and there's a lot of people hanging around—not all of them can be trusted. I was mugged six months ago, walking through this shopping centre."

Ava's mouth dropped open. "Here?"

Ellie nodded and pointed out of the window. "Up there, by the mobile florist stand. Middle of rush hour, this guy snatched my phone and pushed me to the floor. There were loads of people around, but it happened so fast that he got away. So, you know, you have to be careful."

Ava seemed to digest the story and nodded to herself before continuing to take another bite of her sundae.

"So, what's up?" Ellie asked, pushing aside the unsavoury memories of the theft.

"Nothing," Ava said.

"Try again. You look like someone cancelled Christmas, and you're eating the biggest sundae they serve."

Ava looked up at her shyly. "I'm kinda dealing with something."

Ellie tried to maintain her smile while she shifted a little uncomfortably in her seat. She wasn't the best person for anyone to confide in. Her advice-giving skills were mediocre at best. And this was her boss's daughter—was she crossing a line? The last thing she wanted to do was drive a wedge between the new relationship she was developing with her boss. Since Ellie had grown a backbone and started to answer back to Rosalind, things had been going really well. The aloof ice queen persona had quickly slipped away, and Ellie was now seeing the real Rosalind, the one who was a woman and not just a corporate genius. Ellie had been allowed a glimpse of Rosalind as a person, an individual with unique idiosyncrasies that fascinated her. It was as if she'd been allowed into the inner circle, a peek behind the curtain. She imagined that very few people had the opportunity to know the Rosalind she was privileged enough to see. She didn't want to put that at risk. Then again, Ava looked like she needed a friend.

"I'm a good listener," Ellie said. "If you want to, no pressure."

The waitress placed a coffee in front of Ellie, and she mindlessly stirred it while Ava decided what she wanted to do.

"It's just, I'm worried about what my mum will say about something. We're really close, and I don't want to ruin that," Ava said, her attention on her ice cream.

"Well, I don't know your mum very well," Ellie admitted. "But she seems to be fair and open-minded. And she adores you—that always helps."

"Yeah, I know. It's just hard sometimes. To tell people stuff, you know?"

Ellie's mind raced about what it could possibly be that was weighing so heavily on Ava's mind. She wondered if she should leave it be, wait for Ava to approach her, or gently coax the subject from her. It was a hard situation to be in.

On the other hand, she did know that Rosalind would unapologetically rip Ellie's head clean from her shoulders if she upset Ava. Or if she later found out that Ellie had been aware of something that blew up into a real problem.

Ellie's mind flashed through some unlikely, though horrifying, scenarios and she knew she couldn't leave it be.

"You can tell me, if you'd like," Ellie said. "I promise it will stay between us. I might be able to give you some advice."

Ava kept her head tucked down as she whispered, "I think I'm gay."

Ellie nearly sighed in relief that it wasn't drugs, depression, or—worse—a boy.

"Why do you think that?" Ellie asked, sipping at her coffee.

"There's a girl in school, I think I like her. But before that, I thought I might be gay. Mum won't like it."

Ellie pushed down the anger that welled up within her. She couldn't believe in this day and age that some people were still homophobic, especially someone as forward-thinking as Rosalind Caldwell. Not to mention how hypocritical the CEO was, considering Ellie knew the company frequently donated to many LGBTQ organisations.

She bristled in her seat at the very thought that Ava worried that she couldn't count on Rosalind's support.

"Well, then your mum will just have to learn to like it," Ellie said. "She adores you, and she'll learn to accept it, I'm sure. And if you need someone to talk to her about it, then I'll happily do that. No one should feel embarrassed about coming out. It's hard enough as it is without having to worry about the people you really should be able to rely on, through thick and thin. Honestly, I'll speak to her if you want me to. Or I can be there when you tell her, if you like. Whatever you need."

Ava's eyes widened at Ellie's speech. "Oh no. No, I don't think that she won't accept me," Ava explained. "It's just that I know Mum worries about me copying her. When I said I wanted to go into recruitment, she said that I should wait until I'm older and see how I feel about it then. When I said I didn't want to get married, she said I should wait and see if I meet someone when I'm older. She doesn't want to think I'm copying her."

Ellie felt her brows knit together as she attempted to process what she was hearing. Her thought process felt sluggish as she tried to pull all the data together.

"Your mum is gay?" Ellie asked, feeling like a fool for even asking the question.

"Yeah," Ava replied, thankfully too distracted by an escaping stream of chocolate sauce from her ice cream sundae to catch the confusion in Ellie's tone. "And if I tell her that I think I'm gay, she'll probably think I'm just copying her."

Ellie had never had anyone adore her so much that they would copy everything she did, but she had been on the other side of the coin. She had done everything she could to fit in with her two best friends at school, trying to match their cool behaviour no matter the cost. She'd changed her hair, make-up, clothing, and even the way she walked to fit in with the two girls.

Looking back, it was embarrassing. But it had taught her some valuable lessons. Lessons that she hoped would now help the next generation.

"Can I be honest with you?" Ellie asked.

Ava nodded. "Sure."

"Everyone changes as they grow older," Ellie said. "Sometimes it's a little change, sometimes it's their entire personality. My best friend in the world literally turned into another person while she was in university—her sexuality, her politics, everything about her. It was as if she'd had her eyes opened to the world around her and discovered who she really was."

Ellie took a sip of coffee, remembering her former best friend's dramatic transformation. Every time they'd met up, they were further apart. It had been a bitter pill to swallow, but Ellie knew it was for the best in the long run.

"Sometimes people hardly change at all," Ellie continued. "I have another friend who knew what she wanted to do for a career when she was five. She said to her mum that she was going to be a librarian. She's thirty-two now and has been a librarian for years, will probably be one her entire life."

Ellie turned to face Ava, who was looking at her curiously, obviously wondering what her point was.

"The thing is, we don't know how much people will change, and so we tell them not to lock themselves down. Because we've all done it. We've all said that we feel one way, to find out a year later that we feel the exact opposite. That might be about a pop band or about something as important as your sexuality. I don't know your mum very well yet, but I bet she's only saying those things because she wants to give you an exit strategy if you change your mind. Maybe your mum changed a lot from when she was your age to now, and she wants you to be comfortable doing the same. Thing is, I think you should tell her. Especially if it's something as big as this. She'll be supportive and may be able to help you and guide you. And if she does say that you might change your mind, then that's just because she loves you and wants you to have that freedom. It's not because she wants you to be wrong and her to be right. Does that make sense?"

Ava quickly nodded and threw her arms around Ellie's neck. "Thank you, Ellie. That's really helped." She sat back and kept nodding, processing the words.

Ellie couldn't help but feel pleased with herself. It wasn't always the case that her advice hit the spot. And really, she had no idea if this advice had either, but it felt right, and Ava seemed a lot happier for having heard what Ellie had said.

"You're right. Mum just doesn't want me to sleepwalk into copying her," Ava said. "I really do want to be like her, but I'm not gay because she is. I'm sure of that."

"Then tell her. If she doesn't listen right away, it's just because she cares, and she's trying to protect you." Ellie finished her coffee. "Do you have any friends who are younger than you?"

Ava frowned at the question. "Um, yeah, I guess, a few."

"Do they ever say things that make you roll your eyes? Like they haven't quite matured as much as you have?"

Ava chuckled. "Yeah, all the time."

"Well, people older than you will do that to you for the *rest of your life*. And people older than your mum will do it to your mum. There's something about humans—we feel like we become wiser as we become older. We look back on people who are younger than us and roll our eyes at the mistakes they're making, because we've already made them." Ellie gathered her things and stood up. "The sooner you learn that people are only doing it because they care and are trying to stop you making the mistakes they made, the better all round."

"You're really smart," Ava said with a lopsided grin.

"Tell your mum," Ellie said. "I have to get back to the office. Are you going to be okay?"

"I am now, thanks, Ellie." Ava smiled and picked up her sundae spoon to finish her treat. Ellie gave her a final once-over to assure herself that she was fine before leaving. On her way back to the office, she hoped she'd done the right thing by getting involved. She supposed that time would tell.

CHAPTER THIRTEEN

Rosalind could sense Eric entering her office. She looked up and saw that he held a piece of paper in his hand and wore a confused expression on his face.

"Ros?" he said without looking up, his attention entirely on the piece of paper.

"Yes?" Rosalind replied, putting her pen down and giving him her full attention.

"I just had the new invitation proof through to be approved, but I can't find the address on a map. Well, I can, but they don't have an event space. Is this right?" Eric turned the piece of paper around for her to look at.

Rosalind let out a small sigh and took the piece of paper. She glanced over the details and nodded. "Yes, that's all in order. It's not an event space as such."

"Not an event space?"

"No." She purposefully didn't explain, hoping to not have the conversation right then. She'd neglected to mention the finer points of Ellie's Christmas party plans to Eric in lieu of simply telling him that everything was going ahead with no issues.

"Then…what is it?"

"A roof."

Eric blinked. "Come again?"

"The roof. Apparently they have a very nice rooftop garden. Very large, and apparently very suitable for us." Rosalind handed him back the invitation proof. She hoped but sincerely doubted that would be the end of the conversation.

He stared at her, not taking the invite back. "The roof."

"Yes." She waved the piece of paper until he took it out of her hand.

"But…that will be…the roof. In December. What about the cold? And rain? It's bound to rain." Eric looked at Rosalind as if she had completely lost her mind and he was worried about his business and livelihood. She couldn't blame him. If their positions were reversed, then she would have been just as concerned, but not nearly as calm.

"Ellie says to trust her," Rosalind said.

"And do you?"

Rosalind nodded. "I do."

Eric's mouth opened and closed a few times before he shook his head in despair and left the office.

Of course she had her own concerns about the party arrangements—she'd be foolish not to. But she'd stuck her head in the proverbial sand and ignored everything in the hope that it would all be okay. Ellie seemed to be getting on with everything and didn't seem too worried, which had soothed Rosalind's own concerns a little. For some reason, Ellie's calm determination had pacified Rosalind and prevented her from asking too many questions about the questionable decision to hold a Christmas party on a roof.

But now that Eric had highlighted his own anxieties, she couldn't ignore that niggling feeling at the back of her head any longer. There was the possibility that Ellie was calm because she didn't know any better or because she simply didn't care if everything went wrong.

Maybe Rosalind had been wrong to trust Ellie with such a large job. She might be obsessed with Christmas, but she didn't seem to have any event-planning experience. Rosalind's heart started to pound against her ribcage as panic started to rise within her.

Ignoring an incoming disaster was always preferable to actually dealing with it, but now she was thinking that maybe she should have asked a few more questions rather than just overlooking the potential catastrophe on the horizon.

She waited a few moments to be sure that Eric had returned to his office. Once she was certain that he was out of earshot, she called to Ellie. A few moments later, Ellie stood in her traditional spot in the middle of the room, notepad at the ready.

"I've been thinking about the party on the roof," Rosalind said. "What about the cold weather? Or rain? Surely we're not counting on an unseasonably warm winter's evening."

Ellie lowered her notepad upon realising it wasn't that kind of conversation.

"There will be plenty of shelter, and there will be windbreaks and patio heaters," Ellie explained.

Rosalind blinked. "Windbreaks and patio heaters, on a roof." It had been a long time since she'd ignored a problem and hoped it would go away, but it seemed the trait was back, and she didn't like it in herself. It was time to get more involved and see what Ellie was planning. She couldn't just ignore the truth any more. They were walking blindfolded into an unmitigated disaster.

She'd become relaxed with Ellie's presence in the office and the way she had managed to quickly slip into her new role. After a shaky couple of days at the start, Ellie had blossomed into a perfect assistant.

In many ways, she was much more than an assistant. She was intelligent, astute, and willing to go the extra mile. Things ran like clockwork, often before Rosalind even needed to say a word about what was coming up next on the schedule. Her office had become calmer since Ellie's arrival, and Rosalind looked forward to seeing Ellie's cheerful face, expressive eyes, and lopsided grin when she arrived for work in the morning. They worked well together, a magical formula she wished she could bottle.

But now she wondered if she'd allowed Ellie a little too much independence and was now risking the event of the year.

Ellie held up a finger to indicate Rosalind should wait a moment. She dashed from the office and reappeared with a large notebook that was stuffed with pieces of paper.

"So, I did the calculations. The average temperature that time of year is three degrees at night—for safety, I'm going to predict just one degree. The wind speed is roughly twelve miles per hour, and obviously that increases when you're above the ground. I've calculated for the height, the lack of taller buildings around, and the usual wind direction coming from the river that will make it feel colder. Because, obviously, wind chill and actual temperature are different things."

Rosalind slowly removed her glasses as Ellie read from her notes.

"I mean, we're lucky that the jet stream has moved a little further north, but I'm calculating for it returning, just in case," Ellie continued, flipping through pieces of paper. "New Providence Wharf faces south, and it slants at around ten degrees and has multiple levels. But you have to factor in that we're on top of all those apartments. Heated apartments. Even at fifty per cent occupancy, you can calculate for a certain amount of warmth coming up. Because, obviously, heat rises."

Rosalind couldn't believe what she was hearing. It appeared that Ellie had performed complicated mathematical equations to calculate the temperature on the roof of a specific building in the middle of December.

Ellie pulled out a sheet of folded paper and placed it on Rosalind's desk.

"Here's a map of London—sorry, I've drawn all over it, but it will make sense when I explain. Here"—she pointed—"is New Providence Wharf, and you can see that here"—she indicated some arrows she'd drawn—"is the wind direction. These two towers"—more pointing—"will give the space some protection from the majority of the wind, but clearly, wind will go around the towers making four wind streams, so I'll be adding more heaters in the locations I've highlighted in green."

Ellie continued to talk, not noticing that Rosalind had stopped listening and was instead staring up at her in shock. Ellie spoke with such intellect and passion about the weight of the various gazebos she was planning to erect and the methods that would be used to ensure they were weighted down, before moving on to large, themed windbreakers that would easily deflect the worst of the gales from the partygoers.

She'd thought of everything, and Rosalind simply couldn't believe her ears. The level of detail was staggering and not far removed from what she imagined would be required for a mission to space. Complex calculations were jotted down on the map, from temperature, to windspeed, to weight distribution. Ellie had thought of everything on a scientific level.

Rosalind wanted to jump up and call Eric back into the office and show him that her faith in Ellie wasn't misplaced. But the truth was that she'd had no idea that Ellie was this well-prepared. She'd just avoided talking about any details of the whole party situation and had hoped that Ellie would be able to fix her mistake in driving Vanessa away. The fact that Ellie *was* able to fix things was sheer dumb luck and nothing that Rosalind would have the gall to boast about.

"Ellie." She placed her hand atop Ellie's as she was gesturing towards the positioning of patio heater number seven.

Ellie stopped talking and looked down at Rosalind with wild, tired eyes. It was the first time Rosalind had actually stopped to look at her, and she was surprised to notice just how exhausted Ellie looked. She supposed she couldn't blame her—she wasn't just organising the impossible party, she was calculating whether a client's complicated hairdo might be affected by winds if the windbreaker was five foot eight rather than the full six feet. Rosalind removed her hand and gestured for Ellie to take a seat.

Once Ellie was sitting, Rosalind carefully folded up the map.

"Ellie, I had no idea you'd gone to this much detail. You're clearly massively overqualified to be working as my assistant, something I'd been mildly aware of, which is now hitting me with quite the force of realisation."

Panic sparked in Ellie's eyes, and Rosalind chuckled. "Don't worry—I'm not firing you. I just hadn't realised that we had a genius in the building. Your talents are wasted here. But I'll happily use them while you're here. I'd be a fool not to." She handed the map back to Ellie. "Excellent work."

"Thank you," Ellie replied softly.

"Don't burn out," Rosalind told her seriously. "If you need help, let me know, and I can draft someone in to assist."

Ellie looked surprised but nodded her understanding. "Okay, I'll let you know."

Rosalind's phone rang, and she knew it was an important call she'd been expecting. Ellie seemed to sense the same and got to her feet and started to leave.

"Ellie?" Rosalind called after her.

She stopped and turned around.

"Why don't you head home a little early today. It's Friday, and there's only another hour left. Get some rest, and have a nice weekend. You deserve it."

Ellie's face lit up with gratitude. "Thank you, I appreciate that."

Rosalind watched her go, surprised that she hadn't seen the extraordinary depths sooner. She wondered if she'd lost her edge at spotting talent.

Chapter Fourteen

Ellie closed her eyes and allowed the sounds of her favourite choral ensemble to wash over her. She'd never been religious, but the sound of a choir singing carols caused the hairs on the back of her neck to stand to attention. There was something so other-worldly in the style of music. And something so undeniably Christmas.

She knew she drove her housemates mad by constantly listening to Christmas tracks on repeat in her room. But she didn't care. While she would never leave laundry lying around, the kitchen in a mess, or be late with her rent, she would play her music loud and often.

No one said anything. Which was good because none of the boys had a leg to stand on. The boys acted like animals in a zoo for the most part.

A knock on her closed bedroom door had her opening her eyes and letting out a sigh. It was Saturday afternoon, and she'd slept most of the day away and had only been out of her room for supplies to keep her going through lunch. Never did she think organising a party, or being a PA, would require quite so much hard work.

"Come in," she called out.

Theo poked his head around the door. "Hey, got a minute?"

Ellie dragged her laptop closer to her cross-legged position on the floor, lowered the volume of the music, and nodded. "Sure, come in."

Theo entered the room, closed the door behind him, and took a seat in the chair at Ellie's desk, considering she was sitting on the floor. "I was just wondering how the party stuff was going. We didn't really talk about it again," he said, picking up a Funko figure from Ellie's desk and looking at it.

"It's...well, there will be a party," she said. "Whether or not it will be any good, who can say? It's going to be interesting, that's for sure." Ellie looked down at her laptop, her screen showing the bulk order of large cardboard sheets, glue, and spray paint she was about to purchase with her company credit card.

"You found a venue?" he asked, putting the figure down and picking up a Christmas elf stuffed doll.

"Kinda."

He looked at her and frowned. "What do you mean, kinda?"

"It's going to be on a roof," Ellie said.

Theo laughed. "A roof? Are you mad?"

"Maybe. There's a good chance that I lost my mind when Rosalind promoted demoted me," Ellie said. "There's not a single indoor space available in the entire of London, unless I hired twenty small venues and split all the guests between them, which I'm pretty sure would get me fired."

"And organising a party on a roof won't?"

Ellie shrugged. "Rosalind seemed okay with it, once I'd explained my plan."

"What is your plan?"

"Well, I'm still working on bits of it. But I've booked a rooftop garden area that stretches over a really big apartment block. It's huge and will have plenty of room. Then I'm going to build a sort of winter wonderland up there, out of gazebos."

Theo put the elf down and looked at Ellie seriously. "How high up is the roof?"

"Really high." Ellie shuddered at the very thought of it. "I'm not going."

Theo balked. "Not going to your own party?"

"No. It's on the roof. I'd probably have a heart attack and die on the spot. What kind of Christmas present would that be for my parents?" Ellie made light of the situation, but even considering stepping foot in the elevator that *led* to the roof was making her hands shake. "I have it all planned out. I have floor plans, and a team of vendors who will do what I tell them, including taking pictures and showing me what they have done. And I have Will—he said he'll help. I never need to go up there."

Theo was looking at her in a way that clearly said he didn't think her plan was workable. But Ellie had no choice. It was this or nothing, and nothing wasn't an option.

She just needed to rely on other people to build her vision.

"What's your boss said about you not being there?" Theo asked.

"She's fine with it." Ellie ducked her head to focus on her laptop.

Of course, she hadn't told Rosalind that she wouldn't be attending. Because then she'd have to admit to her fear of heights, and that wasn't happening. Not to mention that Rosalind was bound to say that Ellie couldn't possibly organise a party if she'd never stepped foot in the event space.

Which might just be true, but Ellie was hoping it wasn't.

Her rapport with Rosalind was growing each day. Ellie was enjoying the odd smile here and there as well as the occasional vote of confidence in her abilities. The boost to her rock-bottom self-confidence was welcome, and she didn't want to roll the clock back to the early days when Rosalind barely looked at her other than to call her Christmas Girl.

When Rosalind gave Ellie her attention, or when she managed to make her laugh, the world seemed a little brighter. Ellie didn't want to dwell on that realisation too much—she knew what it meant and how dangerous it could be. Developing a crush on your boss was never a good idea.

"Are you okay with it?" Theo asked, jolting her from her thoughts.

"It is what it is." Ellie shrugged. "There will be other parties. Parties on ground level, where they should be."

She heard Theo sigh softly. "I'll leave you to it," he said. "Oh, what's for dinner tonight?"

"Casserole," she replied without looking up.

"Cool, looking forward to it."

When she heard the door click shut behind him, she let out a long sigh and leaned back against her bed. Of course, she wasn't okay with not going to the Christmas party, and for such a ridiculous reason as well. Her fear of heights had ruled her life for as long as she could remember, from not being able to play on the climbing frame with her friends as a child, to not being able to experience tourist attractions as an adult.

But now it was robbing her of Christmas. Specifically, *her* Christmas. Because Ellie had done everything she could to cram every sensation of the season into the event. This was her one and only chance to show other people how she felt about Christmas by way of an enormous event. The decor, the music, the food, the whole feeling—she could finally share it with others. She could create the very essence of Christmas out of thin air and share it with people and allow the unique spirit of the season to flow from person to person.

Except she wouldn't be there.

She'd have to experience it vicariously through others, which, she reminded herself, was another part of the joy of the festivities. She remembered watching Christmas through the eyes of her friend's toddler a couple of years before, enjoying how the wide-eyed delight from the young boy had translated to fun and happiness for everyone who saw him as he stared at brightly decorated Christmas trees and unwrapped his gifts.

Christmas was shareable. It was one of the greatest things about it. The gift of giving wasn't just a saying—it was a lifestyle. People found joy in giving gifts to people they loved. The giver often took a percentage of joy as part of the present-sharing transaction. And so, everyone was a winner.

Now Ellie was going to have to share the experience from afar. She knew that Will would be her man on the ground, or her man in the air if she was going to be precise. He'd help her coordinate and keep her in the loop of what was going on. She wondered if he'd be willing to wear a wire, or a camera…

She turned to her laptop again and started to search for surveillance equipment. She hoped Rosalind wouldn't get an itemised bill of what she was putting on the company account because that would be difficult to explain.

Someone knocked on the door. “Hey, Ellie, what time will dinner be?” Neil’s voice thundered over the calm choral music.

She sucked in a very long breath before blowing it out again. She looked at the clock on her laptop and realised that if she wanted to eat the casserole at a decent time, she’d need to start preparing it soon. She cursed her decision to agree to prepare meals for the house for the umpteenth time. Why did she have to open her big mouth?

“Be there soon,” she called back.

Chapter Fifteen

Rosalind stepped out of the elevator, her mind still full of details from the client meeting she'd just come from. There were two types of businesses in December—those who started winding down for the Christmas period, and those who had deadlines and targets and who suddenly realised they were running out of year.

Unfortunately, most of her clients fell into the latter category, and that meant very busy days in the run up to the end of the year.

She walked through the office, noting that Ellie had expanded the island of boxes that had grown over the last week. Every time Rosalind looked, an additional row of boxes appeared. She'd not said anything, instead taking a few more calls and dealing with her own diary while Ellie got on with whatever it was that she was doing.

Ellie appeared from behind a large flat package, her eyes widening as she saw Rosalind.

"Um," Ellie said, nervously looking around at the mess she had created.

"It's fine," Rosalind said, stepping over a number of smaller boxes that blocked the walkway to her office. "By all means, take over the entire floor. Is there any chance that I could have my second meeting room back soon?"

"No, I'm still using it." Ellie bit her lip and looked around the space. "I could try to move some things."

Rosalind held her up hand. "No. Carry on. Just…do whatever it is you're doing." She paused and looked at the variety of boxes.

Some were large, flat rectangles taller than she was, while some were much smaller and more conventionally box-shaped. She had no idea what was in any of them. For all she knew, her assistant was running her very own drop-shipping operation.

"What *are* you doing?" Rosalind asked, curiosity finally flowing out of her.

Ava stormed into the office, fire in her eyes, and Rosalind immediately forgot about her conversation with Ellie as maternal worry washed over her.

"Sweetness? What is it?"

"Why did you cancel my piano lesson?" Ava demanded.

Rosalind let out a small sigh of relief at the realisation that there was nothing seriously wrong. "Your tutor is sick," she explained. She'd known Ava would be unhappy, but she was hoping that particular battle would wait until they'd gotten home, mainly in the hope that Ava might have calmed down a little by then.

"It's a sniffle," Ava argued.

"It could be flu for all we know," Rosalind said.

"That's ridiculous," Ava shot back. "How am I supposed to keep up with my lesson schedule? This always happens."

"We have to be careful," Rosalind said, lowering her voice so Irene and Eric weren't disturbed by what was clearly about to become a rousing mother-and-daughter argument in the middle of the office.

"You always do this—you hold me back," Ava said. "I'm fed up with it. I can't do anything. I might as well just be locked in my room forever. In fact, I bet you'd prefer that, wouldn't you?"

Rosalind felt embarrassment creep up inside her. She didn't want to have this fight now, not at work and with people around. It was a fight she'd never win. She knew that she was overprotective but knew that she had good reason for being so. Ava was just too young to understand that.

The only way out now would be to play the *I'm your mother* card, and she hated doing that. It would only lead to many hours of angry silent treatment, something she really didn't want to deal with.

"Ava," Ellie piped up, "are you any good at drawing?"

Ava blinked in confusion. She looked around the boxes before spotting Ellie. Rosalind watched the anger seep away from her, not all that surprising as her daughter seemed to like Ellie. Apparently, Ellie was cool and funny, the implication clearly being that Rosalind was neither.

She hadn't failed to notice Ava stopping off at Ellie's desk whenever she came into the office. Rosalind had no idea what they talked about, but seeing Ava happy, and seeing Ellie frequently using hand sanitiser, meant Rosalind saw no need to put a stop to it.

"Drawing?" Ava questioned.

"Yes," Ellie said. "I need help for the secret Christmas project I told you about."

Rosalind snapped her head towards her daughter. "*You* know about the secret project?"

Ava nodded as if it were obvious. "Yeah, sure."

"Why does she know and I don't?" Rosalind asked Ellie.

"Because she's been helping me with stuff," Ellie said, then turned from Rosalind back to Ava. "Drawing? Can you?"

"Yeah, sure." Ava dropped her schoolbag off by the desk and headed into the maze of boxes.

Rosalind shook her head in amazement. It had taken Ellie a few short seconds to distract Ava and defuse a potentially explosive argument. Now they were talking in hushed whispers, looking at pieces of paper and then pointing at various boxes.

She briefly closed her eyes. The drama had passed. Ellie had yet again swept in and solved an issue before it really became one. But the way in which she'd done it was what really impressed Rosalind.

Ellie had taken the time to develop a real friendship with Ava, not something that Rosalind expected or required of her. And it didn't seem at all fake. Ava would be the first person to detect any bogus attempt at friendship—she'd done so in the past with previous assistants who had tried to gain Rosalind's favour through her daughter. Ava was far too perceptive for that.

She took a few seconds to watch the two interacting, enjoying watching them together while also trying to work out what the secret project was. She still couldn't figure any of it out. Multiple boxes, drawing, the need to take over an entire meeting room. If it was a drop-shipping company, she'd have to ask to be cut in on the profits.

❖

Rosalind looked up. She'd been so engrossed in her work that she didn't see Ava enter her office. She only realised that Ava was standing there and must have been calling her for a while by the tone of her voice.

Ava looked at her with a frown. "It's seven, Mum."

Rosalind checked her watch, sure that it couldn't be true. It wouldn't be the first time that Ava played a prank of that nature on her. Unfortunately, it wasn't the case today. Her usual time for stopping work had flown by, and then some.

"I'm sorry, sweetness. I completely lost track of time." Rosalind slammed her laptop lid closed, preparing to leave as soon as she could.

"I know. You looked busy, so I told Ellie not to bother you," Ava replied.

Rosalind looked out of her open office door to see that Ellie had, unsurprisingly, packed up and gone home. "Still, I'm sorry. This will mean a late dinner."

"It's okay, we could stop by Angelo's and get a pizza?" Ava suggested.

Rosalind packed her belongings up and laughed. "Ah, was that part of your grand scheme? Let me work late so we'd have to get pizza on the way home?"

"I'm not that sneaky," Ava replied, but the large grin on her face said otherwise.

"Angelo's it is." Rosalind checked her desk for anything she might have forgotten, before grabbing her coat and gesturing to the door for Ava to leave first. They crossed the quiet office floor, both flicking off the light switches as they went. "So, do you want to tell me about this secret project Ellie is working on?"

Ava pressed the button for the elevator, and Rosalind put her thick, long winter coat on and plucked the leather gloves out of the pockets.

"Do you want me to break a promise?" Ava asked.

Rosalind shook her head. "No, I'm just worried about all the boxes. Is it a drugs empire? She doesn't seem the type, but you never know."

Ava chuckled at her mother's joke, and they both stepped into the elevator. "No, Ellie's not a drugs lord, Mum. And the boxes are decorations and stuff for the party. It's cool. You'll like it."

"Then why is she keeping it a secret?" Rosalind asked, selecting the ground floor.

"Because she's worried you *won't* like it," Ava replied.

"Which doesn't fill me with confidence," Rosalind said.

"It's…unconventional. But you'll love it, I promise," Ava said. "You're her boss. You could order her to tell you if you really wanted to know."

"I could."

"Why don't you?"

Rosalind didn't really know why she hadn't forced Ellie to tell her every aspect of her plans for the Christmas party. She suspected that an element of it was fear. This was the woman who had decided to have a party on a roof in winter. What other ideas could a mind like that come up with?

But the bigger part of it was trust. For some reason, Rosalind trusted Ellie to know what she was doing. There was a confidence in her that lurked beneath a quiet exterior. Ellie was clearly extremely bright, a talent hidden beneath some degree of lethargy.

Rosalind still hadn't gotten to the bottom of why that was and what Ellie's story was. She'd been far too busy to investigate, but it was on her to-do list.

"I trust her," she replied simply.

The doors slid open, and Rosalind draped her arm around Ava's shoulders as they walked through reception, saying goodbye to the night security guards on their way.

"I trust her, too," Ava said.

"Good." Rosalind waited for the guard to unlock the door and let them out, as was the practice in the late hours. She thanked him, and they stepped out into the bitterly cold evening. Rosalind let go of Ava and made sure her daughter's coat was fully done up and adjusted her scarf so there wouldn't be a chill.

"I..." Ava's voice trailed off.

Rosalind looked up from the scarf to her daughter's panicked eyes. "What is it?"

Seeing Ava's sudden change in mood frightened her, and Rosalind was overcome with a need to understand and fix whatever the issue was immediately.

Ava swallowed visibly. "Can we talk?"

Rosalind no longer felt the cold. Her heart thudded against her chest at such a pace that she nearly started to feel faint. "Of course, you can always talk to me. Always."

Ava leaned in to her, and Rosalind wrapped her arms around her, no idea what was happening but holding her tightly regardless.

"Can we get pizza to go?" Ava asked, her voice becoming impossibly soft.

"Of course," Rosalind said. "Let's go home and talk."

CHAPTER SIXTEEN

Ellie stared at the screen of her company-issued iPhone and swallowed hard. She hadn't arrived in the office yet, having stopped to get herself a new cinnamon flavoured hot chocolate from a cafe on the way to the office. Rosalind was clearly already in and inexplicably sending Ellie a meeting invitation.

To dinner.

Ellie read the invitation again, and again. She was tired and it was early. Surely she had it wrong, and it was a meeting invitation, which she was supposed to organise between Rosalind and someone else. Or Rosalind had invited her by mistake. Maybe she was meant to invite Eric? Or anyone else because it couldn't possibly be that Rosalind had invited Ellie to dinner that evening.

"Cinnamon special for Ellie?" the barista shouted in a way that suggested she'd called out a few times before.

Ellie jogged over to the counter. "Sorry, sorry." She picked up her drink and stepped away from the busy pickup area and resumed staring at the message.

She couldn't possibly imagine why Rosalind would like to have dinner with her. She opened the meeting request and saw that the location wasn't filled in. It simply said *anywhere you like*, which just made Ellie all the more confused. Her thumb hovered over the accept or decline buttons, but she didn't know which to pick. Was this even for her?

In the end, she closed the email down. She could pretend she hadn't seen it. Maybe, by the time she got to the office, Rosalind would have realised her mistake and retracted the invitation.

She exited the coffee shop and walked the short distance to the office. Rain was in the air, and she desperately wanted it to go away. Usually, she'd love rain at this time of year because a tiny drop in temperature could mean snow. But as the organiser of a rooftop party, she was now very much anti-rain.

As was customary these days, she took a few deep breaths to compose herself before getting in the elevator that whizzed her to the top of the building. She hated the sensation, but her breathing exercises and clutching the handrail like a lifeline meant she managed to get up there without too much trouble. It helped that the express elevator took no more than thirty-five seconds to get her to the top floor. Much more than that and Ellie didn't think she could hold back the panic attack that hid inside her, waiting for a weak moment.

The elevator doors opened, and Rosalind stood in front of her, bag in hand and coat on, presumably heading out.

"Good morning." She greeted Ellie with a smile.

Ellie left the elevator as Rosalind stepped in. "Morning," she said hesitantly, not expecting to be face to face with her already.

"I've sent you a meeting request," Rosalind said from inside the elevator, reaching forward to press the button to keep the doors open. "I thought you and I could have dinner tonight, as a thank you for all the work you've put in recently. And so I can wheedle secret information out of you, obviously."

Ellie smiled at Rosalind's cheeky grin. "You don't have to do that."

"I know. It will be nice for us to relax and get to know each other outside of these four walls. Feel free to pick wherever you like—you know what I like to eat."

"What about Ava?" Ellie asked, hoping that somehow Rosalind had forgotten her own daughter, and the whole terrible idea would be called off as a result.

"Who?" Rosalind frowned in mock confusion before laughing.

"She's spending the evening with my brother. Book the table for six o'clock. That will give us plenty of time to get to wherever you choose." Rosalind stood back, and the doors slid closed.

Ellie stared at the closed doors for a moment. She was having dinner with Rosalind. For some reason, that both terrified and excited her.

She had to admit that she'd looked at Rosalind in a different way since Ava had outed her mother. For reasons that Ellie couldn't quite bring herself to admit yet, she'd spent a few minutes trawling through Rosalind's calendar for any sign of a love interest. Upon finding nothing she'd felt strangely happy before quickly and firmly reminding herself that Rosalind would never be even remotely interested in someone like her.

But that didn't mean that Ellie couldn't enjoy the secret fantasy of it. A fantasy that was suddenly becoming a bit too real for her liking. She'd dreamt of a successful, mature woman taking an interest in her and inviting her for dinner, but she'd never expected it to actually happen. That was the point in dreaming about it. It meant not having to worry about the reality of not knowing what to say, what to order, what to wear.

Ellie looked down at her boring black trousers, white blouse, and berry-red cardigan. She looked like her grandmother.

"Great, just great," she muttered.

The rest of the working day passed in the usual blur for Ellie. She still wasn't quite over the shock of how quickly her days passed in her new role. Often, she stared at her watch dumbfounded and wondering where on earth the hours had slipped away to.

She'd booked a table for six o'clock at The Wharf. It was one of Rosalind's preferred lunch venues and sat somewhere between casual and smart casual. Ellie still didn't know why they were eating dinner together, only that Rosalind wanted to get to know her, whatever that meant. Ellie would much rather jot down some answers to questions on a piece of paper and silently slip it under Rosalind's office door than have a dinner like two grown-ups, but it seemed she had little choice in the matter.

Ellie wasn't good at talking about herself. Or really very good at talking at all. She'd never been able to sit and just chat like other people seemed to. On her way home from work, she passed the countless bars, cafes, and restaurants in the busy financial district and wondered how people could possibly be so casual while conversing with work colleagues and clients over drinks and food.

Simply talking was something so natural to some and yet so monumentally difficult for others. When to speak and when to listen, what topics to choose and which to avoid, and attempting to seem relaxed while doing it all was utterly impossible for Ellie.

Rosalind was effortlessly personable. Ellie had seen glimpses of her talking with colleagues and clients and was impressed at how Rosalind could so easily pick up any conversational thread and put others at ease. Ellie wished she had such a skill set, but she'd been blessed with a head for numbers rather than social skills.

It was five thirty, which meant they would have to leave soon in order to make their dinner reservation. Rosalind had been locked away in her office all afternoon poring over contract details for a renewal deal for the next year. Ellie secretly hoped that Rosalind would lose track of time and miss their dinner. And then not have time to reschedule a new one. Or forget about it completely.

"Shall we go?"

Ellie jumped when Rosalind appeared by the side of her desk, coat on, bag in hand, and apparently ready to leave.

So much for that, Ellie thought. "Um. Yeah. Sure, let me just pack up my things."

Rosalind nodded. "I'll just be talking to Eric. See you in a moment."

Ellie turned her computer off and put her belongings in her bag. She wondered if maybe she should have spent her last half an hour at work checking Google for conversational pieces. Surely someone had created a list of topics for dinner with your slightly intimidating boss who you didn't know very well.

Realising that she couldn't waste any more time, she put on her coat, scarf, and gloves, and walked towards Irene's desk. Rosalind noticed her approach and finished up her conversation with Eric.

"Ready?" Rosalind asked.

"Absolutely." Ellie tried to smile but didn't know if she'd quite managed it. If she hadn't, Rosalind was too polite to say anything.

They walked to the corridor, and Rosalind pressed the call button for the elevator. As always, Ellie's heart rate spiked. Heights were awful, but elevators were worse. So far, she'd managed to be the sole occupant of the elevator on all her journeys up and down the tower. While she'd never had a panic attack, she worried that it would happen one day and would rather an embarrassing incident like that had no witnesses.

Now she had no escape. She'd have to try to mask her panic while sharing a journey with her boss. Ellie always attempted to hide her fear of heights from people right up until the moment it became obvious it would be impossible to do so. It was humiliating to have a debilitating fear of something that most people didn't even notice, something that some people got a thrill from conquering. She'd also encountered her fair share of people who thought it would all just go away if she faced her fears. Ellie had tried and failed in the past to do just that. Attempting to conquer her fears never worked. In fact, it seemed to make things worse.

The elevator arrived, and they both stepped inside. Rosalind selected the ground floor. Ellie gripped the handrail as subtly as she could and held her breath as they plunged down. She counted in her head, trying to take her mind off their free fall towards the ground.

"What made you choose The Wharf?" Rosalind asked.

Ellie didn't want to admit it was solely because she knew Rosalind liked it. "They have a good menu," she said.

Thankfully, Rosalind didn't say any more and was instead engrossed in something on her phone. The distraction allowed Ellie to continue her silent half panic attack alone.

The elevator doors opened, and Rosalind gestured for Ellie to go first. She hoped her jelly legs would hold up to any scrutiny. She stopped a few steps forward, under the guise of waiting for Rosalind to join her, but really to get her breathing and shaking under control.

They walked together and exited into the chilly night. Rosalind bristled at the cold wind. "Let's hope the weather improves before the party."

"I've calculated for stronger, colder wind than this," Ellie explained to put Rosalind's mind at ease.

Rosalind chuckled. "I'm still not entirely sure how you managed that, you know."

"It's all just math. Most things can be figured out with math."

"Please share that piece of advice with Ava."

"Does she not like math?"

"Not in the slightest. She's very creative and sees no use for math in her life. I'm trying to convince her that there's always a need for it. Sadly, my own math skills aren't the best, and so my words are obviously ignored."

They crossed the road into the garden square that hosted Cabot Square fountain. Rosalind gestured towards the doors that led into one of the shopping centres. "Maybe we should cut through, so we can get out of this wind for a bit."

Ellie nodded her agreement, and a few minutes later they were entering the tall glass doors and passing under heaters that blew blissfully warm air atop them.

"That's better," Rosalind said. "I've never been good with the cold. In fact, I could do without winter as a whole."

"I love winter," Ellie said. "Especially if there's snow."

Rosalind shuddered. "Not for me. I'm old, and if I fall on ice, then I'm in rehab for six months."

Ellie burst out laughing. "You're not old. And walking on ice is easy—you just walk like a penguin."

Rosalind raised an eyebrow. "A penguin?"

"Yes, little steps." Ellie stopped her normal walking and started demonstrating exactly how to walk like a penguin.

Rosalind stopped and looked at Ellie's feet with amusement. "I see."

"It stops you slipping," Ellie explained. "Penguins do it."

"Well, I hope I don't have the opportunity to try it. But if I do, I'll report back."

Ellie felt her cheeks heat in a blush at the realisation that she was showing Rosalind a deeply unflattering impression of a short-legged bird stomping on ice.

"Okay," Ellie mumbled. She continued walking towards the restaurant and was relieved when Rosalind fell into step beside her without another word on the matter.

"I wanted to apologise," Rosalind said.

"What for?"

"For dumping you with organising the Christmas party."

"Oh, it's fine. I'm managing."

"So I see. But I still wish to apologise. Vanessa and I had been finding it harder and harder to communicate with one another, and she clearly carried a very large chip on her shoulder to do what she did."

Ellie didn't say anything. She'd often thought about Vanessa's over-the-top actions and wondered if Rosalind could have really deserved such a kick in the business teeth. Ellie hadn't seen any indication that Rosalind was unfair. Sometimes she was a little short, sometimes she wanted things done a little quicker than could be done, but on the whole she was fair enough. Certainly not as bad as Ellie had expected.

"What happened?" Ellie asked.

"I'm not entirely sure. She'd been missing things, and I'd been less than easy on her as a result. The final argument was about the tea tray, of all things."

Ellie chuckled. "Did she not heed your speech about the importance of the tea tray?"

Rosalind stopped dead and stared at Ellie with a lopsided grin. "I do not give a *speech* about the tea tray."

Ellie took in Rosalind's smile and felt relaxed enough to laugh. "Oh, you do. It's very stirring."

Rosalind attempted to glare at her but was too close to laughter for it to hold any bite. She shook her head, and they continued walking. "Well, clearly it's not impressive enough because she did ruin Greg Ashton's tea tray. But we were already at odds. The week before she'd picked up a book for me, for Ava. Vanessa seemed to be covering up some sniffles, and the very next day Ava was ill. I had reminded her to give the book a quick clean with antibacterial wipes before handing it to Ava, but I'm almost positive she didn't."

"That's terrible," Ellie said, furious that Vanessa would be so careless.

"I have no evidence, just a hunch. But, anyway, the fact of the matter is that I shouldn't have left you with that mess to clear up. It was just a very stressful time, and I wanted it off my plate, so I put it onto yours. And I apologise for that," Rosalind said.

Ellie couldn't remember the last time a person in a position of power had apologised to her like that. She suspected never. At university her professor had once lost her paper that she'd handed in ahead of a deadline, and rather than admit it, he'd asserted that she had never given it to him. She could tell by the shame in his eyes that he was lying, shifting the blame from himself to her. Years later, Ellie hated that he had lied to her, but more than that, she hated how the interaction had shone a spotlight on how weak she was for not standing up to him.

"Thank you," Ellie said. "I appreciate that."

They approached the exit to the shopping centre and braced themselves for the cold winds again. A few moments later they were in the restaurant and being led to their table.

Ellie was alarmed to notice that The Wharf of an evening was very different to during the day. Lights had been dimmed, candles appeared on the tables, and the ambiance was a lot darker and softer, almost romantic.

Ellie wanted the earth to swallow her up. She'd been in The Wharf during the day, and it looked like a perfectly safe place to suggest a dinner with your boss. Now it looked like a date-night restaurant.

Rosalind didn't seem to react to the dramatic change in decor so presumably knew of The Wharf's night-time transformation.

No wonder she asked why you picked here, Ellie thought.

The waiter showed them to a table, handed over some menus,

and left them to it. Ellie shifted uncomfortably in her chair, mentally berating herself for picking completely the wrong restaurant. She could barely see the menu because of the dim lighting. A quick glance around confirmed her worst suspicion that everyone else in the restaurant were couples.

"Have you been here for dinner before?" Rosalind asked.

"Nope," Ellie said quickly.

"I like what they do with the place. Makes it more relaxed and informal." Rosalind opened her menu. "I do recommend the steak, and obviously this is on me."

Ellie was going to argue but saw the prices and felt her eyes water a little. Lunch at The Wharf wasn't cheap—nowhere in Canary Wharf was—but dinner was far worse.

"I also wanted to thank you for what you said to Ava," Rosalind said, her nose still in her menu.

"About?"

"About her sexuality."

Ellie froze. Ava had told her mother. Not only had she told Rosalind that she thought she was gay, but she'd also clearly mentioned that she'd spoken to Ellie about it first.

Ellie quickly apologised. "I'm sorry if I overstepped." She had no idea how Rosalind would feel about her PA giving such personal advice to her daughter.

"You didn't," Rosalind said. "In fact, I'm glad she told you because whatever you told her encouraged her to tell me."

Ellie sagged with relief. She had felt pretty good about her conversation with Ava until an hour or so later when it suddenly hit her that she really ought not to be meddling in someone else's life. She didn't know anything about children or teenagers, and she was hardly a great role model for anyone. But she just couldn't let Ava be so miserable in the dessert shop that day.

"I'm glad she told you," Ellie said. "A little surprised that she told you that she told me."

"Did you expect an emotional twelve-year-old to keep quiet?" Rosalind grinned.

Ellie chuckled. "I suppose not."

"She didn't go into detail about what you said, just that you were very helpful and spoke a lot of sense." Rosalind returned her attention to her menu. "But then, she was emotional."

Ellie smiled at the gentle ribbing. Rosalind was trying to put her at ease, and it was working.

"May I ask what you told her?" Ellie asked. She'd been curious to know if Ava had told her mother, and if so what the reaction had been. Rosalind seemed to be in a good mood and opening up to her, so Ellie was going to take full advantage of that.

Rosalind marked her place in the menu with a finger and closed the hard-backed leather book. She fixed Ellie with a serious look. "I told her that she can be whatever she wants to be, and that she'll receive no judgement from me. As long as she approaches things with an open mind and an open heart, with the understanding that how she feels now might change and to be ready to embrace that change, then I'll be the proudest mother there is."

Ellie swallowed. She wished she'd had that kind of reaction when she'd come out to her own parents. They hadn't *not* been supportive, but it wasn't a fun experience.

"Have I upset you?" Rosalind suddenly asked.

Ellie realised that her heart was on her sleeve, and Rosalind had easily picked up on her change of mood. She could either brush it off or be honest. Ellie would usually brush it off, but there was something about the dim light and how Rosalind looked at her with kind, earnest eyes.

"No," Ellie reassured. "I was just thinking about how my own parents took the news."

Rosalind looked confused. "About Ava?"

"About me. That I'm bisexual," Ellie clarified.

"Oh!" Rosalind blinked. "I'm sorry that your parents weren't accepting of that."

Ellie shook her head. "It wasn't that. They were accepting. Sort of. It was just all very...British. Stiff upper lip and a nod of understanding, and then, that was it. We never really spoke of it again."

"Never?" Rosalind questioned, surprise obvious in her tone.

"No. They seemed to accept it, and I know they love me. We just never talk about it in any detail." Ellie leaned back and let out a sigh. "I would have loved to have someone say to me what you said to Ava. To tell me that it was okay, and to tell me to follow my heart. I spent a lot of time after that wondering if I was making a mistake. They weren't happy about what I had told them, that was clear. Not unhappy, but not happy either. If that makes sense?"

"It does." Rosalind nodded. "I'm sorry, Ellie. That must have been very hard."

Ellie shrugged. To her mind, it was what it was. Her parents were old-fashioned and a little stuck in their ways. They weren't homophobic, but they weren't exactly embracing of it either. She'd accepted that fact, but now that she was faced with the idea that it could have been so very different for her, she felt slightly bereft of a chance at a more open conversation with the people who meant the most to her.

"It was fine." Ellie brushed it off. "It just would have been nice to have more of a chat about it with them. Ava's very lucky."

Rosalind smirked. "Ava would say that she has a *very* interfering mother."

"Don't all twelve-year-olds think that?" Ellie asked.

"I'm sure Ava would paint me as most interfering ever," Rosalind said.

"And are you?" Ellie asked.

Rosalind paused and gave the question some thought. "Probably," she confessed with a grin.

The waiter came over and asked if they were ready to order. Ellie was surprised that she felt a little irritated by the interruption. Since they'd sat down, she'd gone from mortification at booking a table at a romantic restaurant to actually enjoying herself.

She opened her menu again and quickly glanced down the page for something to panic order.

Chapter Seventeen

With drinks delivered and meals being prepared, the conversation lulled slightly. Rosalind was sipping from a heavenly looking glass of red wine. Ellie wished that she'd ordered something that made her look a little more like an adult, but she'd panicked and gone with an alcopop.

It was clear that the ball was in Ellie's court, and she wondered which topic to bring up. Talking about work seemed inappropriate somehow. She still hadn't quite figured out why they were having dinner but it did seem to be just a simple casual chat as Rosalind had inferred. With work off the table, Ellie thought returning to the previous conversation of Ava would be the safest.

"So, do you think Ava has her eye on a specific someone?" Ellie asked.

"I hope not," Rosalind confessed with a grimace. "She's still a young child in my eyes, even though she hates that I see her like that. The idea of her dating is a little too much for me to process at the moment. I'll have to deal with it eventually, but I'm hoping I have a while longer yet. Maybe ten more years."

Ellie bit her lip. She already knew that Ava was interested in a girl at school and had hoped that she'd told her mother that, but clearly not. Presumably that was phase two of Ava's plan.

"Who knows? It might even be a phase," Rosalind said. "Three months ago, she wanted to be a ballet dancer, until someone told her she really ought to have started out on that career path at the age of four."

Ellie snorted a laugh. "A ballet dancer? Ava?"

"I know, right?" Rosalind grinned. "She's hardly the most graceful."

Ellie recalled Ava's lack of coordination when she'd helped out the other day. "She is a little clumsy."

"Extremely. But she has these flights of fancy, and they come and go like flavours of the month. I don't want to stop her creative mind from working, but I also need her to understand that it's okay to change her mind. There's nothing worse than being stuck in the wrong decision."

"Sounds like you know from experience," Ellie said.

Rosalind took a sip of wine before she nodded. "I dated a man, many years ago. I thought I was bisexual at the time, but in hindsight I realised I'm gay. We were engaged to be married. It had never been an all-consuming love, more of a semi-comfortable arrangement where we spent a little under a quarter of our time together arguing, which I thought was rather successful, considering my own parents."

Ellie giggled. She knew the feeling.

"Anyway, he proposed, I said yes. I wasn't sure, but I said yes anyway. I think I was swept along with everything."

Ellie raised her eyebrow. She couldn't imagine the strong and confident Rosalind Caldwell getting swept along with anything she didn't want to be a part of.

"On the day of the wedding, I was incredibly unwell. I thought I had flu. I had a blocked-up nose, terrible headache, sore throat. You name it. But it had come on so suddenly, the morning of the wedding. I knew in my heart that I hadn't caught anything from anyone. I knew it was my body rebelling against this ridiculous decision I'd made and was continuing to make. My own body was shouting at me that I didn't love him and not to make the terrible mistake of actually marrying him."

Rosalind sucked in a deep breath before taking a sip of wine, her gaze distant with memories.

Ellie was enthralled. Rosalind was openly offering her a doorway into a part of her that Ellie couldn't even comprehend existed. It was fascinating to see this side of Rosalind. She felt fortunate, as she couldn't imagine that Rosalind would have this conversation with just anyone. "What happened?"

"I married him," Rosalind admitted, "and then divorced him two years later when I finally came to my senses."

Ellie stared at Rosalind in shock. "Wow, that's…that's surprising, considering you're very, well, determined."

Rosalind chuckled. "It's a learned behaviour. I made a terrible mistake. Wasted some good years of my life, wasted good years of his, too. Even though I knew it was wrong. I made myself sick with worry about it. But I didn't want to disappoint him, my family, everyone who was coming to the wedding. Ludicrous when I look back at it. I don't recognise myself."

"At least Ava came out of it," Ellie said.

"No, Ava was later in my life." Rosalind shook her head and toyed with the stem of her wine glass. "Just medical science and me. I didn't allow myself to have a child with my ex-husband. I kept telling him I wasn't quite ready for children. The fact was that I was ready, but I didn't feel that we—as a couple—were."

Ellie was surprised that Rosalind was being so candid about her life and her perceived mistakes. While she knew this was a get-to-know-you chat, she hadn't expected to actually get to know her boss this much. To know that Rosalind had once been as young and insecure as Ellie felt now was unexpected but satisfying. Knowing that Rosalind hadn't been born some incredible being but had grown into one made Ellie feel there was a chance for her yet.

The warmth that Ellie felt bubbling in her chest at the realisation that Rosalind clearly trusted her was uplifting. She was surprised by what she was learning but felt somewhat blessed to be sitting across from Rosalind, absorbing little gems of information that demonstrated how she ticked.

"Have I surprised you?" Rosalind asked, smiling at Ellie's ongoing silence.

Ellie shook the cobwebs away. "No, sorry, I just hadn't ever thought you'd get married to someone you didn't love. You seem so determined and focused."

"We all grow into ourselves, don't we?"

"I suppose we do." Ellie wondered when she had stopped growing. About the time she'd settled for a job in marketing at Caldwell & Atkinson, she imagined. "So it's just you and Ava?"

"Yes, just the two of us. Although, since she was five she's been trying to set me up on dates, but there's never been anyone serious. I'm married to my job." Rosalind took another sip of wine, and for a split second Ellie wondered if she saw a hint of sadness through the briefest crack in Rosalind's facade.

"Are you seeing that young man I saw you with, or was that just a casual thing?" Rosalind asked before Ellie had too much time to consider what she had observed.

Ellie wondered if the blush she felt warming her cheeks could be seen in the dim lighting. She'd nearly forgotten about Rosalind seeing her and Will coming out of the bathroom. Now the mortification hit her hard once again.

"We're not anything—we're just friends," Ellie explained, hoping but doubting that would be the end of the conversation.

Rosalind raised an eyebrow and looked at her teasingly. Ellie knew then and there how easy it would be to get lost in Rosalind's eyes. She swallowed the thought away. She couldn't afford to become so easily distracted by her boss, not when there was nothing between them and no chance of there ever being anything.

"Really. There's nothing going on there," Ellie insisted.

"Then why were you in the ladies' with him?" Rosalind asked playfully, swirling her wine glass.

"I wanted to talk to him in private," Ellie said, hating how stupid it sounded.

Rosalind looked at her with an expression that obviously said she didn't believe a word of it. "You can tell me if you're interested in him. Pretend I'm not your boss."

"He's not my type," Ellie said, badly wanting Rosalind to erase any images of her and Will engaging in any kind of inappropriate moment in the bathroom.

Rosalind shrugged playfully. "He seems handsome enough to me."

"He's too young," Ellie blurted out. "I like people older than him. Older than me. Much older."

Rosalind blinked at Ellie's sudden declaration. "Oh, really? How much older?"

Ellie took a swig of her alcopop and wished she'd ordered something much stronger. How did she manage to get herself into these predicaments? And how would she avoid confessing that her ideal romantic partner would be around Rosalind's age? Not to mention that her bisexual tendencies definitely leaned towards woman. Woman in power. There was something about an older, authoritative woman that set Ellie's heart racing.

"I'm sorry, that's too personal," Rosalind said, clearly noticing Ellie's discomfort.

"No," Ellie said, "it's fine." She wanted to kick herself. Rosalind had given her a way out, and Ellie was refusing it to save her blushes, only to put herself back into the original undesirable situation. She decided the only way out was to be honest, speak from the heart, and to be as casual about it as possible.

"My gran used to call me an old soul," Ellie said, picking at the label of her alcopop bottle. "People who hardly know me have said that I have a wise head on young shoulders. Basically, I act and feel a lot older than I am. I always have. And I like being with people who are older than me, especially if I'm dating them. There's something comforting about people who have been there and done it or have good advice to give. People who have settled down and know what they want from life. It's sexy."

Ellie took a breath and looked up to meet Rosalind's gaze. Especially sexy in women, she mused. Though she wasn't about to utter that particular thought out loud while sitting in a romantic restaurant with her gorgeous boss.

"So, no, Will isn't my type. Just a friend from when I worked downstairs in marketing. And for reasons I can't even explain to myself, I thought it was a good idea to have a private conversation with him in the ladies' bathroom," Ellie continued, chuckling at herself.

"And on that note, explain to me how a statistician ends up working in my marketing department." Rosalind deftly changed the subject. "I checked your CV. It seems you're the most overqualified marketing assistant in London. How does that happen?"

"Desperation," Ellie admitted, thankful for the conversational pivot.

Rosalind laughed. "None taken."

Ellie winced. "Sorry, I didn't mean to be rude. It's a great company, and I was lucky to get a job here."

"I'm just teasing," Rosalind said. "I'm just not sure how someone with your qualifications ends up as a temp in a marketing department of a recruitment firm. I'm very glad to have you but can't help but feel that it's a waste of your potential."

"After I left education, I tried to find the perfect job," Ellie explained. "And then a slightly less perfect job. Then any job in my field. And then any job at all. I applied for so many jobs, failed interviews for some, and didn't even get a callback for others. It was soul-destroying. In the end, I needed the money. Any job would do."

"How many statistician jobs have you applied for since working for me?"

Ellie shook her head. "None."

"You can tell me the truth. I don't mind if you have," Rosalind pressed.

"I haven't. Really. I just kinda stayed here."

Rosalind cocked her head to the side in confusion. "You're telling me that you had access to our database, a list of nearly all the jobs available in London and beyond, and you didn't bother looking for a role that might fit you better? Might pay you more?"

Ellie shrunk a little in her seat, suddenly feeling very stupid. "No, never."

"I think you must be the only person in the company who doesn't browse through the lists of vacancies and picture themselves in a better job." Rosalind chuckled and shook her head a little.

"I never thought of it," Ellie said. She frowned. "I don't know why I never thought of it." It seemed ridiculous to have not used the very large, very easily accessible list of vacancies to her advantage.

She wondered how many potential roles had come and gone while she had been doing a job she didn't even enjoy.

"I think that maybe you lost your confidence," Rosalind suggested. "Being out of work and looking for jobs can be extremely stressful. Not getting callbacks, not hearing after applications, not getting through to the second stages—it can all be very disheartening. People think it's them, but it's like dating. The right match takes time."

"Except you can live without a date, but you need a job to pay for food and shelter," Ellie pointed out.

"True, and we all date a lot of duds before we find the right one. We all take a lot of temporary jobs before we find the right career path. The trick is to make sure you don't get too comfortable being uncomfortable. If your partner isn't right for you, you shouldn't waste your life sticking with them because it's better than nothing. Same goes for jobs." Rosalind's gaze pierced into Ellie's soul. "Life is short, Ellie. We shouldn't waste time being unhappy if we have it within our power to change things. Even if that can be extremely uncomfortable in the short term."

Dinner arrived, and they both thanked the waiter. Ellie reflected on Rosalind's words. She was absolutely right that Ellie had become comfortable with being uncomfortable. She was in a job she didn't enjoy, in a house she hated, and living with the boys who she loved but would prefer to love from afar rather than being their pseudo-nanny.

She didn't know how she'd managed to slip so far into a life she didn't enjoy, but she had, and she'd been in that place for a long time. The problem was, she had no idea how to get out.

"Why do they have to play Christmas songs all the time?" Rosalind complained as a festive tune started playing through the restaurant speakers.

"Because it's Christmas?"

"Not yet, it isn't. Christmas is but one day, and yet we hear it for weeks. All day. Every single day." Rosalind picked up her napkin and placed it in her lap. She raised her hand and tilted it in the light, peering at the back of it. "And everything is covered in glitter—one of the cards I received today had a glittery snowman on it, and I've washed my hands countless times since, and I *still* have glitter on me."

"It's festive," Ellie said.

Rosalind sighed. Ellie knew the sound well. She'd heard it before from a very select group of people. She looked knowingly at Rosalind.

"What?" Rosalind asked.

"You don't like Christmas," Ellie said with certainty.

Rosalind looked like a deer caught in the headlights. "What? No, I mean, I'm not the most enthusiastic—it's not like I don't actually like it. I mean, it's nice. It's festive, as you said. Festive."

"You don't like Christmas," Ellie repeated, enjoying Rosalind's sudden floundering. "Admit it."

Rosalind licked her lips nervously and looked around. "Well, I'm not the biggest fan. But of course, it's…well, it's Christmas."

Ellie chuckled at the backtracking. "You hate it, don't you? Go on, you can tell me."

"Did Ava say something?" Rosalind demanded.

Ellie laughed outright. "No, but you've just confessed by asking. Wow, you really hate it, don't you?"

Rosalind sighed and slumped a little in her chair. "Loathe it. How did you know?"

"I'm Christmas Girl—I can sense it in people." Ellie picked up a piece of bread and took a bite.

"Seriously, how did you know?" Rosalind asked. "I didn't say anything."

"You sighed."

"Did I?"

"Yep."

"And that's all it took?"

Ellie nodded. "I've heard that sigh time and time again. It's a very particular sigh, comes from people who think the compulsory enjoyment of all things associated with Christmas is too much. It's okay—you're not alone."

"Really?" Rosalind asked, clearly disbelieving. "I've never met anyone who would willingly admit that they dislike Christmas."

"Oh, no one says it out loud," Ellie agreed. "Then you get called Scrooge or a humbug."

Rosalind rolled her eyes. "It's as if everyone loses their senses for a whole month. And the day itself, good grief. You're not allowed to be anything other than ecstatically merry all day."

Ellie grinned. "Do you often find it difficult to pretend to be happy for a whole day?" she teased.

Rosalind picked up a bit of parsley garnishing her plate and threw it at her. Ellie watched it fall limply in front of her and smiled at the unexpected immature reaction.

"No," Rosalind said. "But I do take issue with everything needing to be perfect. And God forbid anyone who ruins Christmas by being late, or not wanting to watch a terrible movie, or isn't feeling like dancing a jig every five seconds just because it's Christmas Day. We're all supposed to have a wonderful and perfect day, but if your most picture-perfect day is anything other than eating dry turkey, getting toiletry gift sets from people who clearly don't know you hate lavender, and watching bad television, then you are condemned to have a terrible time."

Rosalind hates lavender. Ellie made a mental note. She didn't know why she did—it wasn't as if she was ever going to be lucky enough to be in a position to buy Rosalind toiletries or perfume. "Christmas doesn't need to be like that. It's what you make it. Doesn't matter how you do Christmas, or who with, or where. Just as long as you're happy. Christmas spirit lives inside us."

"Tell the masses," Rosalind grumbled.

"No, it's about you and how you see it," Ellie pressed. "Seriously, I know that Christmas can feel super stressful and like everything has to be perfect, but it's not like that. It's about finding your own version of Christmas spirit that makes you happier, which makes the people around you happier, too. That's the real meaning of Christmas, finding something inside you. It doesn't have to be like the movies, it doesn't have to be covered in glitter, or be religious, or have Santa on it. It's what's inside your heart, what makes you happy. People get too wrapped up in the idea of Christmas, and there's this weird idea that we're all the same and we should all feel the same, but that's wrong. Some people want some cinnamon in their coffee at Christmas. Some want to exchange the coffee for hot chocolate. Both are fine. Don't let the masses tell you otherwise."

A smile crept across Rosalind's features, and Ellie wondered if she was about to be ribbed for giving a speech on the true meaning of Christmas.

"I'll take that under advisement," Rosalind said. "Thank you, Ellie. You've given me a lot to think about there."

"I didn't mean to lecture," Ellie said.

"You didn't. I think I needed to hear that." Rosalind took a sip of wine. "Though, don't expect me to be taking your Christmas Girl crown just yet."

Ellie chuckled. "Deal." She raised her glass in a toast, and Rosalind lifted her wine glass, and they met in a chink across the table.

Ever the expert at casual conversation, Rosalind promptly moved on to talk about Ava's adorable speech impediment when she was a child and the opening of an exciting new restaurant nearby.

It had been a long time since Ellie had comfortably conversed with someone who she didn't know all that well. Often there were uncomfortable silences and awkward jokes that didn't manage to hit the mark. But talking with Rosalind was easy.

They laughed and shared stories until the evening ended, which came far too soon for Ellie. Rosalind walked her to the Tube station, and they parted ways like old friends. Nothing felt strained or awkward, and Ellie simply couldn't recall a time that had happened before.

On the journey home, Ellie replayed every part of the evening over and over again with a smile on her lips and familiar butterflies in her stomach. Nothing would ever come of it, but it was nice to fantasise.

CHAPTER EIGHTEEN

Ellie took a mouthful of the festive turkey and cranberry baguette and moaned at the delicious pops of flavour. The little coffee shop on the corner of Westferry had outdone themselves.

Every year, each of the local cafes came out with a host of Christmas treats, and every year, Ellie tried them all. There were so many different things to try that she'd created a schedule, culminating in what she suspected would be the best.

Of course, she could make herself a festive tasting treat any time she liked, but having something newly created by professional chefs and bakers was something that only happened in December. Ellie happily took full advantage and thanked her lucky stars for her fast metabolism.

"Ellie," Rosalind called out to her as she returned from the meeting room and approached her office.

Ellie swallowed her mouthful of food and looked up.

"Have you seen the file for Renshaw's?" Rosalind breezed by Ellie's desk and into her own office.

Ellie stood and walked after her. "No, should I have?"

Rosalind rummaged through papers on her desk. "No, not exactly, I'm just hoping that I'm not a complete idiot."

"You're not a complete idiot," Ellie said, reassuring her.

"I have a meeting with Renshaw's in an hour, and I'm almost positive that I left the file at home." Rosalind dropped some papers to her desk with a frustrated sigh. She rubbed at her forehead and groaned. "Okay, could you call Michael and tell him that he'll need to take my meeting with Steven Forrester, so I can head home and get this bloody file."

"Michael's not in the office today," Ellie reminded her.

Rosalind winced. She looked at her watch and then at the papers on the desk in despair. "Right, okay. Um, is Eric back from—?"

"No, he'll be out the rest of the day," Ellie said.

Irene knocked on the door frame. "Sorry to interrupt. Ellie, reception just called. Steven Forrester has arrived."

Ellie looked at Rosalind, who didn't panic but did appear increasingly stressed. It had been a morning of back-to-back meetings and two important deals teetering on the edge. Ellie had come into work floating on cloud nine following the previous evening's relaxing and enjoyable dinner, only to be quickly brought down to earth by a very hectic workday.

"I can go and get the Renshaw file if that helps," Ellie offered.

Rosalind looked at her. "I can't ask you to do that. It's not in your job description to have to fetch things, especially because I was a fool and forgot a file at home. You know, I've never done that before. Had to happen eventually, I suppose." Rosalind checked her wristwatch again and sighed.

"You're not a fool. I'm happy to go and pick up a file," Ellie said. She turned to Irene. "Would you mind asking him to come up and showing him to the meeting room? The tea tray is ready, I just need to—"

"Say no more," Irene said kindly. "I'll deal with everything."

"Thanks," Ellie said.

"Thank you, Irene, I'll be along in a moment," Rosalind added. She turned to Ellie. "Thank you for this. I'll owe you one."

Ellie felt a tingle go through her body at the increasing realisation of exactly what she would like Rosalind to owe her. The thought of soft lips and sensually whispered requests had kept Ellie warm on the journey home the night before. Of course, it was all a fantasy but one that she'd happily continue to enjoy in the privacy of her own imagination as long as Rosalind kept providing her with kindling for the bonfire of her musings.

Rosalind picked up her handbag and handed over a set of keys, indicating a fob and a silver key. "This will get you into the building and the lift, and this opens the door. I'll text you the address so you can use the map on your phone. It's only fifteen minutes away. It's literally right there on the dining table—I can see it in my mind."

Ellie took the bunch of keys and smiled. "Not a problem. Don't worry about it."

"Thank you, Ellie. You're a star," Rosalind said as she gathered some papers for the meeting she was about to have.

Ellie beamed with pride at being able to do something so little but so meaningful for Rosalind. She turned to exit the office. "Don't forget to send me the address."

"I'll send it in a moment, just printing out these documents," Rosalind replied.

Ellie walked over to the coat stand and pulled on her coat, hat, gloves, and scarf. She grabbed her bag from her desk and headed over to the dreaded elevators.

She'd already decided that she'd stop off and get a couple of cinnamon cake pops on the way back. One for her, one as a gift for Rosalind to hopefully ease her afternoon a little. The cafe was on the way back and wouldn't have much of a queue at that time of day. It would add a couple of minutes to her outing but hopefully make the rest of the day a little better for Rosalind.

She called the elevator and made her way down to the ground floor, gripping the handrail tightly and squeezing her eyes closed while counting slowly under her breath. Usually, she wouldn't want to suffer through an extra elevator trip up and down unless it was for something important, but being the knight that saved Rosalind from potentially having a meeting without all her notes was worth a little extra stress.

She exited onto the street and pulled her phone out of her bag. Rosalind had sent a text with an address, which her phone automatically converted into a link for her. She clicked the link and requested directions from her navigation app and started walking in the direction of the arrow.

If she was honest, the thought of having a look at Rosalind's home was tantalising. Ellie thought of her like an exciting new book, so much to find out about, and no way to race ahead without reading each page. Rosalind couldn't be considered a closed book—she was far too transparent for that. But, as with all relationships, it took time to get to know someone, and sometimes that seemed like an unfairly long process.

Ellie ached to know more about Rosalind, even if she ultimately did nothing with the information. In many ways, it would just be fodder for her own imagination. In her dreams, Ellie could pretend that the night before was a date. In her dreams, she could pretend that she had dared to press a soft kiss to Rosalind's cheek before they parted ways at the station.

Ellie smiled to herself. It was madness to think that she would ever have such courage. Or that Rosalind would be interested in someone like her. But that didn't matter when it was a fantasy. In her daydreams she was different—confident, unafraid of heights, desired by all.

But sometimes daydreams were pushed to one side as reality made itself known like a huge black cloud ruining a summer's day. As Ellie walked down the street towards her mystery destination, she had a sinking feeling that she knew exactly where she was going. The towering building at the end of the road seemed to go on forever, up and up into the clouds.

It made the Caldwell & Atkinson building look tiny by comparison.

Ellie stopped dead and looked at her phone again. Sure enough, her final destination was the behemoth, soaring into the sky. She looked at Rosalind's text message to read the entire address. Her heart sank. Rosalind, for reasons Ellie could not fathom, lived on the forty-sixth floor.

A wave of dizziness came over her. She held out her hand and leaned on a nearby wall to stop herself falling to her knees there and then.

"You can do this, you can do this, you can do this," she whispered to herself.

She wasn't even at the building, and already her knees couldn't straighten properly at the very thought of going up to such a height. She leaned fully against the wall and hurriedly rang Will.

"Caldwell and Atkinson, Will Hampton spe—"

"It's me," Ellie cut in. "I need your help. Rosalind lives in the fucking sky."

"What?"

"I said I'd get something from her house. But she lives on the forty-sixth floor. Who lives that high up? How am I supposed to get up there?" Ellie sucked in a deep breath to stop the panic from overwhelming her.

"I…I'm sorry, Ellie. I have a meeting in a couple of minutes, or I'd come and help you," Will said. "Can it wait an hour?"

Ellie rubbed her eye with her free hand. "No," she whined. "She needs it now. I said I'd do it."

"I'm sorry—I really can't get out of this. It's with Cath."

Cath was Will's boss and the single most grumpy woman to work in the whole of London. She never had a nice thing to say about anyone, and everyone feared her. Ellie had once hid under her desk from Cath's laser beam stare upon hearing the formidable woman's heels thudding across the floor.

"Maybe you need to tell Rosalind you can't do it," Will said in a soft tone. "She should know about your issue with heigh—"

"No!" Ellie stood up straight. "No, she doesn't need to know. She can't know, okay?"

"Okay, okay," Will replied, clearly sensing her panic and seeking to reassure her. "I won't tell her—of course I won't tell her. But maybe you should consider that you should."

"No, I don't…" Ellie sighed. "I don't need her to look at me like that."

"Like what?"

"Like she pities me."

"Do you know she'd do that?" Will asked.

"Everyone does it, Will. Everyone. I'd just rather keep it to myself. Please?" She felt bad for suggesting that he also did it, but he did. She knew he tried to hide it, but he couldn't. No one could.

When you admitted that you had a fear of heights, people changed. They either pitied you, wanted to fix you, or both. "Will?"

"Of course, you know you can trust me." He paused. "And, for what it's worth, I don't pity you."

Ellie took a couple of deep breaths. Whether he realised it or not, he did. Pity was such a strange emotion. It essentially meant to feel sorrow for someone else's misfortune, which seemed fine on the face of it, but to actually see pity in someone's eyes was an entirely different matter.

But she knew that he meant well. Most people did.

"I know. Don't worry. I'll be fine. I'll come up with something," she told him. "Good luck with Cath."

He thanked her and they hung up. Ellie turned back towards her nemesis and took in a deep breath. It was time to see what she was really made of. She'd almost conquered the twenty-second floor, as long as she didn't think about it, listen to it creaking in the wind, go near a window, or think about the floor unexpectedly giving way. Okay, so she hadn't conquered it at all, but she'd managed to survive it.

Deciding that it was time to test herself, she hummed "Joy to the World" to herself as she approached the building. She hoped the uplifting tune would distract her from what she was about to do—or at least try to do.

The thought of letting Rosalind down was the only thing that pushed her along. Rosalind had been so genuinely happy and relieved when Ellie had offered to do this one little thing for her, so Ellie would damn well try her best to do what she had promised.

She used the fob Rosalind had indicated to open the door and crossed a smart-looking lobby, smiling at the concierge and the security guard as she did. The last thing she needed was to be flagged as suspicious and kicked out. They smiled and nodded back to her.

The building was new and had a smart elevator bank that asked users to enter their floor number to call the elevator. Ellie continued to hum her happy tune as she called for an elevator to take her to the forty-sixth floor. She felt mild irritation that the doors opened immediately for her. She'd hoped for a little more time to prepare herself for the ascension to a nauseating height.

She double-checked Rosalind's text message once more to make sure she wasn't misreading and only needed to brave the fourth or even the sixth floor. Sadly, she'd been right the first time. She stepped into the elevator and held her breath.

Nothing happened.

She waited and waited, but still nothing happened.

"You need to use the fob," the security guard called out to her. "On the panel."

"Oh yeah, of course." She tapped the fob to the panel, and the display lit up. "Thank you."

The doors slid closed, and she felt the elevator start to move. At great speed. There was no handrail to hold on to, just three mirrored walls and the mirrored doors. Ellie leaned her back against one of the walls and realised that she was now humming her tune at twice the speed.

She glanced at the display screen which showed the floor numbers whipping upward so quickly that they were just a blur. It was then that she realised she was in an express elevator, one dedicated to the higher floors and travelling at an absurd speed.

Her acute fear meant that the journey felt as if it was taking forever, despite the fact she knew she was travelling at excessive speeds for a metal box suspended by some cables.

Suddenly the elevator bounced to a stop. Ellie felt her breath catch in her lungs. This was it—the elevator was broken, and she was going to be trapped. Or worse, it was about to collapse to the ground. She'd seen it in movies, and now that vision constantly played over in her mind if she allowed it the slightest opportunity to do so.

The doors opened, and Ellie almost fell out of the elevator and gratefully gripped the wall. She'd made it to the forty-sixth floor. She had no idea how she'd make it back down, but she was halfway to achieving her goal.

She kept the palm of her hand pressed to the wall as she made her way from the elevators towards the apartments. She checked her phone again and found Rosalind's apartment number. Thankfully, it was just around the corner from the elevators.

She pushed away from one wall and quickly fell into the other, holding her flat palm against a new solid surface. She sucked in a few calming breaths. Time was ticking by, and she knew that she had to hurry if she was going to get back without Rosalind or Irene wondering what had taken her so long. She simply didn't have time to panic, which was problematic as that fact was certain to make her do just that.

With a shaky hand, she got the set of keys out of her pocket and opened the door. She stepped into the hallway and closed the door behind her.

Her panting breaths echoed through the empty apartment, and she tried to focus her attention on what she was doing and not on the desperate desire to have a full-blown panic attack.

"You're okay," she reminded herself. "Everything is fine. Just get the file. It's all good."

She lowered her hand from the death grip she had on the door handle and looked around. The decor was stunning—dark wood floors and chic furnishings. She could smell Rosalind's perfume in the air and smiled to herself despite the situation.

The living area was visible through the hallway to her right, and she stumbled towards it. Through an archway she saw a comfortable sitting area, where she pictured mother and daughter curled up on the corner sofa watching movies. On the other side of the room was a glass door that led out onto a balcony.

Ellie swayed a little at the thought of sitting out on a balcony so high up in the air. She tore her gaze away and focused instead on finding the dining table. The airy open-plan layout led to a modern kitchen and then to a dining area. She saw a stack of papers on the table and rushed over to pick them up.

As she grabbed the folders, she realised the table was next to floor-to-ceiling windows. This time there was no balcony to prevent her from seeing straight down to the ground.

The papers slipped from her hand, and she squeezed her eyes

tightly closed as the familiar feeling of horror washed over her. She fell to the floor and crawled away from the window, gripping the legs of the chairs as she pulled herself along. Tears streamed down her face, and she wondered how on earth she would ever get out of there.

In fact, right then, she wondered how she would even survive.

Her breaths were coming in short, shallow pants, and she didn't think she'd ever catch a full breath again. She was shaking so much she couldn't control her limbs as she desperately attempted to get away from the perceived danger of the windows. She felt for certain that the floors were bending and she would suddenly slip and end up pressed against the glass. Nothing felt secure or solid any more. She was falling, even though she was lying on the ground.

Her vision went from blurry to dark around the edges, and she fought to stay awake. She found a solid wall by the kitchen and leaned her back against it, trying to shut out the unsteady feeling. In the back of her mind, she knew she needed to perform her breathing exercises, but she was too caught up in the icy grip of pure panic to even attempt it.

Her eyes drifted closed, and she felt the fight be pulled away from her.

CHAPTER NINETEEN

Rosalind entered her office, took one look at her desk, and then turned around again. She stood by Ellie's desk and examined that for a moment before deducing that her file wasn't there either. She looked up to Irene.

"Have you seen Ellie?"

Irene turned and shook her head. "No, not since I was in your office an hour ago."

Rosalind looked at her watch. She only had ten minutes before the meeting with Rebecca Oakes of Renshaw's. She went back into her office and picked up the phone to call Ellie and ask where she was.

"Hey Mum," Ava said, stepping into her office with a file in her hand.

Rosalind recognised the file immediately. "Hello sweetness, is that the Renshaw notes?"

"Yep, Ellie asked me to give them to you." Ava handed the folder over. "She has a couple of important Christmas party things to sort out. I saw her outside, and she asked me if I could bring this up to you."

Rosalind's lie detector rang loud and clear. Ava wasn't the most accomplished liar in the world, but Rosalind had long ago decided to not let her daughter in on that fact. It was far easier to let Ava think that she'd pulled the wool over her eyes and try to figure out the truth at a later time, than to tip her off and risk her improving her subterfuge skills.

"Thank you, do you know what Ellie was doing?" Rosalind asked casually, flipping through her notes to reacquaint herself with the details. For some reason, Ellie had vanished, and now Ava was covering for her.

"Nope," Ava said. "Just, you know, party stuff."

"I see. Do you know when she'll be back?"

"Nope."

Rosalind looked at her daughter. Try as she might to appear casual, she was failing dismally. Something had obviously happened, and the two of them were going to try to keep it to themselves. Ava didn't look injured or upset, a little shifty but nothing that caused Rosalind much concern. Whatever was going on was obviously centred around Ellie or possibly the Christmas party itself.

Rosalind took a deep breath to stop herself from demanding information from Ava. Doing so was the quickest way to ensure the gateways of communication slammed closed. The best thing she could do now was pretend that she was satisfied with the flimsy excuse and unaware that there was anything to investigate. And then do precisely that as soon as her schedule allowed.

"Okay, darling, thank you for the file. I better go and prepare for this meeting. Will I see you at home, or are we meeting somewhere else?"

Irene knocked on the door. "Rebecca Oakes is here. Would you like me to get her settled?"

Rosalind looked gratefully at Irene. "Yes, please. I'm sorry, Ellie's off running errands."

"It's no trouble," Irene said.

"Can I meet you in Influence?" Ava asked, referencing a cafe on the opposite side of the wharf that Rosalind had once upon a time okayed.

"I thought their hot chocolate was below par?" Rosalind asked.

"You should always give things a second chance," Ava replied. "Influence, okay? What time? When will you be leaving work tonight?"

Rosalind ducked her head into her folder to attempt to hide her smile. Her daughter was clearly trying to discover exactly when she would be leaving the office, something she ordinarily cared little about. Ava spent the waiting time on her mobile phone and rarely noticed when her mother had arrived, anyway. Rosalind decided to not help Ava with whatever situation she was keeping from her.

"I'm not entirely sure yet, sweetness. How about I text you nearer the time?" Rosalind picked up a couple of items from her desk. "I really must get to this meeting. I'll contact you later."

As she passed Ava, she gave her a kiss on the forehead. Ava mumbled a farewell, and Rosalind headed towards the meeting room. She didn't know what her daughter and her assistant were up to, but she was determined to get to the bottom of it quickly.

She tried to push aside the unwanted memory of her evening with Ellie the previous night. As much as Rosalind hated to admit it, the supposed working dinner had quickly turned into something much more intimate. She wished she could blame the setting but knew in her heart that was only a part of it. Dim light and soft music weren't all that was required to turn a dinner into something bordering on romantic. She'd done that herself.

Ellie had been nervous at first, an adorable trait that Rosalind had enjoyed soothing away. Soon enough she had become comfortable, and they'd spoken casually about a range of topics. To Rosalind the entire experience had felt like a date. A very good date, better than any she'd had for a long time. But the fact of the matter was that she shouldn't be going on dates with members of staff, certainly not her own personal assistant. The ethics were as bad as the optics.

Unfortunately, it wasn't going to be easy to step back from it. She'd felt something she hadn't felt for a long time, an indescribable warmth combined with anticipation and a good dollop of nerves.

However, as she kept reminding herself, she shouldn't be having near-candlelit dinners with members of staff, so whatever she was feeling was frankly irrelevant as Ellie was entirely off limits. But try as she might, telling her heart that was a completely different story.

Dinners with staff were a tactic Rosalind frequently used to get to know people and allow them to speak freely outside of the office. Last night was the first night such a dinner had become more than that for her. Thankfully, Ellie hadn't seemed to notice. In fact, she had seemed no different that morning, maybe a little more relaxed, but that was to be expected.

The success of the dinner coupled with the new mystery of Ellie's sudden disappearance spiked Rosalind's curiosity. What had happened over the course of the last hour? Where was Ellie? And why was Ava covering for her?

She entered the meeting room to await her client and tried to push the questions from her mind. She was only partially successful, knowing that the questions would linger until she managed to find answers.

❖

The meeting with Rebecca Oakes lasted forty minutes more than Rosalind had allocated. With no meeting after to allow her to make her excuses, the two women ended up chatting for far longer than Rosalind would have wished.

Fortunately, the meeting had gone well, and Rosalind had achieved everything she wished. Unfortunately, Rebecca was clearly winding down her work output for the Christmas period and was content to sit and drink coffee, eat biscuits, and chat to Rosalind about the upcoming ski season.

Rosalind managed to extract herself from the meeting room, only to end up having another ten minutes of chatting in the corridor by the elevators. She thought it would never end, but luckily Rebecca received a phone call and said she had to leave. Hoping she didn't sound too relieved, Rosalind said goodbye and added that she was looking forward to seeing her at the Christmas party.

She returned to her office feeling weary, having spent far more time than she desired speaking about things that simply didn't interest her. Part of the job was being sociable to all, no matter the topic of conversation, but that didn't mean that Rosalind didn't find it utterly exhausting sometimes.

Seeing Ellie back at her desk instantly brightened her mood. She carefully looked Ellie over from a distance to see if she could detect anything out of the ordinary. Her heart clenched as she noted that something was clearly wrong. Ellie was pale and drawn, her eyes wild as she hunted for a piece of paper on her desk. The relaxed and calm assistant from the morning had completely vanished.

"Good afternoon," Rosalind said, stopping by Ellie's desk.

"Hi, did you get the folder from Ava?" Ellie asked, ducking her head and declining to meet Rosalind's gaze.

Rosalind frowned. "I did, thank you. Everything go okay?"

"Yes. Absolutely." Ellie turned her chair and was now supposedly looking for something in her desk drawers. Rosalind guessed that it was a merely convenient excuse for Ellie to put her back to her. "Do you need anything?"

Ellie was clearly very uncomfortable, and while Rosalind was desperate to find out what had happened and figure out how she could fix it, she could also tell that now was not the right time. Whatever had happened, Ellie wasn't ready to talk about it and most certainly wasn't ready to deal with it.

"Not at the moment. I'll be in my office." Rosalind glanced at Ellie one final time before heading into her private sanctuary and closing the door behind her.

Of course Ellie was allowed to have secrets, everyone was. Rosalind didn't have any control over what Ellie told her and what she kept private. But in that moment, Rosalind positively ached to know what she had missed.

She briefly considered putting a little pressure on Ava to get that part of the puzzle but quickly pushed the thought aside. If she was to know, then she'd find out. She had no professional reason for demanding answers. Ellie had vanished for a short period of time, but it wasn't as if Rosalind demanded her staff remained chained to their desks throughout the day.

She had to accept that her curiosity wasn't because a member of staff had gone missing for a short period of time and returned visibly upset. It was specifically because it was Ellie.

While Rosalind would love to pretend it was simply her proximity to Ellie that made her desperate to know what had happened, she wasn't about to lie to herself. She was smitten with Ellie Pearce, and that was the only reason she yearned to know every detail of what had happened, and to be the one who offered comfort.

Which was all the more reason she had to stay back and leave the situation to resolve itself. If she needed to know, she would eventually.

CHAPTER TWENTY

Ellie sat in the coffee shop with both hands wrapped around the mug containing her peppermint mocha. Usually such a treat would cheer her up, and her feet would be doing a little dance beneath the table. But not today.

"Hey." Will sat in the chair opposite her and looked at her with concern. "I got your S-O-S. What happened?"

Ellie looked up at her best friend and tried to keep herself together. It had taken every last bit of strength she'd had to come back into the office that afternoon and finish up her work. Rosalind had left early, which meant that Ellie had been able to slip away on time, something she hadn't done for weeks.

Part of her wondered if Rosalind suspected something was up and had left the office early to allow Ellie to do the same. The thought mortified her. She didn't want Rosalind to know what had happened and how weak she was.

"Ellie?" Will was seated now, looking at her with compassionate, though worried, eyes.

"I had a panic attack. A big one." Ellie pulled the mug a little closer and stared at the liquid.

"What happened?"

"I got into the apartment okay. I mean, I hated it, but it was okay. But the folder Rosalind needed was on a table by a window, and I…I froze. It felt like the floor was slipping away. I—" She stopped and shook her head before the memory took her over again. "Ava found me."

"Ava?" Will asked.

"Rosalind's pre-teen daughter," Ellie explained.

"What did she say?"

"Nothing much. She obviously wondered why her mum's assistant was alternating between blacking out and hyperventilating in her dining room. When I got myself together, I told her that her mum couldn't know. She helped me. Now I feel terrible because I've asked a child to lie for me. And I'm sure Rosalind knows what's up."

"Are you okay now?" Will asked, cutting through Ellie's overall worry about the situation and zoning in on her well-being, there and then.

"I'm…getting there," she admitted. She wasn't okay, and she knew she wouldn't be for some time yet. But she wasn't having a panic attack on the plush carpet of her boss's luxury apartment, and that was something. "I need you to do something for me next week."

"Sure." Will nodded before even knowing what it was.

Ellie smiled. His kindness really knew no bounds. She was so lucky to have found a friend like him.

"Can you go up to the party venue and FaceTime me, so I can see some of the arrangements? They're going to set up the areas and build and tether the gazebos now, so they can be given clearance by the council. Apparently I need a permit to have a party on a roof." She rolled her eyes at the prospect of extra red tape that she could really do without, especially considering her tight deadlines.

"Good," Will replied. "If they just let anyone have a party anywhere, I'd be worried."

"Well, it's a massive inconvenience for me because it means I need to be ready a couple of weeks earlier than I thought. And any notion I had about possibly going myself is now well and truly out of the window, after what happened this afternoon. I just have to accept that I can't do heights." She took a sip of her drink, sad that the peppermint didn't bring her the joy it usually did.

"You're really not going?" Will asked gently.

Ellie shook her head. "I can't, Will."

"I know—I just thought that with all you're building up there, you might be able to, I don't know, pretend you weren't as high up as you were."

She looked at him and smiled sadly. "It doesn't work like that. I'll know I'm really high up. It's an irrational fear, and it can hit at any time. And I can't take the risk that I'll have another panic attack, especially when I'm at a busy party. What would the guests think? What would Rosalind think?"

"She'll probably wonder why you didn't tell her," Will pointed out.

Ellie rolled her eyes. "You know I can't tell her."

"You keep saying that, but I don't understand why you can't. The possibility that she might pity you shouldn't be enough to make you suffer like this, Ellie."

"Will," Ellie said in a warning tone.

"If she knew, then we wouldn't have to be so cloak-and-dagger about everything. It would make things easier. And it's not like you'll work for her forever—who cares what she thinks about you?"

"I do!"

"Why? It's just Rosalind." Will shrugged.

"I just...want her to like me," Ellie spluttered before realising what she had said.

Will frowned. "Why? I'm sure she'll help you get a new job whether she likes you or not. She'll get a pretty decent commission for placing a qualified statistician like you in a new job."

"It's not that." Ellie lowered her head and let out another big sigh.

"Then what is it?"

Ellie blew out a breath. How did she explain to Will something she hadn't really been able to explain to herself yet? It was lurking at the back of her mind, the daydream fantasy that had no right being fed the oxygen of reality.

But Will needed some kind of answer. He was doing so much for her, he was her best friend, she just wished she could explain without admitting what she was trying to keep buried in her subconscious.

"I'm Christmas Girl, right?" Ellie started to explain. At Will's nod, she continued, "And to the boys at the house, I'm basically the cleaner, cook, and maid. My parents love me, but they fundamentally think of me as some neurotic Christmas obsessive with no real friends and certainly no love life. Rosalind isn't like that. I'm charging all this money to her company credit card and getting all kinds of things delivered, and she has no idea what I'm doing, but she trusts me. I can see it in her eyes, Will. She just trusts me. She speaks to me like I'm a real person. Like she actually wants to know what I think about things."

She saw the smile slip from Will's face and reached out to take his hand. He was her best friend and meant so much to her, but she needed him to understand that she needed more than just one person in her life. It wasn't that he wasn't enough, it was that she wanted to be accepted by more than just one person in a planet of nearly eight billion.

"Rosalind and you are the only two people who see me as a real person. I appreciate you—you know I do. But Rosalind is different. I need someone like Rosalind in my life and to see me as something more than just Christmas Girl."

Ellie was always mindful of the small crush that Will had once upon a time harboured for her. While they had swiftly moved on and become good friends, she was always cautious to never do or say anything that hurt him or unintentionally encouraged him. She knew that her befriending someone new would hurt Will, but she needed him to understand that she needed this. She needed Rosalind to see her as a normal person, not some Christmas obsessive who couldn't climb a stepladder without fainting.

Will held on to her hand and nodded his understanding. "You like her."

"Of course I do. She's successful, intelligent, funny—" Ellie stopped as she realised what Will meant. "Oh no. Nothing like that. I mean, well, she's exactly my type but only in my wildest dreams. Someone like Rosalind would never, *ever* be interested in someone like me. I just want her to like me as a friend. Or even just as a work colleague who actually knows my name and doesn't just see me as Christmas Girl."

He gave her hand a small squeeze and then released it. He sat back in his chair and smiled softly. "Okay, so no telling Rosalind. I don't understand it, but I respect it. Is Ava going to be able to keep this quiet from her mum?"

Ellie let out a small sigh. "I don't know. She says she will. I hope she will. I was in quite a state when she found me, so I think she gets how important it is to me."

"How are you going to explain not being at the party?" Will asked.

"I'm not." Ellie took another sip of her mocha.

"Isn't Rosalind going to expect you to be there?"

"Yep. And she'll think I am there."

Will blinked. "You're, what, going to pretend you're there when you're not? I'm not carrying a carboard cut-out of you around the roof, Ellie."

Ellie laughed. "Don't worry, you won't have to."

"So what's the plan?"

"Think about it logically. Rosalind will be super busy, and I'm going to be doing party stuff, or supposedly doing party stuff. It's perfectly reasonable that we won't see each other that night. There are two hundred and thirty-six people coming to the party. Why would we see each other? It will be fine."

"You think?" Will asked, clearly very sceptical.

"Sure. Especially with you helping me." Ellie batted her eyelashes a few times.

He laughed. "I just don't know how you expect to be able to pull it all off."

"I have a plan." Ellie nodded knowingly.

"A plan that you're sure will work?" Will asked.

"Of course." Ellie gestured towards the counter of the coffee shop. "Can I get you something?"

Will looked at his watch. "Sure, I'll have a filter coffee, thanks."

"Sandwich? My treat," Ellie offered. She'd already decided

she was going to have a melted cheese and ham toastie with a bag of crisps and another mocha. She'd need the sugar and fat to get over the horrors of the day. She texted the boys and told them that they were on their own that evening. The chef was taking the night off.

"Go on, then, can I have—"

"The beef and horseradish, I know," she said. "You have the same thing every time you come here."

"It's the best sandwich they do. Why mess with perfection?" he asked with a grin.

She grabbed her purse off the table and went over to the counter to get them some food so they could talk over their strategy. She hadn't exactly lied to Will—she did have a plan. Or parts of a plan, to be accurate. So what if a part of that plan was crossing her fingers and hoping that Rosalind wouldn't notice her absence at the party of the year?

CHAPTER TWENTY-ONE

Rosalind poured a generous amount of gin over the large ice cubes that sat in the glass tumbler. She added a small amount of tonic water and softly swirled the two together. Ava was deep in concentration at the dining table, focused on science homework that went well over Rosalind's head.

She took a small sip and regarded her daughter, wondering the best way to bring up the topic of conversation she was hoping for. Ava was no fool. The days where Rosalind could wheedle information out of her were long gone. She was just as wily as her mother.

The direct route was preferable but sadly out of the question. As the afternoon had worn on, it had become abundantly obvious that something was terribly wrong with Ellie. So much so that Rosalind had decided to leave the office early solely to allow Ellie an escape from whatever it was that was clearly bothering her.

"Can I get you a drink, sweetness?" Rosalind asked.

Ava pulled one earpiece out of her ear. "Sorry?"

"Can I get you a drink?" Rosalind repeated.

"Can I have a Coke?"

"What do you think?" Rosalind asked. Ava was aware of the one fizzy drink per day rule and had already consumed it on the way home from school.

"Can I have a gin and tonic?" Ava asked playfully.

Rosalind walked into the dining area, placed her drink down

on a coaster, and pulled up a chair beside her cheeky offspring. "On the rocks?"

"What does that mean?" Ava asked.

"The fact you don't know means you're too young to be ordering a gin and tonic. What are you working on?" Rosalind looked at the open textbook and held her breath, hoping that Ava wasn't in need of any help.

"The life cycle of plants," Ava said. "Which is about two minutes, around you and me."

Rosalind chuckled. She couldn't deny it—her lack of green fingers was notorious. Plants wilted as she held them. Ava had never shown an interest in plants, and Rosalind had nothing to offer her by way of advice, anyway. Between them, they were the most efficient of horticultural assassins.

"Shouldn't take you long to complete the module," Rosalind mused. "Did you speak to Ellie today?"

"Only in passing." Ava turned back to her work.

Rosalind took another sip of her drink and regarded her. She was clearly lying—her shoulders had hunched slightly, her lips were pursed, and she refused to make eye contact. As Rosalind had suspected at the start, Ava knew something.

"How did she seem?"

Ava shrugged. "I don't know, like normal."

"Ellie's not normal," Rosalind teased.

"True, okay, she seemed like Ellie."

"Did she say anything out of the ordinary?"

Ava lowered her pen and turned to face her mother. "No. Why do you ask?"

"Just asking." Rosalind took another sip of her drink.

"Seems weird that you're suddenly asking these questions about your assistant," Ava said. She narrowed her eyes at her mother. "Do you fancy her, Mum?"

Rosalind nearly choked. She coughed a couple of times and swallowed to clear her throat. "What? No, of course not. What a thing to say, Ava!"

"What? She's cute, she's into women. You're into women." Ava kept a keen focus on her.

"You think she's cute?" Rosalind asked, her pulse rate going through the roof. The last thing she needed was for Ava's sudden declaration about her sexuality to be in any way tied to Ellie's presence.

"For an old person, yeah, she's okay." Ava's eyebrows rose as she realised what her mother was asking. "Oh, ew! Mum! No, not for me. For you! Ellie's, like, ancient! Oh, ew, I need to bleach my brain now. Thanks a lot."

"She's much younger than me, Ava," Rosalind pointed out.

Ava stopped her fake retching. She stared at her mother, her eyes twinkling. "So you do like her."

"What? No!"

"Then why are you asking about her so much?"

"I've barely said anything."

"You quizzed me when I dropped off the folder, you asked me on the way home, you asked me over dinner, and now you're casually asking me again. Do you fancy her? It's okay if you do—you can tell me stuff like that, you know. Besides, I think you'd be good together."

Ava's gaze pierced her thoughts, and Rosalind sat stock still, hoping that any faint traces of attraction could somehow escape the barcode scanner of her daughter's gaze.

"Ava, it would be completely inappropriate for me to think of Ellie that way. We're not discussing it." Rosalind stood up, grabbed her drink, and stalked back to the kitchen.

"Why inappropriate?" Ava asked.

"Because she works for me." Rosalind tossed the rest of her drink down the sink, not wanting to say anything she'd later regret because of alcohol.

"So what? Darren McKenna and that woman in accounts… Lauren? They got married. They work together." Ava followed her into the kitchen and sat at the breakfast bar.

Rosalind opened the dishwasher and pulled out the tray.

"That's different. Darren is a client manager, and Laura works in accounts."

"I don't get it."

Rosalind put the glass in the dishwasher and closed the door. She pinched the bridge of her nose and let out a sigh. She didn't feel emotionally ready to have the discussion but knew that was irrelevant. Ava needed to understand the importance of give and take and, more importantly, power imbalances.

Rosalind couldn't not have such an important conversation just because she didn't feel like it, or worse because she felt guilty for even involuntarily considering bending the rules she had in place for herself. Rules she wished all people in positions of power had for themselves.

"It's frowned upon for bosses to date assistants. Or for anyone with some kind of authority over another to ask them out."

"Why?"

Rosalind leaned back against the worktop and folded her arms across her chest. "Say a boss asks an assistant out for dinner—there's a chance that the assistant might feel that their job is at risk if they say no. Worse, they may feel coerced to do something they don't feel comfortable doing because it's their boss asking. Then there's other employees to think of. If someone is dating the boss, then other employees may think that person is getting preferential treatment. It's a bad idea all round."

"If you asked Ellie out, I think she'd say yes," Ava said.

"It's irrelevant. I shouldn't be asking Ellie out. It risks there being a power imbalance in our relationship. Can you see how that could be awkward?"

Ava thought about it for a moment and nodded. "In some situations. Like, if you had a really gross boss, and he asked you out, and you didn't want to, then that could be weird. But that's not you and Ellie."

"You can't be sure of that. I wouldn't want to put Ellie into an uncomfortable situation. I wouldn't want her to do something she didn't want to do just because I, as her boss, asked her."

Ava sniggered.

"What's funny?" Rosalind demanded, wondering why her daughter was being so flippant about something so important.

Ava waved the question away. "Nothing, it's just funny that you think you have any control over Ellie. She's her own person, Mum. If you said she had to go to dinner with you or you'd sack her, she'd probably pack up her Christmas lights and all those plastic elves and give you the finger as she left the office."

Rosalind grinned. "Well, yes, that's probably true."

"It's cute that you think you have authority over her." Ava chuckled. "Crazy, but cute."

"Well, I'm glad I can amuse you with my delusions of grandeur." Rosalind laughed in return.

Ava was right, of course. Ellie might have appeared to be meek at first, but time had proved that she was anything but.

"Why haven't you asked her about any of the secret Christmas party planning?" Ava asked.

She shrugged. "I suppose I trust her to figure it all out."

Ava slipped down from the breakfast bar stool. "Yeah, you do trust her. And you hardly ever trust anyone, definitely not with anything important." She pointed towards her schoolwork. "I better get back to learning about how to not kill plants."

Rosalind swallowed and nodded. Ava knew her well, sometimes far too well. She watched Ava return to her homework before making an escape to her bedroom. The fact-finding mission hadn't gone very well at all. All she had done was trigger Ava's curiosity, and that was never a good thing.

She sat at the vanity table and stared at her reflection. Feelings for Ellie had been niggling at the back of her mind for a little while, but knowing something had happened that day had brought them flooding to the surface.

Ava seemed almost happy about the idea of her and Ellie being together. Not entirely surprising considering how quickly Ava had taken to Ellie. But Ava was a good judge of character, quick to size someone up and decide whether or not they were worth her time. It was a skill that Rosalind had taken into her professional life and one that Ava seemed to have inherited.

"You'd be good together." Rosalind whispered Ava's words to her reflection. Ava had spent some time with Ellie and was probably one of the best people to make that pronouncement.

She shook her head. It was silly to give the idea more than a second of thought. Ava's aspiration of having her cool new friend and her mother together was nothing more than a childish fantasy. It would never work. Primarily because it was *wrong*. Rosalind couldn't date her assistant.

"Don't be ridiculous," she chided her reflection. "It's a little crush, nothing more."

She stood up and looked at her watch. Leaving the office early had left her with a little extra work to do that evening. She knew her time would be much better spent getting on with that rather than thinking about things that would never—*could* never—be.

Chapter Twenty-two

Ellie felt someone watching her and stopped typing. She turned to see Rosalind standing by her desk and looking distastefully at a garland of tinsel that Ellie had used to decorate the top of her in tray. Ellie chuckled. Rosalind made no effort whatsoever to hide her dislike of Christmas decorations, which some would consider kitsch. Or *tacky*, as Rosalind would no doubt label them.

"There won't be any of that at the party, I take it?" Rosalind asked, pointing at the tinsel.

"Tons of it," Ellie said. "I've placed a bulk order with a warehouse in China. I just hope it gets here in time. Ideally, I want the rooftop to be seen from space."

Rosalind narrowed her eyes. "You mock me?" she asked in jest.

"I do." Ellie returned to her typing. "I know you well enough to know not to have any tinsel—don't worry."

"And how do you know that I don't like tinsel?"

Ellie paused typing and slowly turned her head. "Oh, don't you worry. I know someone who doesn't like tinsel when I see them."

Rosalind smiled, folded her arms, and sat on the edge of the desk. "Oh, really? Am I that transparent?"

"Yes. You don't like glitter or tinsel. I'm going to guess that you're also against tacky fairies on top of Christmas trees, probably hate inflatable snowmen. Oh, and Santa. I bet you loathe him."

Rosalind laughed loudly, and Ellie smiled internally at being the cause of such a wonderful sound. "You think I don't like Santa?"

Ellie nodded. "You're more an Old Saint Nick person. I can't see a commercialised depiction of Santa being your thing at all." She picked up a Christmas card that had arrived that morning and had a cartoonish, jolly Santa on the front. She held it up for Rosalind to see.

Rosalind rolled her eyes and playfully sighed. "Fine, you're right. On all counts. I better go back to work and mumble *bah, humbug* under my breath while I work by candlelight."

"It'll all be over in a couple of weeks," Ellie said.

"Thank goodness." Rosalind winked. She stood up and walked into her office, closing the door behind her.

Ellie grinned. Their relationship was growing by the day, from slightly scary boss to something so much more. Ellie both loved and hated the transformation. Sharing playful banter and getting to know more about how Rosalind ticked was wonderful. On the other hand, the closer they got, the more uncontrollable Ellie's crush became.

A calendar note popped up on her screen, and she realised she was running late. She grabbed her phone and hurried towards the ladies' bathroom. The moment she entered the room, a FaceTime request popped up on her screen from Will.

It was the third time he had agreed to go up onto the roof of New Providence Wharf and see to the party arrangements. She knew she owed him big and had already managed to secure what she was sure would be the best Christmas present ever for him.

"Hi Will," she said, turning on the camera on her phone.

"Hey. Can you see everything okay?" Will flipped the camera from front-facing to show the roof space.

"I can—it looks great!" Ellie leaned against the washbasin and looked at her plans coming together before her eyes. The gazebos were now fitted in place and created the labyrinth she had designed. The space was long and wide, so Ellie had decided early on to make a number of separate zones to hide the shape of the space, protect against the winds, and create a storyline for guests to move around.

"Is the forest finished?" she asked.

"Yep. George got the last walls installed today," Will said. The camera shook a little as he walked through the labyrinth. "Honestly, Ellie, it looks incredible up here."

"It will look even better when I get my decorations up," Ellie said. "That needs to be last-minute though, just in case of poor weather. Don't want my reindeer getting wet."

Will walked into the large space that would hold Ellie's winter wonderland forest, and she gasped with delight at how perfect it looked. It was the middle of the day, and the sun shone a little through the hard canvas, but even so, the effect of the small fairy lights illuminating the way through the dark space was not lost. All Ellie needed was her fake snow and her decor, and it would be magical.

Her heart clenched at the knowledge that she'd never see it in person.

"George says his photographer is coming tonight to get the pictures," Will said.

"Great, tell him he owes me." Ellie chuckled.

"I did. He agreed."

George was one of the property managers and had taken a keen interest in Ellie's designs from day one. Hesitant at first, he was now her biggest cheerleader as he understood that he would be able to use promotional photography from the event to advertise the space year-round. Ellie's plans and vision had given the property a whole new income stream, which had bought her a lot of goodwill, and Ellie was determined to use it.

"Tell him that the furniture will be delivered on Friday—ask if he can have his team take it to the roof and secure it."

"Yes, I think he said he'd already heard about the delivery. I'll double-check. Hey, you and I should open an event-planning company. We're getting good at this."

"We are!" Ellie smiled. "Who says you actually have to visit locations to organise events? You just need a good friend and a whole lot of planning."

"Yes. This is easy. Oh, we have that extra heater installed. Want to see it?"

"Yes, please."

The camera started to shake again as Will walked through the various temporary rooms. Ellie again began to wonder if she just might be able to get herself up there, but the thought was quickly pushed away by the memory of her most recent panic attack. She couldn't risk that happening again.

It had taken a long time to learn her limits. As a child, she'd pushed herself too far and frequently ended up in a debilitated state. As she got older, those panic attacks started to have real physical and emotional side effects, which made her fear worse, rather than better. She'd learnt, over time, that pushing herself further than she was able to go was damaging to her health. In the long run, she was making herself worse.

The solution was to identify her limits and stay within them. That rule wasn't going to make it onto a T-shirt design or be used as an inspirational poster. But sometimes the boring, practical statements were the most accurate.

"By the way, are we still on for dinner tomorrow?" Will asked.

"Absolutely, there's a full turkey dinner with my name on it."

"Don't you get sick of roast turkey?"

"Do you get sick of oxygen?" Ellie asked.

Suddenly, she heard the door to the bathroom start to open. She ended the call and leaned against the basin, attempting to look casual, but the look on Rosalind's face told her she wasn't managing it at all.

"Busted," Rosalind said, grinning.

Ellie continued to lean against the basin, knowing that she looked ridiculous, but her brain couldn't seem to come up with any other suggestion.

Rosalind looked her up and down before turning and half-heartedly looking around the room. "Oh Lord, don't tell me I've caught you at it again? Is he here?"

Ellie rolled her eyes at the teasing. "No, I told you what happened."

"Well, so you claim," Rosalind said, goading her, looking

into the cubicles to continue her joshing. "But you can never tell. Sometimes people seem so innocent, but they are actually completely the opposite. Is this a weekly rendezvous?"

"I'm not even going to justify that with an answer," Ellie replied, finally finding her foothold in the conversation.

"Daily?" Rosalind asked in mock surprise. "My, my. Always the quiet ones." She looked down at the phone that Ellie still gripped in her hand. "You seem awfully flustered. What were you up to, really?"

"Nothing, just...checking the news."

"I see. What's been happening in the world?"

"Stuff." Ellie held her head high but knew she had all but lost any possibility of fooling Rosalind.

"Comprehensive." Rosalind smiled and bit her lower lip in amusement. "You really are terrible at this."

"I know. I was making a call," Ellie admitted.

"There's a phone at your desk."

"A private call," Ellie added.

"Finally looking for a job that matches your experience?" Rosalind asked without a hint of concern. "You don't have to run off in here to make those calls. Feel free to take them at your desk. I know you won't be staying here forever. Just don't leave me in the lurch."

"I wouldn't."

"I know you wouldn't." Rosalind's face softened from teasing to gentle.

Ellie's phone started to ring again, the screen clearly showing Ellie's saved picture of Will's smiling face. She turned her phone away but knew it was too late and Rosalind had already seen him.

"Ah, Bathroom Boy it is," Rosalind said.

Ellie froze, having no idea what to do next. The sound of the call echoed around the tiled room. Rosalind took a step closer and whispered in Ellie's ear, "Maybe you ought to, you know, answer that?"

Ellie nearly moaned.

A hundred fantasies of other times Rosalind might whisper in her ear flashed through her mind.

"I…have to go." Ellie slid past Rosalind and made her escape into the hallway. As she hurried down the corridor, she nearly tripped over her own feet in her haste to escape.

"Oh, boy," she muttered to herself.

Chapter Twenty-three

Rosalind's desk phone rang. She glanced up to Ellie's empty desk and frowned for a moment before recalling that Ellie had gone home early. She looked at the display on the phone and saw that it was reception.

She picked up the phone.

"Hi, sorry to bother you, Miss Caldwell. We have a visitor in reception for Ellie, but she's not answering her phone."

"She's left for the day, who is it?" Rosalind asked.

"It's a gentleman from New Providence Wharf. He says he urgently needs a certificate. Something about the Christmas party," the receptionist said.

"I see. Send him up, please."

She put the phone down and finished up her email. When finished, she quickly crossed over to the elevator to meet the visitor. She arrived just in time.

"Hello, you're here to see Ellie?" Rosalind asked.

"Yes, I'm George Ward."

"Rosalind Caldwell." She held out her hand.

"Thanks for seeing me, sorry to interrupt your day, but I have a bit of an issue. The council have issued a certificate to confirm the roof space can be used for an event. I have a copy, and I sent that to the insurance company, but they want to see the original. Don't ask me why." George threw his hands up like a man who'd had enough of red tape for one day.

"That shouldn't be a problem. Come with me, and we'll dig it out." Rosalind gestured for him to follow her back to Ellie's desk.

"I tried to call Ellie, but I couldn't get through," George said.

"She's left early for the day—she has a meeting with the catering company and then something else over the other side of town. She's probably in a meeting."

Rosalind sat at Ellie's desk and looked for the black folder that she knew held all the paperwork for the party. Ellie clutched the folder like a lifeline and was forever adding to it or using it to find phone numbers or other details. Rosalind had made a joke or two about Ellie probably sleeping with it.

She opened the desk drawers and looked through some paperwork. "Ah, we may have a problem. She might have the folder with her, and I'm certain the certificate will be in there."

She picked up the phone and dialled Ellie's mobile number. It only took a second for Ellie's voice mail to kick in.

"Ellie, can you give me a call when you get this?" She hung up before turning back to George. "I'm sorry, I'm not sure what else I can do to help. I'm judging by the fact you've come over here in person that this is urgent."

George nodded. "Yes, we need to have insurance in place immediately, or we have to take all the preparation work down again. That will put us behind, not to mention we'd need to get the council out again to approve everything we've done and then issue another certificate. And that's if the council will even be able to get out to us. Ellie pulled a few strings to get them out the first time."

Rosalind held up her hand to slow George's panic. "I see. Can we negotiate with the insurance company? Who are the insurers?"

"It's Greysons—they're based just over the road. They said they need to see the original today, or they will have to pull cover."

Rosalind had a number of contacts in many businesses throughout the city but, sadly, no one at Greysons. "Is there any chance that we can get an extension on that?"

"I doubt it. Let me just give them another quick call, just in case." George pulled his phone out of his pocket and dialled a number.

Rosalind stood and walked to Irene's desk. "Do you know if Ellie had the party folder with her when she left?"

"I think so." Irene cocked her head to the side as she tried to recall. "Probably, she has it with her most of the time. Is there a problem?"

"Apparently the insurance company wants to see an original certificate, not a copy."

Irene rolled her eyes. "In this day and age?"

"You know insurance—they're about fifty years behind the curve," Rosalind mused. She noticed George was off the phone and walked back to him. "Any luck?"

"They said they need it today, but they're open until ten o'clock this evening." George looked apologetic. "I'm sorry, they literally let me know this an hour ago."

Rosalind gestured for him to follow her into her office. She plucked a business card from her desk drawer. "It's not your fault—these things are sent to try us. Could you email me the name of the person I need to see and their address, and then advise them to expect me later tonight? I'll go to Ellie and bring the certificate back here. I live just around the corner anyway."

George took the business card. "Thank you, I really appreciate your help."

"I appreciate the use of your roof." Rosalind smiled. "And what's a party without a last-minute hiccup? If this is all it is, I'll be happy."

George thanked her again, and she accompanied him back to the elevator to show him out. While she didn't relish the idea of traipsing across town so late in the day, she also knew that Ellie was no doubt at her appointment in Hammersmith by now, which meant she was at the opposite end of the city. Coming back into Docklands to deliver the certificate would be a very long journey, and even longer for her to get back home again.

And that was if Rosalind managed to get hold of her before she turned her phone off for the night. Not that she imagined Ellie did such a thing without checking her messages first, but there was always a possibility, and that could be the end of the Christmas party.

Rosalind had a remarkably clear afternoon, and she walked past the insurance offices on her way home anyway, so it just made sense to go and get it herself.

She couldn't ignore that part of her enthusiasm to help out was that she would be able to get a peek at Ellie's home. She knew it was wrong to be so curious—some might say nosy—but Rosalind enjoyed teasing her and watching the adorable blush touch Ellie's cheeks.

Turning up on her doorstep would surely be a fun outing.

She grabbed her things from her office and approached Irene again.

"Irene, could you call HR and get Ellie's home address and email it to me? I'm going to go and get that paperwork rather than dragging her all the way back here. Do you have any idea roughly where she lives?"

Irene picked up her phone. "She lives over Clapham way, I think."

"I'll head into the city then, thank you. I've put us through to voice mail, but if there's anything urgent, you know how to contact me."

"No problem, I'll hold down the fort," Irene said. "See you tomorrow."

❖

Rosalind walked down the residential street, peering into the darkened gardens to see if she could note a door number. The closer she got to her destination, the more she worried about whether or not she was doing the right thing.

She'd deliberately quashed down any thought as to why she was visiting Ellie at home. As the boss, it was perfectly within her rights to demand that an employee returned to the office with essential paperwork that they had removed from the premises.

For some reason Rosalind didn't want Ellie to go out of her way, and the opportunity to see Ellie's home life was tantalising.

She'd tried to push away the sinful thoughts of Ellie that had been slowly filling her brain, but to no avail. She was hooked on knowing more about the mysterious, complex, and fascinating woman who sat outside her office every day. It was fast turning into an obsession.

The prospect of seeing Ellie's home was too good a chance to pass up. The insight would be interesting, to say the least. And catching Ellie unawares would be a little treat. Ellie's nervous blush was becoming one of Rosalind's favourite things to see. It was also the reason she did things that were probably a little unwise, like whispering in Ellie's ear or turning up at her home unannounced. But the real joy was when Ellie rose above the nerves and confronted her head-on. Rosalind enjoyed the teasing that soon became a two-way street. Maybe she enjoyed it a little too much.

Of course, she'd called and emailed Ellie a couple of times along the journey. But it had become very clear that Ellie's phone was off for some reason. Ordinarily, that would have frustrated her, but as she drew closer to her goal, she was thankful for it.

She found herself in front of number thirty-eight and entered the small front garden. The pathway had more slabs that were broken than were intact. A couple of dead bushes filled the rest of the small space. No one on the street seemed particularly green-fingered, and Rosalind certainly wasn't one to cast stones. But even so, it seemed like a sad frontage to somewhere called home, unloved to say the least.

She rang the bell and waited patiently, wondering if Ellie was already home or if she was in for a wait. A light sprang to life in the hallway. Heavy footsteps approached, and a large shadow filled the frosted glass of the door.

Definitely not Ellie.

The lock clicked open, and the door was pulled open, with some effort. A tall young man looked at her in confusion.

"Er. Hi?"

"Is Ellie in?" Rosalind asked.

"Um. No."

The lumbering great lad in front of her was clearly not one for small talk. She took in his sweatpants, torn T-shirt, and dishevelled hair and hoped that this was not some secret love interest that Ellie was keeping hidden. Ellie deserved better.

"Do you know when she'll be back?"

"Dunno."

"Who is it, Charlie?" another male voice called from inside the house.

Good Lord, Rosalind thought. Another one.

Charlie looked at her in confusion.

"I'm Rosalind, Ellie's boss."

That did the trick. Charlie stood a little taller and cleared his throat. "Oh, right. Um. Do you want to come in?"

Rosalind thanked him and stepped into the hallway.

"It's Ellie's boss," Charlie yelled.

Two more young men appeared in the hallway.

Three, Rosalind noted. A notion skittered through her mind that Ellie might be part of a very interesting…arrangement.

One of the men held his hand out politely. "Hi, I'm Theo."

Rosalind smiled at him and shook his hand, relieved that one of the lugs had some manners. "Nice to meet you, Theo."

"This is Charlie, and this is Matt." Theo introduced the two others.

She heard footsteps and looked up to see yet another man coming down the stairs.

"That's Neil," Theo said.

"Are there any more of you lurking?" Rosalind asked.

Theo laughed. "Nah, just the four of us. And Ellie. She's not home yet, not sure when she's due."

Matt folded his arms and leaned against the wall. "Yeah, she used to be home like clockwork, but these days it's impossible to know when she'll be back."

Charlie stood beside him. "Yeah, she's doing a lot of overtime for you."

Rosalind tried to hide her smirk. The two were doing a terrible job of trying to mildly intimidate her.

"Yeah, we hardly see her these days. And she had to cancel her Christmas carol rehearsal because she was too busy," Neil added.

"If you have something to say, by all means say it," Rosalind challenged.

The hallway was narrow and the men were strapping, rugby-playing types who filled the space. Someone else might have felt unsettled, but Rosalind could easily tell that they would scuttle away at the very idea of conflict, though, she had to confess their attempts to play protective big brother were adorable but, sadly for them, woeful, as fear was clear in their eyes.

Theo, who seemed the most sensible of the bunch, said, "We're just worried about her. She's working very hard—"

"Too hard," someone interjected.

"And she's really stressed out," Theo continued.

"Since she was promoted demoted," Neil added.

"Promoted demoted?" Rosalind asked.

Charlie elbowed Neil in the ribs.

"When she gets home, she can hardly keep her eyes open," Matt added.

"I'm worried about her," Neil said. "She needs to rest."

Charlie nodded quickly. "She does. She's exhausted."

The sound of a key sliding into the lock on the front door stopped the conversation dead. The front door was shouldered open by someone a lot more petite than the men that towered around Rosalind and blocked her view of the door.

"Hey guys, sorry I'm late," Ellie said. "My phone died, uch! I was sure I had charged it, but the cable wasn't in properly, and then it died and I couldn't find anywhere to charge it. One meeting overran, and I was late for another. Then my Tube stopped in a tunnel for, like, twenty minutes. I'll get dinner started in a minute. I got milk on the way home."

Rosalind's eyebrows rose, and she noted that each of the lecturing men suddenly seemed half as tall as they had been.

"Matt, are you still doing gluten-free? If so, I can try to do some different dumplings for you. Dinner will be ready in about an hour, unless there are no saucepans clean. Then I'll need to… actually I'll need to do the washing up anyway. Say an hour and fifteen to be on the safe side."

Rosalind narrowed her eyes, and each of the men shrank even further back.

"Hello, Ellie," Rosalind said, announcing her presence. "Don't you worry about making dinner. Your delightful housemates were just telling me how they were planning on making you dinner tonight. Weren't you, gentlemen?"

Her words were received by a flurry of nodding heads.

"And you'll be leaving the kitchen in a perfectly clean state, won't you? Including doing every. Single. Dish." She stabbed each of them in the chest to punctuate her point.

Given their orders, the men hurried into the kitchen in a rugby scrum in their eagerness to escape Rosalind's glare. She turned around and saw a stunned-looking Ellie standing in the hallway with her coat half off and her mouth open.

"Good evening," Rosalind said, revelling in the fact that she had surprised Ellie so thoroughly.

"Uh. Hi?" Ellie squeaked.

Rosalind pointed over her shoulder to the kitchen. "Four men, Ellie? Really. Does Will know?"

Ellie rolled her eyes and pulled her coat off. "They are my housemates. You know that. Stop teasing me."

"I like teasing you," Rosalind admitted.

"Um. Ellie?" Matt approached, nervously wringing his hands as he looked from Rosalind to Ellie. "How do we make the, uh, the casserole?"

"I'm going to go out on a limb here and assume that you've heard of Google," Rosalind said.

"Yes, right, yeah…I'll…" He hurried away.

"They don't know how to cook," Ellie said.

"What a wonderful learning opportunity for them this is, then."

Rosalind looked around. "Is there somewhere we can talk?"

Ellie nodded and pointed to the stairs, picking up her bags and climbing to the first floor. Rosalind fell into step behind her, shaking her head in despair at the confused noises coming from the kitchen.

A moment later Rosalind realised she was standing in Ellie's bedroom. The wall-to-wall Christmas imagery was the first clue. The bed and desk sealed the deal. She was again struck by the recognition that Ellie was more or less just starting out in the big city and could only afford a tiny room in a houseshare for herself.

Rosalind had been in a similar situation once herself but had all but forgotten this stage of her life. Too eager to get up the employment ladder and on to better things, she'd quickly moved beyond this stage.

"It's not much, but it's home," Ellie said. "Am I in trouble?"

"Why would you be in trouble?" Rosalind asked.

"It's not every day the boss comes to your house." Ellie unbuttoned her cardigan and threw it on the back of her chair. She opened a drawer and pulled out a cosy sweater and pulled that on.

"The insurance company that the venue is using need to see the original of the council's permit," Rosalind explained. "I believe you have it with you. I couldn't get hold of you, and I was in the area for a meeting anyway, so I thought I'd drop in." She didn't know why she lied, especially about something that the person who managed her diary could so easily check.

"Oh! They said a copy would be fine." Ellie put her bag on the desk and started rummaging through pieces of paper.

"Well, it's not any more. They would like the original by this evening."

"I'll get it to them now. I'm so sorry, Rosalind. My phone died and—"

"It's fine, Ellie," Rosalind said. "And I'll take it back. It's on my way. No point in you going all the way back to Docklands and back here again."

Ellie looked up at her, all big doe eyes and confusion. "You'll take it?"

"Of course." Rosalind wondered if it really was so unlikely that she'd do such a thing. Ellie was looking at her as if she'd grown a second head.

You wouldn't have done it for Vanessa, she reminded herself.

Some shouting erupted from downstairs. Ellie looked embarrassed and sighed. "Sorry about them. They are sweet enough, just a bit useless."

"So I gathered," Rosalind said.

"It's just that house prices are mad and…"

"You now cook dinner for four men?" Rosalind asked playfully. "I'm hoping you take it in turns, and I've just arrived on your night to cook."

Ellie's face said it all.

"Please tell me you don't do all the cleaning."

Ellie handed Rosalind the certificate, then sat on the edge of the bed. "It's do the cleaning or live in a dirty house."

"Okay." Rosalind put the certificate into her bag. "But you get a reduction in rent, surely?"

Ellie looked down at her feet in embarrassment.

"I see." Rosalind looked around the room. It was modest, though comfortable. Ellie clearly took pride in her surroundings. Photos of her family sat alongside fascinating woodcarvings of festive elves. "What are these?"

Ellie looked up. "Nisse, from Norway."

"Nisse?"

"They are little men with long red stocking caps who are supposed to reside in barns in Norway. If you care for them, they will bring prosperity to your barn. If you ignore them, then they become troublesome." Ellie stood up, plucked one of the ornaments, and handed it to Rosalind. "I picked these up in Norway a few years ago."

Rosalind looked at the decoration with interest. "I've never heard of them. How do you care for them?"

"You leave them a bowl of rice pudding on Christmas Eve," Ellie explained.

Rosalind handed back the elf. "And your barn is prosperous?"

Ellie laughed. "Hardly. Maybe I need to give them more rice pudding?"

"Maybe you create your own prosperity," Rosalind mused. "Although it certainly can't hurt to appease these…What are they called again?"

"Nisse."

"Hmm." Rosalind realised she was out of small talk. It now felt strange to be in Ellie's bedroom with the door closed and in such close proximity with not a lot to talk about. Ellie was embarrassed and exhausted, and Rosalind knew that she should probably take her leave.

But she didn't want to go. She wanted to be there for Ellie, wanted to hold her and talk about how to get her into a job that was worthy of her. Start her on a career path where she'd be able to use her incredible intellect, where she'd be happy and earn a decent salary. One which meant she didn't have to live with four toddlers.

The only problem was that wasn't her responsibility, and there was a very real possibility that her input would be unwelcome. Rosalind could see that Ellie wasn't happy, but saying that and asking to help fix it were completely different matters.

Her gaze fell upon the bed, and out of nowhere she wondered if the archives boy had been in the room. Possibly even in the bed.

Was there anything between him and Ellie? It was none of her business, but she ached to know. Twice she had caught Ellie engaged in some secretive conversation with him, and twice Ellie had launched a nervous denial of anything between them. She tried to tell herself that it didn't matter, that it was irrelevant to her, but she couldn't shake the feeling.

She looked at the window and realised that some kind of opaque film had been applied to it. Curtains hung neatly on either side of the window, and Rosalind wondered why the glass had been covered.

"Is your view so bad you had to block it out?" Rosalind asked.

Ellie chuckled. "Our garden is a state. I'm sorry about the certificate," Ellie said. "Really, I did check, and the person I spoke to said a copy was fine."

"I don't doubt you. Insurance companies are fickle. No harm done." Rosalind smiled. "As I said to the building manager, parties always have a last-minute problem, and if this is ours, then I'll be very happy. All the other arrangements have gone well, yes?"

A flicker of something flashed in Ellie's eyes for a second before it was gone again.

"Yes, everything is going great," Ellie said with a tired enthusiasm that Rosalind could see right through.

"I look forward to you showing me what you're creating in my meeting room," she said lightly, attempting to get a smile out of Ellie. "Considering you keep the door locked."

"That's just to make sure nothing gets damaged," Ellie explained.

Rosalind knew that was the case, and she had a master key to every door in the office, so it wasn't like she couldn't take a look if she wanted to. But she'd decided to let Ellie have her privacy and reveal whatever she'd been working on when she was good and ready to do so.

Again, a luxury she would never have afforded Vanessa. She looked at Ellie and wondered what it was, exactly, that was creating an invisible pull for her. She knew it was wrong to desire Ellie in the way she did. Age and position meant that a relationship was impossible. And there was the not-so-small matter that she was positive that Ellie would never be interested in someone like her. Yes, she kept herself in shape and maybe didn't feel all of her many years. But she was still much older than Ellie.

Then again, Ellie had indicated she liked the company of older people. Maybe the age gap wouldn't be such a big problem.

But the fact Ellie was her assistant most definitely was.

The thought depressed her.

Finally, she'd found someone she was actually interested in, and it wasn't possible. And even if it was possible, it wouldn't be right. She wouldn't date an employee. Others might, and that was their choice. But Rosalind had worked in recruitment for a long time and had heard the horror stories. People being fired, people being sued, and worst of all people feeling coerced to do something they weren't comfortable with.

"I better be going," Rosalind said. She knew that staying any longer would only pull on her already strained resolve.

"Thank you for coming all this way. I wouldn't have minded dropping off the paperwork," Ellie said.

"Oh, I know. As I say, I had a meeting over this way."

A slight frown started to form on Ellie's face, presumably as she wondered what sudden meeting in an unlikely part of town had caused Rosalind to be local.

"Anyway, have a lovely evening," Rosalind said before Ellie could question her. "I'll see myself out. I want to say goodbye to those delightful young men before I leave."

Ellie smiled. "What are you going to say to them?"

I'm going to tell them to pull their weight and stop treating you like a slave. I'm going to let them know that I saw right through them. I'm going to suggest that they insist on a fairer division of labour. And I'm going to suggest that I'll be back to check up on them.

"Nothing, just a polite farewell," she said. "See you in the morning."

Try as she might, Ellie wasn't able to eavesdrop on the whispered words that took place in the kitchen. After a short exchange, she did hear the sound of heels clicking on the tiled floor of the downstairs hall and the door closing, with some help from one of the boys, indicating that Rosalind had left.

Ellie went back into her room, closed the door, and flopped on the bed. She couldn't believe that Rosalind had been in her house, in her bedroom. Her dreams that night would be uncontrollable.

But Ellie was ashamed that Rosalind had seen her at her worst, in a house that needed more than a little repair and surrounded by men who took her for granted. At least her bedroom was relatively clean and tidy, which wasn't always the case.

She covered her face with her arm and sucked in a deep breath.

She couldn't believe she had allowed her phone to run out of power. And now Rosalind had come all the way across town to recover an important document. It was mortifying.

Ellie didn't recall seeing any external meetings in Rosalind's diary for that afternoon, and she'd seemed a little reluctant to talk about it. Ellie wondered if it was a private meeting, maybe a date. The thought caused her stomach to turn.

Of course Rosalind would date. She was an attractive and successful woman. Ellie just hated the idea of it. Jealousy was an ugly emotion, but Ellie wasn't above admitting that she had it in spades.

The idea of someone else seeing Rosalind was nearly as painful as the knowledge that soon Ellie wouldn't be able to see her on a daily basis any more. While she was happy to be on a trajectory that meant she'd be working in her desired field and meeting her full potential, the thought of not seeing Rosalind was eating her from the inside.

Ellie had two countdowns happening in her mind these days. The first was the number of days until Christmas. The second was the number of days until the first working week of the new year, when she would be actively seeking new work.

For the first time in her life, she wished time would slow down.

CHAPTER TWENTY-FOUR

Rosalind lowered her mobile phone when she felt as though she was being watched. She looked up to see Ava and Ellie standing in the doorway to her office.

"Oh, dear," she said good-naturedly.

Ava looked excited while Ellie looked more than a little nervous. With two days to go until the Christmas party, Rosalind assumed that the two were finally about to let her in on the secret project they had been working on.

"You'll love it, Mum," Ava reassured her.

"I'll have to. I notice you've left it to the very last minute, so I can't possibly change anything." Rosalind leaned back in her chair and grinned.

"You, of course, have the power to veto whatever you like," Ellie told her. "But if you do, then it will be a pretty plain Christmas party."

Rosalind wasn't too concerned. She knew they had a venue, shelter, heat, music, food, and drink. The essentials had been covered, and everything else was decoration and theming. She knew that was important—often the little touches were the reason a party was a success. But she'd come close to having no party at all, and so her usual standards had dropped dramatically.

Over the last few weeks, she'd taken calls from many people to confirm that, yes, the party was taking place on a roof, and yes, she had thought it through, and no, she hadn't lost her mind. In many ways it had been quite fun to show a daring and edgy side to the company. Their Christmas party had become a staple in the recruitment industry calendar, and no other company could come close to creating a party anything like the Caldwell & Atkinson one, and so no one bothered any more.

It would be like a group of musical enthusiasts trying to go toe to toe with the Proms. No one would dare.

But such success meant an expectation to improve year on year, and that had become difficult. Having a party on the roof was just the kind of wow statement that would get them noticed and hopefully generate a lot of positive press.

If it all worked out.

Negative thoughts had nagged at Rosalind now and then as the date drew nearer. While she did trust Ellie, she didn't trust the British weather in the slightest. There was a very big chance that they had gambled too much. The weather reports looked positive, and Ellie had remained confident and upbeat. But Rosalind couldn't help but worry. Organising something in the hope that the weather would hold was a risky proposition in Britain at any time of year, but doing so in December was foolhardy at best.

On the other hand, she'd be lying if she said she hadn't enjoyed Ellie's and Ava's sneaking around to work on whatever the project entailed. Ava's playful ribbing that she knew what was going on and her mother didn't was actually quite amusing.

"I'm reliably assured I will love it," Rosalind said, gesturing to Ava. "Shall we?"

She followed the two of them towards the meeting room at the other end of the building. She was now pleased that she hadn't checked on the progress earlier and could enjoy the grand reveal properly.

Ellie stood back, nerves still obvious, while Ava shoved the door open with a dramatic gesture and beckoned her to enter the room. Rosalind hadn't put much thought into what to expect, but notions of tacky tinsel and Santa characters lingered at the edge of her mind. While neither was her style, she was more than aware that others enjoyed them.

She hesitantly stepped into the room. The moment she saw

the designs, she couldn't help but smile. Classic and elegant large white cut-outs filled the room. Reindeer, Christmas trees, stars, and presents were presented for inspection, with many more stacked against the walls.

"We cut them all out ourselves," Ava explained. "Ellie had some templates, but some we free-formed ourselves. How cool is that?"

"Extraordinary," Rosalind said with feeling. "Honestly, I'm so very impressed."

She approached a reindeer, its horns making it taller than she was. The material was thick and appeared to be foam-backed. It was two-dimensional, a stylish stand at the back ensuring it would stay in place.

Looking around the room, she could easily count more than fifty of the pieces. All different shapes and sizes, but all classic white. Simple and yet so striking.

"The gazebos are black," Ava explained. "Which will really make these stand out. And look at this." She opened a box and pulled out a roll of cotton-wool-like material. "This is the fake snow we're using. It comes in rolls and clumps, and we can make it look like a landscape. All over the place."

Rosalind could easily picture it in her mind's eye. Black fabric, stylish lighting, faux snow, and the figures would create a wintery scene. It was perfect, and very much like the shop windows on Oxford Street that year.

"I didn't want to go over the top," Ellie explained, hesitantly stepping into the room. "Doing it this way meant we could create scenes in the different areas on the roof. With Ava's help, I had time to create loads of them, and I think they are definitely on-trend."

"They certainly are," Rosalind said. "Honestly, both of you have done an excellent job. And I'm glad you didn't tell me because if you told me you'd be cutting out bits of cardboard, I'd have worried."

"I want to do something like this in my bedroom," Ava announced. "With some more colour. Now that Ellie has shown me how to make them, they are so easy."

"Sounds like a good idea." Rosalind knew that Ava was already sick of the plain white rooms that new builds favoured. A few coloured accents throughout the room weren't enough to satisfy her daughter's need for pleasing design.

Ava put her arms around Rosalind's middle, looked at the decorations, and sighed. "Isn't it all so Christmassy?"

Rosalind remained silent. She never felt Christmassy, and some, admittedly tasteful, cardboard cut-outs in her meeting room weren't about to change that.

Ava gave her a squeeze and stepped back. "Oh, come on. Even you have to admit that this is Christmassy."

Rosalind chuckled. "I've told you—I just don't get that Christmas spirit. I'll admit it's very nice and very on-trend. But it's not likely to change the habit of a lifetime and make me understand the supposed joys of Christmas."

Ava looked towards Ellie for help.

Ellie shrugged. "She can't be helped. She's a humbug."

"A proud one," Rosalind added.

"Can I go to Ellie's Christmas carol concert tonight?" Ava asked. "It's at six. It will only be an hour."

"I can walk her home after, if you like?" Ellie added.

Rosalind felt a little hurt that she hadn't known about the concert. She tried to maintain a neutral expression. "A concert?"

"Yes, we do it every year over at the Wintergarden. Not professional or anything, just keen amateurs," Ellie explained. "It's nothing much. Just some fellow singing and Christmas enthusiasts from local businesses. I didn't mention it as I know it's not your thing."

Rosalind could hardly deny that. Simply the idea of going to a carol concert bored her greatly, but the thought of missing Ellie perform at one was a completely different matter.

"Can I, Mum?" Ava pleaded.

"Of course, do you need a ticket?"

"It's all free," Ellie said. "First come, first served for seats. Standing room until we're full. Which never happens."

Rosalind knew the space well. It could easily hold a thousand people, and so she wasn't surprised they never managed to fill the venue.

"Very well. But I can't ask Ellie to walk you home on top of everything else, so I'll attend as well," Rosalind said casually. She looked at her watch. "In fact, let's call it a day. Maybe we can all have a quick bite to eat together before we go to the concert."

Ava squealed happily and then dashed out of the door to get her things. Ellie looking a little surprised at the sudden offer.

"Are you sure? You have a lot of paperwork to do," Ellie said.

"I can take it home. Besides, the party is tomorrow evening, so I doubt I'll get to see much of you before then. Consider this a thank you." Rosalind hoped she didn't look as nervous as she felt. She was suddenly overwhelmed with fear that Ellie might decline the offer.

"Are you sure you want to come to a carol concert? I really don't mind walking Ava home," Ellie said.

"Maybe it's what I need to find my Christmas spirit."

Ellie chuckled. "Maybe. It's an hour long."

Rosalind laughed. "I used to say the same thing to Ava when she was a child and didn't want to go to the bathroom before we went somewhere."

Ellie just continued to look at her silently, seemingly still not convinced that Rosalind really wanted to attend.

"I'll be fine," Rosalind said. "I'll even turn my phone off and applaud after every little tune. I'll be the model audience member. Unless there's audience participation—that's where I draw the line."

"I'll be sure to ask you to come onstage and help us with 'Jingle Bells' at the end."

"Only if you don't want to live to see Christmas Day," Rosalind joked.

"You need me. I'm the only person who can deliver your Christmas party tomorrow evening." Ellie grinned.

"I didn't say I'd exact my revenge immediately. I'm not stupid." Rosalind winked.

Ava reappeared, coat on and schoolbag on her back. "Come on, you two."

"I have a couple of quick things to do before we go," Ellie said.

"As do I." Rosalind wrapped her arm around Ava's shoulders. "You can use the time to come up with some suggestions of where we can eat."

Ava's eyes lit up at the prospect of free rein to choose a restaurant. Rosalind knew the thing Ava enjoyed the most about living in Canary Wharf was the ample supply of eateries. Ellie walked over to her seat while Ava joined Rosalind in Rosalind's office.

"Way to go, Mum," Ava whispered. "Proud of you!"

"What do you mean?" Rosalind frowned.

"Asking Ellie on a date and going to her concert. It's cool."

Rosalind closed the door behind them. "It's not a date. Why on earth would I ask you to come along if it was a date? And I told you before, it's not appropriate—"

"Yeah, okay, uh-huh," Ava said in a way that Rosalind knew meant that she had already very clearly lost interest in the conversation.

She considered forming another attack of denial but decided it would be met with disbelief anyway and instead took her seat to quickly complete her remaining tasks.

In the back of her mind, she had to wonder why she was tormenting herself. While she'd framed the meal as a thank you, she knew it was simply a way to spend more time with Ellie.

She even found herself looking forward to the carol concert, something that she'd ordinarily go out of her way to avoid.

You're in deep. This could be a problem, she told herself.

❖

Ava chose an independent cafe with an extensive menu of both hot and cold food, perfect for sandwiches, soups, and light meals. Rosalind had to admit that her daughter was good at planning meals and events and wondered if a career in event planning was in her future.

Ellie ordered a turkey pot pie that was apparently on some kind of list she had to get through before the end of the working week.

Ava ordered the same, and Rosalind chose a chicken salad with every intention of having a couple of bites of Ava's meal.

Ava's comment in the office had caused Rosalind to worry that she was perhaps displaying a little too much interest in Ellie. She decided to try to hold back a little, not to the point of being unfriendly, but certainly not joking as much as she had been. She'd always struggled to hold back when she was interested in someone. Talking turned to bantering, turned to flirting, every single time.

Not that it happened often.

In fact, Ellie was the first person in a long time that Rosalind had given a second glance to. Her interest in Ellie was increasing all the time, and she knew it wouldn't take much for that interest to spill over into something inappropriate.

The last thing she wanted was for Ellie to detect the flirting and feel obligated in some way to reciprocate in order to keep her job. Ava was convinced that Ellie was strong enough not to be coerced into anything of the sort, but Rosalind wasn't about to take that gamble. If Ellie took even the slightest action because she thought she had to, rather than because she wanted to, Rosalind wouldn't be able to look herself in the mirror ever again.

"Don't you think, Mum?"

Rosalind looked up from her salad, realising that her desire to step back had taken her a little far and to the point of not even listening to what was being said.

"Sorry, sweetness, I was miles away. What were you saying?"

"I was saying that the new houses down by Greenwich are very nice," Ava said.

Rosalind blinked, wondering why on earth her daughter was discussing real estate. They'd only recently moved, and any property in Greenwich was most definitely out of Ellie's price range.

"Yes, I suppose they are. I hadn't really thought of it."

"What are you two doing for Christmas?" Ellie asked, seemingly eager to change the subject.

"Going to see my brother," Rosalind said.

"Mum would prefer we didn't," Ava added.

Ellie smiled as Rosalind glared at her daughter.

"She doesn't like Auntie Gwyneth," Ava added, ignoring Rosalind's continued pointed look.

"I don't dislike her. I just don't agree that Christmas has to be a regimented schedule where we all do the same thing, at the same time, year after year," Rosalind explained.

"I think they call that *tradition*," Ellie said teasingly.

"Mum got told off for not wearing a silly Christmas sweater last year," Ava said.

"That's true," Rosalind admitted. "And I'll likely be told off again this year."

"It's not very festive to tell someone off on Christmas Day," Ellie said.

"That's exactly what I said," Rosalind replied.

"To her face," Ava added.

"Well, it's not worth saying it behind her back," Rosalind mused.

"Do you enjoy going to your aunt and uncle's?" Ellie asked Ava.

"Not really," Ava said, pushing away her mother's roaming fork that was aiming for a particularly succulent-looking piece of turkey.

"You don't?" Rosalind asked.

"Not particularly."

"Why didn't you ever say something?"

Ava shrugged. "I thought you liked it."

"Did I ever do anything to give you the impression that I liked it?" Rosalind asked.

"No. I just thought it was one of those things that we had to do. Like when we had to see Great-Aunt Lucille who no one liked."

"This isn't like that at all. We go because I thought you enjoyed it, which I now discover you don't," Rosalind said. "You mean I could have spent the last few Christmas seasons in Cancun? I let that woman scold me for not wearing a sweater for you, Ava."

Ellie chuckled. "See? This is what I mean when I told you that Christmas lives inside us. Of course you don't like Christmas if you spend it doing things you don't enjoy. If you both want to go to

Cancun and sit on a beach and eat…whatever they eat in Cancun, then do it. Christmas isn't about snow and Father Christmas. It's about empathy and kindness to others, and even to ourselves. If you're the kind of person who likes things a certain way, then maybe you might not want to allow someone else to control your schedule."

"Can you tell Auntie Gwyneth that we don't want to come over?" Ava asked.

"You're on your own there." Ellie gently bumped Ava's shoulder.

Rosalind wondered if she was doing the whole Christmas thing wrong. Other people seemed to adore it, and every year she dreaded it. She'd decided that she just didn't get it, but maybe there was more to it. Maybe she focused too much on the details and not enough on the overall picture.

Ellie and Ava started to discuss the merits of their turkey pot pies, and Rosalind allowed herself to consider the time when she had started to dislike Christmas. It was as a child when she had been forced to go and see her miserly grandfather. Her mother had claimed that it was essential that they see him one day a year, and that day was Christmas Day.

In hindsight she knew that was simply her mother's guilt forcing her to spend some time with a man she loathed, purely because of a date on the calendar. Unfortunately, she'd dragged Rosalind along with her. Christmas went from being a joyful experience of present receiving and watching her favourite movies to spending the day listening to a grumpy old man complain about the world. Soon after that, Rosalind had to spend time with her own parents in much the same way. Later, she was invited to her brother's home where her sister-in-law would list the rules of Christmas like a general going into battle.

It all seemed so obvious now, but before it had felt like a confusing puzzle. She'd honestly spent years completely baffled by why she hated Christmas so much. Now, it was crystal clear. She'd allowed herself to be at the mercy of other people, having someone else call the shots on food, schedules, budgets, and gifts. Rosalind was the first to admit that she was very particular about things.

Of course it would never work for her to be dictated to by others, especially when those others were so keen that Christmas had to look just like it did in a movie in order to be, supposedly, perfect.

Worse of all, she'd done the same thing to Ava.

It seemed so obvious that Christmas was a feeling and not a set of actions to be performed, but Rosalind was only now really understanding that fact. She wasn't the sort of person who wanted to eat dry turkey with a paper hat on her head while mentally preparing herself to gorge on sweet treats she didn't even enjoy for the rest of the day.

She needed to let go of obligation and do something she enjoyed instead. Something she and Ava would prefer over Gwyneth's idea of perfection.

"What will you be doing for Christmas, Ellie?" Rosalind asked.

"Going to Torquay to see my parents. It's where I grew up." Ellie looked at her watch. "Oh, damn, I better get going. I need to get changed and warm up with the others."

Rosalind felt a pang of sadness that their meal together was over so soon. She smiled as brightly as she could in the hope she would cover up her sorrow.

"We'll see you shortly, then," she said.

"Okay, you know where it is?" Ellie asked, standing up and putting her scarf on. She winced. "Sorry, of course you know where it is."

"I do," Rosalind said.

"Cool, I'll see you both there." Ellie waved farewell and hurried away.

Rosalind watched Ellie leave before realising that eyes were upon her. She turned to see her daughter smirking.

"Yes?" Rosalind asked.

"You really do like her, don't you?" Ava grinned.

"I do, yes, Ava," Rosalind admitted, too tired to bother fighting the truth any longer.

The grin fell away from Ava's face. "Oh."

"There's nothing to be done, Ava. I won't bend or break my

principles. Besides, I'm too old for someone like Ellie. But, yes, yes, I do like her. And I wish things could be different, but they are not, and I have to live with that. If you don't mind, I'd like to not discuss it." Rosalind ducked her head and continued to eat her lacklustre salad.

It wasn't the salad's fault. It could have been the best salad in the world, but Rosalind wasn't in the frame of mind to appreciate any food right there and then. The truth was no longer containable. Her repressed emotions had broken free and were washing over her in waves. Admitting the truth to Ava was the final step, a kindness to herself to put a halt to Ava's teasing. Now that Ava knew she did have feelings for Ellie and understood why nothing could come of it, she would hopefully stop bringing the matter up.

A smaller hand rested on hers. "I'm sorry, Mum."

"Nothing to be sorry for, sweetness." Rosalind placed a quick kiss on her daughter's cheek. "Just…don't meddle. I mean it."

"I won't."

Rosalind knew Ava wouldn't say anything. It wasn't in her nature to share her mother's secrets.

"Do you still want to come to this concert?" Ava asked. "I can go on my own."

"No, it's fine. I said I'd go, and so I will."

Ava just nodded and returned to her meal. Rosalind didn't really understand why she was punishing herself by going to the concert. She had a need to see Ellie, a pull that she couldn't control. It reminded her of a childish crush, which irritated her even further. When did Ellie manage to stroll into her brain and reprogramme her? When did she go from being a strong lone-wolf CEO to a mess who just wanted nothing more than to catch another glimpse of someone she desired?

It wouldn't be much longer, she reminded herself.

Come the new year, Rosalind would find Ellie the perfect job and bid her farewell and all the best with her new career and her new life. Rosalind would satisfy herself with the knowledge that Ellie would finally be in a job she enjoyed and one that paid her true worth. Hopefully it would be the catalyst for her to move out of the playpen she currently resided in with the overgrown toddlers who took advantage of her kind nature.

It wasn't what Rosalind's heart desired, but it would have to do.

It was the right thing to do.

Chapter Twenty-five

Ellie looked at her reflection in the terrible lighting afforded her in the ladies' bathroom and sighed. She felt like a fraud. Essentially because she was a fraud.

She was getting dressed up for a party that she wasn't even attending. All part of her grand scheme, which she somehow looked more and more likely to actually manage to pull off. It had occurred to her woefully late in the plan that she'd need to get dressed up in order to appear like she was going to attend the event.

This year she was mindful that she'd spend most of the evening in a cafe—which she was calling her headquarters—on many FaceTime calls with Will to ensure everything was going to plan. She didn't want to be dressed to the nines and sitting in a cafe for hours on end. That would definitely raise a few eyebrows among the waitstaff.

But she also needed to ensure that she could blend in with the crowd at the party, so she could realistically pretend she had been to the party. If she was wearing something very obvious, Rosalind would know she wasn't there very easily. But if she wore something similar to everyone else, there would be a chance that Rosalind would believe that they just didn't have a chance to see each other as Ellie was lost in the crowd. She needed to be dressed up, but also as bland as possible.

Experience of these parties told her that they'd be awash with black cocktail dresses. With so many parties in the city, most women had a small selection of standard black dresses and suits that they could wear, which made it impossible to tell if they were wearing the same thing party after party. The look was classic for a reason.

Ellie stared at her reflection. It felt strange to be dressing for an event she wasn't even attending. Stranger still to be doing so at three o'clock in the afternoon. If she was supposedly organising the party, she needed to leave early to finish the last-minute arrangements.

In reality, she'd long ago told all her vendor contacts that Will was her assistant and that he would be attending in person. Will had kindly taken a half-day holiday from work and was making his way through Ellie's large checklist. She'd done as much as she possibly could beforehand, but there were always last-minute things that needed to be done and people who needed to be instructed.

She clipped shut her clutch handbag and gave herself one last look-over in the mirror. She hated lying to Rosalind. While she was keeping this a secret by omission, she could convince herself that was okay. But the outright lies she was about to tell were something else.

She sucked in a deep breath and left the bathroom. She passed by her desk and knocked on the door frame to Rosalind's office. Rosalind looked up.

"I have to get going," Ellie said, feeling a cold stone in the pit of her stomach at the lie. "Just the last few things to do before we're all ready to go."

"Thank you, again, for all your work on this party. I'm sure it will be a huge success," Rosalind said. "I'll see you on the roof, words I thought I'd never say."

"It's certainly a talking point," Ellie admitted. "And I might not see you much. I'll be very busy and flitting from thing to thing."

Rosalind smiled. "I'm sure our paths will cross at some point."

"Ellie, my dear, you look wonderful!" Eric enthused as he approached Rosalind's office.

"Thank you," Ellie replied.

"Doesn't she look wonderful, Ros?" Eric asked, slipping into Rosalind's office and placing a file on her desk.

"She does," Rosalind agreed.

Ellie felt a blush prick at her cheeks at the thought that Rosalind might actually think she looked wonderful.

"I'm looking forward to tonight," Eric continued. "Very excited to see how it will all be set up. Everyone's talking about it. I don't think we've ever had a guest list so full, have we?"

Ellie shook her head. "No, we usually have ten to fifteen per cent decline, and we go to our secondary guest list, but not this year."

"Everyone wants to see the mad people who want to stage a party on a roof," Rosalind said. She pushed her chair towards the window and looked up at the sky. "At least the weather seems to be on our side."

Ellie held her breath. Seeing Rosalind so close to the glass made her heart rate spike uncomfortably.

"I better get going," Ellie said.

Rosalind looked back to her and smiled. "Okay, see you this evening."

Ellie knew it would sound strange to repeat her claim that she'd be too busy, and so she nodded. She said goodbye to Rosalind and Eric, grabbed her bag and coat from her desk, and made her way towards the elevators.

If everything went well, she'd be able to hide out in the local cafe and arrange everything from there. It would be a long afternoon and an even longer night, but Ellie had faith that her meticulous planning had accounted for every possible eventuality.

That didn't stop the cloud of depression weighing heavily on her.

It was the first time she'd ever organised a Christmas party, and it was one she wouldn't be able to attend. It had also taken up so much of her time and energy over the last few weeks that she'd had to cancel other functions. She'd never felt less prepared for the Christmas period. It wasn't that she needed to go to parties to feel the Christmas spirit—it was more a part of her tradition. Seeing friends and family, exchanging gifts, going to special events. It all followed a pattern that she was used to and comfortable with.

But this year was shaping up to be very different.

Although she'd undeniably been busy with party arrangements, one of the reasons she'd missed some of her usual parties and events was to spend more time with Rosalind. Even if it meant sitting outside her office late into the evening sometimes, in the hope that a conversation might take place when Rosalind left to go home.

She felt a little unprepared for the festive season, but she wouldn't change a thing. Those brief encounters with Rosalind were worth more than anything. Which was why not seeing her at the party and having to just lie to her face felt all the harder.

She sucked in a breath and stepped into the elevator. It was time to remotely organise a party.

CHAPTER TWENTY-SIX

Rosalind sipped from her champagne flute and attempted to listen to the incredibly boring story that Michael Weatherby was telling. She'd been listening to it for the last ten minutes, which was almost certainly nine minutes longer than the tale actually needed to be.

However, Michael was the HR director of a large financial firm that gladly outsourced all their recruitment needs to Caldwell & Atkinson, and so Rosalind was duty-bound to listen to him and even laugh at his terrible jokes.

Usually it wouldn't be such a struggle, but that evening she found herself terribly distracted.

The party was perfection. The decor was even more elegant in position than it had been in her meeting room. Food, drink, waitstaff, furnishings, everything was exceptional. All she had heard for the last two hours was how wonderful the guests thought the party was and how brave the company was to create something so unique.

As Ellie had promised, guests were warm, dry, and entertained. The various gazebos and patio heaters were all doing their jobs. Not a single person looked perturbed to be on a roof, not a gust of wind rustled a partygoer's hair. It was an amazing feat.

Rosalind had done her best to keep her expression neutral. After all, it wasn't right for one of the hosts to be too caught up in how marvellous their own party was. Her act had faded to nothing by the time she entered the Winter Forest. It was lit by small, twinkling fairy lights and furnished with fake pure white trees of different shapes and sizes.

Essentially, it was nothing more than a hallway connecting three areas of the rooftop. It was also absolutely astounding. Rosalind had gasped when she'd first seen it. Since then, everyone who came to speak to her mentioned the forest and how magically beautiful it was.

Rosalind was desperate to tell Ellie of all the good comments she was receiving. She'd moved from group to group, an eye out for Ellie at all times. It had been two hours since she'd arrived, and she'd not seen her at all.

She couldn't help but wonder if something was wrong. The party seemed to be going smoothly, but Ellie was nowhere to be seen, not even in the behind the scenes areas, which Rosalind had popped into a couple of times under the guise of praising the waitstaff.

On the other hand, she had seen Ellie's friend Will, Bathroom Boy, skittering around the party like a man possessed. Rosalind had seen him more times than she could possibly count, and yet Ellie had all but vanished into thin air. Something was most definitely up, and Rosalind had no earthly idea what it might be.

Being out of the loop was one thing, but being out of the circle of trust when Bathroom Boy was clearly on the inside was more than she could take.

She'd already made the decision to corner him the next time an opportunity presented itself. As much as it hurt to admit, if anyone would know where Ellie was, it would be him.

She knew jealousy was an ugly and petty emotion, but she couldn't help herself. The boy had something she wanted—Ellie's friendship, close and sincere. And possibly more. She couldn't help shake the feeling that there might be something more between Ellie and Will, despite Ellie's protests. Either way, it was a relationship that Rosalind was never going to have. She disliked him, and she didn't particularly care if he knew it either.

Just then, Will appeared, dashing from one side of the gazebo to another.

Rosalind smiled warmly at Michael. "Michael, I'm so sorry, but I have to attend to something urgent. I'll catch up with you later, and you can finish telling me all about it."

"Oh, not a problem, Rosalind. Wonderful party, by the way, just wonderful." He turned and found a new group of people to talk to.

Rosalind slipped away in pursuit of Will. As she entered the second room, she noticed he had his phone pressed to his ear and was engaged in a conversation. She wondered if Ellie was on the other end of the call and picked up her pace a little.

He entered an area reserved for the catering staff, and Rosalind knew this was her chance. She followed him and nodded to the two waitresses in the area to leave. They hurried out, and Rosalind stood in the only doorway, arms folded, and waited for Will to notice her.

"It's done," he said into his phone. "I spoke to Grace and Lucy, and they've topped everything up. Don't worry."

Rosalind cleared her throat. She enjoyed the way Will jumped, spun around, and looked terrified in a split second. He hung up the call.

"Um. Hi, Miss Caldwell."

"What's going on?" Rosalind asked.

Will did a terrible job of looking like he had no idea what she meant. "Sorry?"

"Where's Ellie?"

"She's…around. I think I saw her over by the east bar a little while ago." The lie dripped from him.

Rosalind narrowed her eyes and took a step closer to him. "What are you hiding from me?"

"Nothing?" Will sounded like he doubted himself.

Rosalind remained silent and just stared at him. He was skittish enough that she knew he'd cave in a few seconds. Her best glare was a formidable opponent and had broken far stronger people than him.

It took a ridiculously short amount of time before Will let out a shuddering breath. "She's not here."

Rosalind nodded. "That much I had ascertained myself. Where is she? When did she leave? *Why* did she leave?"

Will swallowed and his eyes became impossibly wilder. Rosalind realised then that she had clearly only scratched the surface of whatever was happening.

He shook his head and muttered something to himself.

"It's not a difficult question," Rosalind said sharply.

"She's never been here," Will replied in a whisper. "She's going to kill me."

Rosalind balked, thinking for certain that she had misheard him. "I'm talking about Ellie."

"So am I," he said.

"What do you mean she's never been here?" Rosalind demanded, not in the mood for any further confusion. She wanted to cut through to the heart of the matter, and she wanted to do it immediately. Being outside the circle of trust was a cold and uncomfortable feeling. Not knowing where Ellie was and having to speak to her go-between made it all the worse. She needed answers, and Will would give them up whether he wanted to or not.

"Ellie has never been up here," Will said.

Rosalind couldn't fathom what he was talking about. She felt her posture start to loosen at the fact she wasn't keeping up with whatever he was telling her. She understood the words he spoke, but they just didn't make any sense.

"I don't understand," she finally admitted.

Will ran a shaky hand through his hair. "She's going to kill me."

"Explain," Rosalind demanded. She didn't have time for his concern about what Ellie might do to him. She wanted him to worry about what she'd do to him if he didn't shape up and give her some answers immediately.

"Ellie has a fear of heights," he said. "She's terrified of them, so she's never been up here. She organised everything from elsewhere. She's not here. She's never been here. I told her it was stupid to think she could get away with it."

Rosalind took in what he was saying and then burst out laughing at the absurdity of it. "Did she put you up to this?"

"I'm not joking."

She stopped laughing upon seeing how serious he appeared. "But that's…that's impossible. How could she have possibly done all this without ever coming up here?"

"She's incredible," Will said simply. "I think she can do anything she puts her mind to."

Rosalind bristled. She knew Ellie was incredible—she didn't need Will to tell her such an obvious fact. Not to mention that she could see right through him. He had feelings for Ellie, that much was very clear to her. Jealousy welled up within her.

"Where is she?"

"She's in a cafe over at West India Quay. She's been using it as a HQ. She's still in charge and organising everything. I'm just her man on the ground. Or in the sky, as she calls me." He dug his hands into his pockets. "And now she's going to kill me for telling you."

Rosalind couldn't feel sorry for him. She was too shocked by the turn of events. Ellie was apparently terrified of heights and had somehow managed to organise an event in a space she'd never even seen with her own eyes.

Ellie'd lied to her, getting dressed up to supposedly go and organise the final details of the event, and was sitting in a local cafe instead. She knew that she should feel anger, but she couldn't because one question loomed over everything.

"Why didn't she want me to know?" she asked the only person who had answers for her, even though she loathed the fact that it was Will who seemed to have them.

"I don't know. She says people treat her differently when she explains her fear. Or that people don't understand it very well," he explained. "But I think the real reason was that she didn't want you to see her as weak."

Rosalind couldn't find a response to that. She opened her mouth, but no sound came out. Her brain scrambled to come up with something, but she had nothing. She was barely catching up with the idea that Ellie had a debilitating fear of heights, and now she needed to wrap her mind around the fact that Ellie thought Rosalind would perceive her as weak for it.

On top of everything was the deeply uncomfortable knowledge

that Will knew all of this. Ellie and Will, best of friends and maybe more, hiding important information from her. Her shock meant that she was struggling to cut through what was genuine upset at being lied to and what was resentment towards the young man in front of her. Jealousy was an ugly emotion, and she was struggling to keep it buried.

"She went through the mammoth task of organising a party in a location she couldn't get to. And then she lied to me, just so she didn't have to tell me of her fear of heights," Rosalind said aloud, more to herself than to Will.

Will wisely didn't reply. He jammed his hands into his pockets and looked at the ground, probably wishing it would swallow him up.

"Hold on," Rosalind said, something occurring to her. "How pronounced is this fear of heights? She works on the twenty-second floor."

Will bit his lip nervously. "She manages that, but only just. Before you promoted her, she'd never willingly been higher than the second floor. She avoids the windows."

An image of Ellie nervously standing in the middle of her office appeared in her mind. Ellie always stood in the centre of the office, she never approached Rosalind's desk, and she certainly never looked out of the windows.

She cupped her mouth, realising that she had unwittingly put Ellie in a horrible position.

She recalled the frosted window in Ellie's bedroom, another innocuous clue she had overlooked. She wondered how many other clues she hadn't noticed.

She shook her head at her stupidity. She noticed boxes of wine stacked in the corner. Spare chairs and tables were folded against the wall.

"You've been organising all this?" Rosalind asked.

He shook his head. "Not organising, just doing what Ellie tells me."

The pieces were falling into place far too slowly for Rosalind's liking, and she felt sluggish. "And she's…"

"In a cafe. On the ground."

"I can't believe you both managed to keep this a secret." She shook her head. "I can't believe you both felt you *needed* to keep this a secret."

"For the record, I wanted to tell you," he said.

"Well, I see you lost that battle."

"Yeah. Ellie wouldn't let me."

Rosalind could feel anger seeping in. She thought she and Ellie had an understanding of one another at the very least, possibly even a friendship. But Ellie had kept perhaps the single biggest detail about herself from Rosalind.

But she'd told him. This boy who could barely meet her gaze. The one with no backbone, a wrinkled shirt, and a haircut from twenty years ago.

"Well," Rosalind said, "I'm glad she has someone like you in her life."

Even she could tell the bitterness and jealousy had leeched into her words and lingered in the air between them. She hadn't meant for her jealousy to be so obvious, but she couldn't help it any more. She was too disorientated and hurt to think straight.

Will held his chin a little higher and met her gaze with a defiance she didn't think possible. "That may be," he said. "But the truth is that she doesn't want someone like me in her life. She wants someone like you. In fact, she wants *you*."

Rosalind swallowed. "What do you mean?" She tried to sound strong, but the waver in her voice was clear.

"I think you two should talk," Will said. "Ellie's my best friend, Miss Caldwell. I just want her to be happy, that's all. If you'll excuse me, I have to make sure there's enough ice at the bars."

Will edged past her and all but ran away, leaving Rosalind with a great deal of questions and no one to answer them. She licked her dry lips and considered her next move.

Chapter Twenty-seven

Ellie pulled her coat tighter around her and let out a shudder. The temperature was dropping and no shops were open. For all her planning, she'd made one grave error, and that was assuming that the cafe would remain open late into the evening.

As it happened, it closed at eight o'clock. Along with every other cafe in Canary Wharf.

Some restaurants remained open longer, but Ellie didn't feel comfortable setting up her HQ in one of them. With the shopping centres closing, she'd had little choice but to walk around.

It was just after nine o'clock, and Ellie had completed several long loops around the district, taking in the park, the outdoor shopping centres, the skyscrapers, and the boat docks. She'd always thought the area was quite large, but attempting to kill time walking around it had quickly disproved that fact. She was sure the security guards were now keeping tabs on her as she looked suspicious.

Cold had set in and the only reason she hadn't gone home was because it meant a Tube journey with patchy reception. If Will needed her, she'd be out of communication for at least fifty minutes, and she couldn't do that to him. She didn't know how long she could continue doing laps of the area before she turned into an ice cube, but she'd do it as long as she possibly could.

Her phone vibrated in her hand. She looked at it and felt a spike of panic at seeing Rosalind's name. She held her breath and opened the text message. *Things are going very well, aren't they?*

I'm heading downstairs for some fresh air and to get some time away from people, meet me in the lobby in ten minutes?

Ellie breathed a sigh of relief that she hadn't tried to head home. She quickly tapped out a reply to say she'd meet Rosalind soon and then hurried towards New Providence Wharf. She'd have to come up with some kind of excuse to not return to the party with her, but she'd deal with that when the moment came.

She thanked her lucky stars she was so close to the building and wouldn't have to run or look terribly out of breath when she arrived. It was just dumb luck that she wasn't on the other side of the wharf. Her meticulous planning had been entirely focused on the party and nothing else, and now she was suffering the result of that.

Her heart beat a little faster, not just from the hurry to get there but from the joy at seeing Rosalind. It was ridiculous to admit, especially as it had only been a couple of hours, but she was already missing her.

She had no idea what she'd do when she got a new job. Not seeing Rosalind every day was going to be hard. Not having an adequate excuse to ever see Rosalind again was going to be downright painful. Ellie had done all she could to push that thought out of her mind, but with time ticking away, the reality grew.

She arrived in the lobby at the same time that one of the elevator doors opened and Rosalind stepped out. Ellie stopped and stared. The long burgundy dress with a plunging neckline that enhanced her cleavage clung to Rosalind's body. When Ellie caught an eyeful of creamy white thigh through the scandalously high slit in the side of the dress, she very nearly considered joining Rosalind at the rooftop party, if only to have more opportunity to stare at her in the dress. Sadly, she knew she'd collapse into a heap the second she got to the top of the building.

Rosalind retrieved her coat from the coat-check area, and Ellie tried not to frown when a long black coat covered up the incredible dress.

Rosalind turned. Her gaze fell upon Ellie, and she smiled. "Shall we head out and get some fresh air?"

Ellie shuddered at the thought of yet more fresh air. The warmth of the lobby was so nice after her laps around the area. She nodded quickly and fell into step beside Rosalind as they went outside.

A few partygoers were hanging around outside, as always happened—people who wanted a quiet chat with someone, or people who were in the process of making an early escape when caught by someone they knew.

Rosalind greeted a couple of people politely but made it clear that she was busy as she passed by. They walked a short distance and were soon on a well-lit walking path by the river. It was completely deserted, and Rosalind gestured towards a wooden bench with an amazing view of the river and the Oxo tented exhibition space across the water.

Ellie sat down and Rosalind sat next to her.

"Ellie, when were you going to tell me that you never attended the party?" Rosalind asked as casually as she might enquire about the weather the next day.

Ellie's heart slammed in her chest. She hadn't expected that question and was now torn between telling the truth and continuing with her lie. Lying was definitely the most appealing, but a small voice at the back of Ellie's brain told her it was futile, and she'd been caught out.

"If you'd told me, I would have helped you," Rosalind continued. "I would have understood. Tried to understand, at the very least."

Ellie swallowed hard. Not only did Rosalind clearly know that she wasn't at the party, she was also aware of her fear of heights.

"You mustn't blame Will," Rosalind added. "He tried his best to keep your secret."

Ellie couldn't find any words. While she'd feared this moment, she had never actively prepared for it. The reality of Rosalind finding her out was so scary that Ellie had pushed the idea deep down inside herself.

Which left her with precisely zero idea of what to say or do.

"I'm sorry you felt you couldn't trust me." Rosalind stared out over the river.

The sadness in her voice prompted Ellie to finally reply. "It wasn't that," she said. "I do trust you."

Rosalind sat back against the bench and slowly turned to look at Ellie. The smile was missing from her face, and her eyes were dull. It was clear to Ellie that Rosalind didn't believe her.

"I trust you," Ellie repeated, needing Rosalind to hear the honesty in her tone. "It's just a hard thing to tell people. It's…kinda personal, you know?"

Rosalind shook her head. "I don't. But I'd like to understand."

Ellie sucked in a deep breath. The last thing she wanted to do was bare her heart on a bench in the middle of the night about the one thing in her life that she felt the most shame about. But then this was Rosalind, and seeing her so hurt by Ellie's deception was heart-breaking.

"I…don't know what to say," Ellie admitted.

"You have a fear of heights?" Rosalind prompted.

"Yes." Ellie nodded.

"Have you always had it?"

Ellie nodded again. "Since I was little. I've been to therapy. My dad once tried to take me on a Ferris wheel to overcome it. I screamed all the way around, hyperventilated until I nearly passed out. A lady from St John's Ambulance taught me how to control my breathing to stop panic attacks."

Rosalind's eyes widened in horror at the tale. "That sounds terrible. I'm so sorry, Ellie."

It wasn't a story that Ellie told very often. Her dad had meant well when he had effectively traumatised her for life. It was hard to explain that all he had wanted to do was fix her, but he hadn't the tools to do so. He'd done what he thought was best in his own clumsy way.

Remembering the incident always meant her eyes welling up, and this time was no different. However, when the tears started to fall, this time they were wiped away by Rosalind's soft fingertips. Ellie revelled in the sensation for the split second it happened. But when she made eye contact with Rosalind, she was surprised to see the tender expression change in an instant to one of concern. Rosalind frowned and placed the back of her fingers against Ellie's cheek.

"You're absolutely freezing. I thought you were set up in a local cafe."

"It closed."

Rosalind got to her feet. "Well, you're freezing. We can't stay out here." She looked around the area, her eyes briefly catching the rooftop at New Providence Wharf and then looking away.

"I'm fine," Ellie insisted.

"We can go to mine," Rosalind suggested, her gaze settling on the enormous skyscraper in the distance.

"I can't," Ellie said, waiting for the penny to drop for Rosalind. The thing about a fear of heights was that the average person just didn't get how prohibitive it was. Every little action had to be considered, even visiting someone's home. Ellie waited for Rosalind to put the pieces together and realise just what a disaster Ellie really was.

"Of course you ca—" Rosalind stopped dead. Her gaze dropped to Ellie. "You can't."

Ellie shook her head.

Rosalind sat back down. She continued to stare at her home in the distance. Ellie could tell that she was starting to figure it all out. "How did you get that folder? What happened? Ava knows something, doesn't she?"

Ellie broke eye contact, the embarrassment building within her. "I…had a panic attack in your apartment."

She felt sick to her stomach for saying the words out loud. Admitting to it meant she could no longer sweep it under the carpet and pretend it hadn't happened. And worse, now another person knew of it. Every extra person who knew was another notch on Ellie's already battered self-confidence.

"Ava found you?" Rosalind guessed.

Ellie nodded. "She helped me. You've raised a good girl there."

"Well, to be fair to her, she practically raised herself," Rosalind joked half-heartedly.

Ellie chuckled. "I know that's not true." She looked up and met Rosalind's concerned gaze.

"Ellie, I am so sorry that I sent you up there," Rosalind said.

"You didn't—I offered," Ellie reminded her. "I wanted to help. I thought I could do it. But it turned out that I really couldn't, and I made a mess of everything."

Ellie tried to look away but gentle fingers reached out and took hold of her chin, encouraging her to look at Rosalind. "You didn't make a mess of *anything*. You're extraordinary, Ellie."

A laugh burst from Ellie's lips. "Hardly."

Rosalind maintained her loose grip on Ellie's chin and shook her head. "You are. I don't know how anyone could possibly organise a party at a venue they'd never seen before. You calculated likely temperatures and wind speed on a roof you'd never seen using data and maps and who knows what else. You then single-handedly organised a party, something you've never done before. You became the perfect assistant in under two days. You got Ava to like you, and that's no easy task. You made each day at work a joy for me, even when I had back-to-back meetings and wondered why on earth I'd bothered setting up the company in the first place. These last few weeks have been more than I ever could have hoped for. You're the most impressive person I've ever met."

Ellie didn't know how to reply to that. She wanted to tell Rosalind that she was wrong, that she was insane, that she was too kind. But the ability to speak left her as her eyes drifted down to Rosalind's lips.

She couldn't be imagining it. The air was charged with something.

Ellie leaned forward slowly, hoping that she was reading the signals correctly and that Rosalind would do the same. Her heart skipped a beat as Rosalind leaned in close to meet her. Their lips met in a gentle kiss. Ellie's eyelids fluttered closed, so she could focus all of her attention on trying to remember every single detail of what was happening. The smell of Rosalind's floral perfume, the warmth of her fingers resting on her chin, the softness of the lips pressed against her. Ellie wanted to capture every single facet and compare it to the countless dreams she had enjoyed of similar situations.

It all came to a sudden end, and Ellie felt a flash of cold come over her. She opened her eyes to see that Rosalind had stood up. She had her hand to her forehead and her back to Ellie.

"Damn," Rosalind muttered.

Ellie's breath caught in her throat. Somehow she'd managed to misread the situation. She'd ruined everything.

Rosalind spun around, a haunted look on her face. "You need a new job."

Ellie's heart sank. She'd hoped they'd be able to ignore the kiss and get on with their lives, but it appeared that Rosalind wanted her gone.

"We can't do this if you're my assistant," Rosalind added. "It would be a conflict of interest. Not to mention a massive imbalance of power. We need to find you a new job before this goes any further."

Ellie frowned. "Wait, what?"

"I'm your boss. It's not a good foundation for this," Rosalind explained. "You must see that. Especially with my position, I can't be seen to be in a relationship with my assistant. Unless you're no longer my assistant. I mean, people will still talk. And, frankly, let them, I say. But it can't happen now."

"Foundation?" Ellie blinked. She couldn't believe her luck, couldn't believe what she was hearing. She thought Rosalind was pushing her away, but that didn't seem to be the case. "You mean, you want this? Us? I mean, you…you want this?"

"Of course I want this," Rosalind said. A trace of fear flittered across her expression. "Do you? I thought this was the start of something. I thought we were on the same page. Maybe approaching a relationship. Am I wrong? Are you looking for something temporary? A one-night thing?"

Ellie quickly shook her head. "No. Definitely not. I want to be with you, I just didn't think it was ever likely to happen. A relationship sounds nice. Really nice."

Rosalind's expression softened with relief. She smiled, a little nervously. "Well, then we're in agreement. I think."

Ellie licked her lips and looked up at her soon to be ex-boss. "We are."

"I thought there was something between us," Rosalind said. "But I obviously ignored it, due to our positions. It's nice to know I wasn't going mad."

"I felt it, too," Ellie acknowledged. "I didn't think you'd be interested in someone like me."

Rosalind laughed sharply. "Whyever not? You're extraordinary, Ellie. Anyone would be very lucky to have you in their lives. Why you'd want to be with me is the real question here."

Ellie snickered. "Yeah. The heart of gold CEO, funny, witty, successful. Not to mention that dress you're wearing."

Rosalind smiled and then swallowed and looked down at her feet. "But you need a new job. I can't, I won't, engage in anything if you're under me…I mean *working* for me."

Ellie chuckled at the slip. She stood up and took Rosalind's hand gently, thrilled at the feeling of being allowed to do something so bold. "You're the boss, Rosalind. I don't want to be your assistant, so fire me."

"I can't fire you. For what possible reason could I fire you?" Rosalind asked. "That's as bad as being involved with my assistant."

"Then move me back to my old job. You needed someone to organise the Christmas party—job done. You can get a temp to manage your schedule for a couple of weeks until you find someone you want. It's quiet now, anyway. Move me back, and then help me get a new job in the new year. If you're any good at your job, I'll be in another company in a couple of months. But start by demoting me." Ellie looked up at Rosalind, trying to catch her gaze.

Rosalind's decency was touching and sexy as hell. Ellie knew that Rosalind's reticence was to protect Ellie and others in her position, and as much as Ellie wanted Rosalind to throw the rule book out of the window, she knew she couldn't ask her to do that. Rosalind had to be comfortable with the situation, and she had to be reassured that Ellie was, too.

"I'll quit if you ask me to," Ellie added. "But I'd kinda like a salary."

Rosalind quickly shook her head. "I don't want you to leave, and I certainly don't want you to be without pay because of this. Whatever this might be. Might become."

"Demote me," Ellie pleaded. She softly tugged on Rosalind's hand. "Demote me and then kiss me again."

A smile tugged at the corner of Rosalind's mouth. "You'd like that?"

Sensing that the mood was turning, Ellie tried her luck and pulled Rosalind a little closer. Rosalind allowed herself to be moved and ducked her head to meet Ellie's.

"Have I been demoted?" Ellie whispered as their lips were millimetres apart.

"Yes," Rosalind breathed.

"Good." Ellie pressed a kiss to Rosalind's mouth, grasping her by the hand and holding her close. Ellie didn't think she could bear the idea of losing Rosalind now. Something she'd never thought was possible was actively happening right there and then, and Ellie was going to do whatever she could to make sure she kept hold of it.

Rosalind intensified the kiss, and Ellie melted into it. Rosalind Caldwell kissed just like she did everything else, with passionate confidence. Far sooner than Ellie would have liked, Rosalind pulled back.

"You're still cold," Rosalind said.

"I'm getting warmer," Ellie replied.

Rosalind threaded her fingers through Ellie's and held on tight, smiling at her and sighing happily. Ellie couldn't believe the turn of events, from thinking Rosalind would be livid at her lie being exposed, to somehow sharing a kiss. Of course, Ellie did believe in Christmas miracles and was fully intending to consider the evening one.

❖

Rosalind gazed back towards New Providence Wharf. "I wish there was a way to get you up there. It's really something. And it's warm. I had a genius calculate where to put patio heaters."

Ellie chuckled. "I've seen pictures."

Rosalind looked at Ellie. "It's not the same."

Ellie shrugged. "I can't go up there. It's just not possible, honestly."

"I don't doubt it. I just wish it could be different." Rosalind let out a small sigh. It was unfair that the person who loved Christmas most was the one who was unable to see the exceptional party that she'd created.

She had a hundred questions, but they'd all wait for another time. She could see that Ellie was shaken by her secret being revealed and had no desire to bombard her with questions. Knowing that Ellie felt something for her was exhilarating, and Rosalind was struggling to understand how someone so youthful, beautiful, and impressive could be interested in her. But the look in Ellie's eyes told her that it was all true.

When Ellie had leaned in to initiate that first kiss, Rosalind thought she was dreaming. Her heart had beaten faster, and her breath had caught in her throat. She'd pushed those feelings to one side as quickly as she could, throwing caution to the wind and taking her chance to kiss the marvel that was Ellie Pearce.

Now Rosalind knew that she would do whatever she could to give Ellie anything she desired. But the first step had to be getting Ellie a different job, one where she was independent of Rosalind and there could be no talk of impropriety.

She sighed to herself. Now that she had kissed Ellie, she didn't know how long she would be able to wait until she could do so again. Questions buzzed around her head, like the practicalities of how they would date. Obviously, Rosalind's apartment was out of the question due to Ellie's fear of heights. And Rosalind had little desire to traipse over to Ellie's houseshare across the city.

"Greenwich," she breathed, the pieces of a previous conversation suddenly falling into place.

"Sorry?" Ellie asked.

"Greenwich. Ava was talking about the new houses being built in Greenwich," Rosalind recalled.

Ellie's cheeks lit up in a blush, and Rosalind knew she was on to something. It had seemed strange at the time that Ava was talking about the homes. Now it all made sense. She knew of Ellie's fear of heights and wanted Rosalind to consider a new place to live, one nearer to ground level.

"Ava might have guessed I had a little crush on you," Ellie murmured.

"She'd mentioned my own crush a couple of times," Rosalind confessed. "In fact, I admitted it to her finally only yesterday."

Ellie's head snapped up.

"What? She's an astute girl, as you know," Rosalind said. "And I like Greenwich."

Ellie shook her head. "Don't give up your sky palace for me, Rosalind."

Rosalind laughed. "Sky palace?"

"You live amongst clouds," Ellie said seriously. "I think it's a different ecosystem up there."

"Well, the lease on my sky palace is up soon. Maybe a move is in order," Rosalind suggested lightly. "Ava has been talking about wanting to walk to school, so I had been thinking of moving a little closer so I could let her."

It wasn't entirely a lie. Rosalind had been giving some thought to how she could give in to Ava's bid for independence and not fret for her safety. A move would solve that issue and allow Ava to walk to school through a less populated route in a more residential area.

She liked the apartment, but it was a little small and definitely a bit impersonal with its white walls and modern look. She'd rented to see what it was like as moving from the house in Surrey was a big move, and she'd wanted to try before she bought.

It was a conversation to be had with Ava. Rosalind knew that Ellie's fear of heights would play a factor in the decision, but it wasn't the only reason for the move. She hoped that would make Ellie feel better about the whole thing.

"Are you just saying that?" Ellie asked.

"No, ask Ava. We moved into the apartment as a trial. It would be nice to be back in a house again. I miss the garden."

"Ava's told me about you and plants," Ellie said, sniggering under her breath.

"Well, obviously I'd get a gardener in again," Rosalind said. "Don't want to have a garden like yours."

Ellie smiled at that. "Hey, there's nothing wrong with…Okay, yes, the front garden is a state."

"Want me to come over and encourage one of those fine young men you live with to give it a makeover?" Rosalind offered.

"They're still quaking since your last visit," Ellie admitted. "They jump every time the doorbell rings."

"Good." Rosalind smiled.

Ellie sighed. "Look, trust me that I really hate to say this, but shouldn't you be getting back to the party?"

Rosalind shook her head. "I think I'd rather be here."

She wasn't about to let the moment end now. She didn't think she could stand the idea of spending the rest of the evening away from Ellie, especially with no idea when she'd see her again.

Ellie rolled her eyes. "I didn't kill myself organising the best party in the world for you to be sitting down here on this bench with me. Don't you always tie up loads of deals on this night?"

Rosalind shrugged. "I've spoken to nearly everyone I needed to. Though, I must say I was woefully distracted by not seeing you. I spent half the night looking for you." Something clicked in Rosalind's mind, and an idea formed in an instant. She got to her feet and looked down at Ellie. "Will you meet me in the lobby at New Providence Wharf in fifteen minutes?"

Ellie frowned. "Why?"

"I want you to see the party," Rosalind said.

Irritation, fear, anger, and disappointment all flashed across Ellie's face as she shook her head and looked away. "I told you, I can't. You can't force this away. It's a real thing, Rosalind. Take me as I am, or just don't bother with me."

Rosalind perched on the edge of the bench and looked intently at Ellie until Ellie slowly turned her head to look back at Rosalind again.

"I know. I promise you that I understand that," Rosalind said.

She realised she'd not explained herself properly in her excitement and wanted to make sure that she was absolutely clear in her acceptance of Ellie's situation. "I won't try to force you towards the roof—you absolutely have my word. Trust me, give me fifteen minutes."

Ellie looked confused but gave a slow nod. "Okay."

Rosalind stood up, shrugged out of her coat, and handed it to Ellie.

"You'll be cold," Ellie said, holding the coat at arm's length.

"You're *already* cold. I'll be inside again in a few moments." Rosalind turned on her heel and walked away. "Fifteen minutes! Don't steal my coat, it's vintage."

CHAPTER TWENTY-EIGHT

Rosalind hurried back to the party, all the while her brain whirring to catch up with what had happened and to fill in the gaps of things she had missed. She didn't like not knowing and had a lot of questions that needed answers, amongst them, what had happened to Ellie when she'd had a panic attack, how much Ava knew, how would their relationship work, and ultimately if it would even work at all.

But all of that could wait. Rosalind was happy to just enjoy the moment before any harsh reality might fall into place and make life a little more difficult.

The fact that she was already toying with the idea of moving told her quite clearly that she was already more deeply infatuated than she had initially realised. The acknowledgement that Ellie was interested in pursuing a relationship had awoken a number of thoughts within her that she hadn't expected. Now she was eager to try to make things work.

It had been a very long time since anyone had excited her in the way Ellie did. Realising that her feelings were reciprocated was the only Christmas present Rosalind needed that year. She felt as if she'd been gifted an opportunity, a new chapter in her life, one she was very happy to start reading.

She entered the elevator and selected the button for the top floor. If she was to have any hope of pulling off her plan, she'd need Will's help. And if she and Ellie had any chance at a happy relationship, she'd need to make peace with him. Her instant dislike of him had been simple jealousy through and through, and she needed to apologise to him.

She'd won Ellie's affections in a way that Will clearly hadn't been able to but only because he had graciously given Rosalind all the clues she needed. His words had echoed in her ears as Ellie had leaned forward for that first kiss. It was then that Rosalind truly believed that there was the chance of something meaningful between them. Which meant that she now had to clear the air with Will.

The elevator doors opened, and she strode out and nearly straight into Eric.

"Ah, Ros! I was wondering where you'd gotten to. Isn't everything going splendidly? I've yet to see Ellie to tell her myself. I imagine she's extremely busy."

"Eric, I need to tell you something." She hadn't expected to have this conversation so soon, but now the opportunity had presented itself, and she wanted it done and out of the way.

She took his arm and led him to a quiet area. He looked at her in confusion, silently waiting for her to fill him in on whatever she was obviously about to drop on him. Eric's calm demeanour was one of the things Rosalind most appreciated about him. She knew she could tell him anything, and the most she would get would be a blink to centre himself before he offered his opinion.

"I'm demoting Ellie back to her old job, then helping her to find a new job," Rosalind said. Starting off with that bit seemed a lot easier than the next bit.

Eric nodded. "Okay." His expression remained confused. Rosalind's staffing decisions were nothing to do with him, and he had clearly yet to catch on to why the change in assistant might be relevant.

"I just kissed her," she admitted. "Well, we kissed. I didn't pounce on her or anything unsavoury. We're at the early stages of a relationship. Nothing happened before this evening."

Eric blinked. "Okay."

Rosalind waited a few seconds for the news to settle and then be processed. Eric wasn't necessarily that good with sudden changes to the scheduled programming. He needed time to fully hear, process, and understand this kind of new information.

A smile slowly spread across his face. "Yes, oh yes, I think that will be rather nice. You two make a good match."

Rosalind frowned. That hadn't been the reaction she'd expected. She'd thought he'd warn her off the idea, not smile and seem happy with it. "You think we do?"

"Oh yes."

"But I'm much older and she's—"

"You make each other smile," Eric interrupted. "That's a good foundation for a relationship. I'm happy for you, Ros. For both of you."

"As I say, nothing happened before—"

Eric brushed the concern aside with a wave of the hand. "I know, you wouldn't."

"But I have. She's still technically my assistant. And I kissed her. In public. People may have seen us." Rosalind suddenly started to realise what she had done. Whether or not Ellie would be leaving the firm, she worked for her when they'd shared the kiss.

"Was it consensual?" Eric asked.

"Yes."

"There you are, then." He shrugged. "Sometimes you can't stop these things. You're doing the right thing now. Don't beat yourself up, Ros. You've not done anything wrong. Where is she anyway?"

The question woke Rosalind up to the fact that the clock was ticking.

"She's, um, getting some fresh air downstairs." Rosalind took a step backwards, checking the area for Will.

Eric looked around with a frown. "Not fresh enough for her up here?"

"I'll explain later," Rosalind promised. She patted his upper arm. "Can you hold the fort while I attend to a few things?"

Erin smiled knowingly. "Of course. Always."

She spotted Will in the distance and said her goodbye to Eric, then crossed the rooftop terraces as inconspicuously as she could. Ordinarily she'd be happy to mingle, but now she was a woman on a mission.

Approaching Will, she gestured to a quiet area where they could talk. He still looked like a rabbit caught in the headlights, and Rosalind knew that their relationship would require a little maintenance if it was to survive and hopefully thrive. Clearly he was important to Ellie, which made him important to her.

"First, thank you for telling me about Ellie's fear of heights," she started.

"Does she know I told you?" Will asked, panic in his eyes.

"She does, but I implied that I forced the secret from you. Embellish the situation as you wish." Rosalind looked away for a moment. "And thank you for telling me about the other matter, too. I understand that this probably isn't easy for you, but I think it's much better if we're friends rather than enemies. For Ellie's sake, more than anything. I really would rather we didn't fight for Ellie's affections. It would be beneath both of us and hard on Ellie."

She forced herself to make eye contact with him, wishing it wasn't so difficult to do so. This man, this scruffy youth, worried her. He had the upper hand, a friendship with Ellie that went deeper than her own. He also clearly had feelings for Ellie. And Rosalind had bouts of jealousy that would only become worse if she didn't resolve this matter with Will right there and then.

"I agree," Will said, surprising her. "Ellie is my best friend, and that means a lot to me. I don't want to ruin that. She only sees me as a friend, and I'm good with that. I want her to be happy. I think you'll do that and…" He swallowed. "You should, you know, treat her right and stuff."

Rosalind realised he was attempting to play some kind of protective role and threatening her with…she wasn't quite sure what. It was cute, and Rosalind did her best to maintain a serious expression.

"I will absolutely do my best," she said. "I do care for Ellie a great deal."

Will nodded. She could tell he was putting a brave face on it, and she appreciated his trying even if the end result wasn't perfect.

"Good. Now, on another matter, I have a favour to ask of you."

CHAPTER TWENTY-NINE

Ellie sat in the lobby of New Providence Wharf with Rosalind's coat wrapped around her. She didn't need it any more. Her heart was pounding loudly enough to be heard by passers-by, and she'd been in the warm lobby for long enough to have thawed out.

But that didn't mean she was going to give it up. Being cocooned by the coat was meaningful, and Ellie wasn't about to remove it so easily. She took another tentative sniff of the collar and smiled to herself at the presence of Rosalind's scent.

She heard footsteps approaching and looked up to see Will rushing towards her, wringing his hands and looking nervous. She stood up, and the moment he was in striking distance, she punched him in the arm.

"Ow!"

"You told her!" Ellie punched him again.

This time Will took the hint that the attack would continue until he was out of harm's way and stepped back. "She's really scary, Ellie. She dragged it out of me. You know I wouldn't tell her unless she forced me. She was all *Where is she?* I couldn't say anything else."

Ellie did know that, but she was still angry that her biggest secret in the world was leaked without her permission or knowledge.

"You could have warned me," Ellie said. "A text wouldn't have killed you."

Will hung his head in shame. "I know. I should have told you. I was just really worried what she'd do. I need this job. She's the boss. And she hates me."

"She doesn't hate you." Ellie sighed.

"Well, no, maybe she doesn't," he admitted. "But I thought she did then."

Ellie was angry, but that anger was easily superseded by her joy at what had followed. The kiss they'd shared lingered in Ellie's mind, and she couldn't wait to share more with Rosalind. She was so happy she felt as though she could burst.

"We kissed," she confessed, needing to tell her best friend about the best thing that had happened all year.

"I guessed," he said, grinning. "I'm glad you two got your act together. Now, you need to come with me. Your new girlfriend sent me on a mission, and if I don't complete it quickly, then she'll probably come over here and eat me alive."

Ellie laughed and elbowed him in the ribs. "She's not that bad."

"She's dead intimidating, Ellie," Will said.

"Not when you get to know her," Ellie replied.

Will took her arm and gestured across the lobby.

"Where are we going?" she asked, slightly nervous despite Rosalind's promise not to try to get her to go up to the party. Her fear of heights was irrational. Being in the vicinity of the party and the possibility of someone trying to push her into an elevator was enough to cause a quiver of tension to run up her spine.

"Trust us," Will said.

Ellie did. Or at least she wanted to.

They rounded the corner to a dead end, where Rosalind was waiting for them.

Ellie started to smile but then noticed that behind Rosalind was an elevator. She took a small step back into Will's waiting arms.

"It's okay," he whispered in her ear.

"We've commandeered the service elevator," Rosalind explained. She held up a key. "When the doors open, I'm going to put this key into the lock and set it to manual. That means that no one can call the elevator, and it will remain here, on the ground floor, with the doors open. It can't move, and the doors cannot close, as long as the key is in the lock."

"The elevator won't go anywhere," Will said. "We promise."

"Why do we need an elevator at all?" Ellie asked.

Rosalind took a step to one side and pressed the call button. The elevator doors clattered, and Ellie took a hesitant step forward. Inside the larger-than-average elevator was a cocktail table with some canapés, champagne, and glassware. The floor was covered in fake snow, and some of the battery-operated fairy lights hung from a white cardboard reindeer. Her pre-approved Christmas playlist filled the space. The lights in the ceiling of the elevator had been disabled somehow.

"It's not quite the same as upstairs," Rosalind said. "But it is a mini-version of the party you organised."

Rosalind stepped in and placed the key in the lock. She gestured for Ellie to take a look. Ellie tentatively stepped closer, poking her head around the door and seeing the key.

"It won't go anywhere now," Rosalind promised. "But if you'd rather stay outside, that's fine."

Rosalind walked over to the table and poured some champagne into three flutes. Will stepped around Ellie and into the elevator, picking up a champagne flute from the table and delivering it to Ellie.

Ellie looked from Will to Rosalind and realised that she felt safe with these two people. She knew they weren't going to try to break her of her fear through shock tactics. She knew they understood as best they could. It was a relief to be in the company of two people who actually got it.

She took the champagne flute from Will's hand and stepped into the elevator.

"To the two people who organised one of the very best Caldwell and Atkinson Christmas parties I can remember, against all kinds of odds. Thank you both," Rosalind said, raising her glass.

"I didn't do much," Will said.

"Nonsense, you were Ellie's man in the air." Rosalind smiled at him.

There was the tiniest tension between them, but Ellie could tell that they were both making an effort to come together. For her. She appreciated the gesture more than she could verbalise to them.

"Will's the best," Ellie said, putting her arm around his shoulders and bringing him into a hug. "He did so much. I couldn't have done it all without him."

Will ended the hug reluctantly and took a small step back. "You're the brains of the operation," he told Ellie.

He nervously looked from her to Rosalind and back again before gulping some champagne. Ellie knew it would take a while for these two to come together but appreciated the effort they were making.

"She's right, Will," Rosalind said. "Can I offer you a couple of extra days of paid holiday? You've certainly earned them."

Will's eyes widened in delight, and he quickly nodded and accepted the offer. Ellie knew that he'd be playing the latest releases on his PS4 all through the holidays, and Rosalind had just gifted him with an extra forty-eight hours to be extra unsociable. He'd love it.

"I better go," Will said. "I need to make sure the food is flowing and all that."

Ellie felt her eyes widen at the mention of the party. While she knew it was happening, she'd completely forgotten that she was supposed to be a part of it.

"Oh, gosh, yes. We need to make sure that the patio heaters have been turned up by one degree. The wind direction is due to change in half an hour," Ellie said, looking at her watch and calculating if they'd missed their deadlines.

"It's all in hand," Will said, reassuring her. "I wrote down everything you told me."

"I couldn't have done this without you," she said.

"That's what friends are for, right?" He lowered the champagne flute to the table and gestured towards the door. "I'll, um, leave you both to it."

"Speak to you later," Ellie promised.

"Thank you for your help, Will," Rosalind said.

Will ducked his head in embarrassment and quickly left. The moment he was out of sight, Ellie turned to Rosalind.

"Are you two going to be friends?" Ellie asked, easily detecting the effort Rosalind was putting in. "Or will you be calling him Bathroom Boy again by the end of the year? Which is two weeks away."

"We'll be best of friends in no time. I'm winning him over with my charm."

"Thank you, you don't have to do that." Ellie walked around the table and adjusted the fairy lights that were haphazardly draped on the reindeer.

"He's important to you. You're important to me," Rosalind said.

"Are you jealous of him?" Ellie asked, already suspecting that she knew the answer.

"I was, a little," Rosalind admitted.

"You know there's no need to be jealous of him, right?"

Rosalind shrugged. "It's an irrational fear."

"Are you still going to see your brother for Christmas?" Ellie asked, changing the subject. A silly thought had entered her head while she had been waiting in the lobby. She had no idea if Rosalind would go for it or not, but it was worth trying.

"No, Ava and I decided that if we wanted to be treated like that, then we could join a military fitness club." Rosalind sipped some champagne. "Why do you ask?"

Ellie took a deep breath. It was a big ask, but she reasoned that Rosalind could always say no. It wouldn't matter. But if she didn't ask, she'd always regret it.

"Come with me to Torquay," Ellie said. "Both of you."

Rosalind's eyes widened. "To meet your parents?"

"Not exactly. To have Christmas with me and my family and friends. We don't have to introduce you as my…partner. Not if you don't want to. The thing is, my parents own a small hotel by the sea. They have a few guests over at Christmas, just some friends of the family. There's usually between fifteen and thirty of us, and there's always room for more. They always tell me to invite friends to join us, and I rarely do. There's space for you and Ava. You can be as involved or uninvolved with the Christmas stuff as you like. You don't even have to eat turkey. I…I'm not suggesting we share a room. You and Ava can have your own room, of course."

Rosalind bit her lip and smiled.

Ellie had no idea what was going on inside her mind, but she hoped she'd consider it. Her parents' standing invitation to bring anyone to the hotel had never been taken up. Every year her mum would call the day before Ellie travelled to confirm the numbers for dinner, and every year Ellie would say it was just her. Two guest rooms were always put aside for her, and space was always available in the large dining room that overlooked the sea from the cliffs.

Ellie looked forward to the large Christmas celebrations, but this year the thought of being so far away from Rosalind, even though they hadn't ever planned to spend those days together, was too much. She knew it could be considered odd to invite her new girlfriend to spend Christmas with her parents on the night of their first kiss, but Ellie didn't care. If there was a possibility of it happening, she needed to explore it.

"You want to spend Christmas with someone you've personally labelled a humbug?" Rosalind teased.

"Yes, I'm willing to suffer the consequences of my actions and be mocked for my Christmas antlers." Ellie nodded, enjoying the easy banter that Rosalind always offered up.

"Christmas antlers implies you have a selection of antlers," Rosalind pointed out.

"You'll have to find that out," Ellie said.

"Are you sure we wouldn't be putting anyone out? It's very late notice," Rosalind said.

"There's room, and my parents always want me to bring someone along. They'd love to meet you and Ava," Ellie said. "Especially my mum. She's the reason they bought the hotel. She loves meeting new people."

"Will there be Christmas sweaters?" Rosalind asked playfully.

"Yes, and we must don them at the strike of eleven or you will be asked to stand outside for an hour as penance." Ellie chuckled. "You can wear Christmas sweaters if you want. But if you don't, no one will judge."

"Sounds nice. But I have to ask, what if I do want to be introduced as your partner?"

Ellie swallowed. "Then I'd be really happy."

"And your parents?"

"Would be happy as well." Ellie remembered her earlier conversation with Rosalind regarding her parents' initial reaction to her coming out. "They're comfortable with my sexuality. They're just not very touchy-feely about these things. Like, they didn't celebrate it or tell me they were happy. Just nodded and carried on eating dinner. But they want to see me happy."

"I'll have to ask Ava," Rosalind said.

"Of course."

"And I'll have to tell her about us," Rosalind added.

Ellie held her breath. It was illogical to be worried. She knew Ava was aware that they had feelings for each other. She'd been a typically unsubtle teenager a few weeks ago when asking Ellie what she thought of her mum. And now Ellie knew that Ava had detected the attraction from Rosalind's end as well. Presumably Ava would have tried to pull them apart if she hadn't liked the idea.

"She'll be fine," Rosalind added, detecting Ellie's concern.

Ellie nodded. "I know. It's just weird, you know?"

Rosalind nodded. "I do. Are you sure about this?"

"Yes, are you?"

"I am." Rosalind smiled.

"Can I kiss you?" Ellie asked.

Rosalind swallowed. "I'd like nothing more than that. But you are technically still my assistant, and anyone could come around that corner by accident and spot us."

"You demoted me, remember?" Ellie looked at the elevator panel. "Can you close the doors and still keep the elevator here?"

Rosalind was over to the panel in a blur of burgundy. "Yes. It's set to manual. We just turn it to close the door. If you're comfortable with that?"

"Do it," Ellie instructed.

Rosalind turned the key and the doors clattered shut.

Ellie lightly gripped Rosalind's upper arms and backed her into the wall of the elevator before standing on tiptoe and kissing her senseless. They'd never get another chance to make out in a winter-themed elevator, and Ellie was about to take full advantage of it.

Rosalind had gasped in surprise at being pushed into the wall but soon recovered and responded, slipping her tongue into Ellie's mouth. Ellie groaned in happiness.

She'd been waiting years for it to happen, but now her Christmas miracle had arrived. She wasn't disappointed.

EPILOGUE

Ellie leaned to the side and looked at the driver's dashboard in front of Rosalind.

"Not yet," Rosalind said.

Ellie looked at the miles to go and grinned to herself. "But so close!"

"You two are ridiculous," Ava said from the back seat.

"We've simply learnt the art of compromise," Rosalind replied.

"Just let Ellie put her music on," Ava instructed.

"Not until we're at a hundred and fifteen miles to go," Rosalind said. "I won't be listening to a Christmas song a mile before I have to. Besides, you have your headphones on, so you don't get a say."

Ellie watched Ava shake her head and put her headphones back on and return to staring out of the car window at the passing countryside. It was their sixth year going to Torquay, their fifth year travelling together. After that first year, when Ellie had played back-to-back Christmas hits throughout the four-hour journey, Rosalind had declared she couldn't take that kind of torture again.

At first, Ellie had suggested two hours of Rosalind's music and then two hours of Ellie's. Then, after some quick calculations, she decided that mileage would be a far fairer way to divide the journey up. Now Ellie waited for the hundred and fifteen mile point, when she could start playing her music through the Bluetooth connection.

"Can you believe it's been five years?" Ellie asked.

"It's flown by," Rosalind admitted with a smile. "Any regrets?"

"Tons," Ellie joked. "If it wasn't for you, I'd still be writing fake reports for the marketing department at Caldwell and Atkinson."

"They aren't fake reports," Rosalind defended. "They highlight the positives in otherwise negative data."

"We have a word for that at the Office for National Statistics," Ellie said. "I think it's…oh yeah, it's *fraud*."

"Remind me who got you that job."

"Some hot recruitment consultant, you don't know her," Ellie teased.

"Clearly I should have got you a placement at the local stand-up comedy club," Rosalind said. She peered into her wing mirror and indicated to change lane. "We're at a hundred and fifteen miles, by the way."

Ellie clapped her hands in delight and unlocked her phone to set up her playlist.

"Do you want to start with the classics?" Ellie asked.

"I'd like to start with earplugs," Rosalind replied.

Ellie smiled. For all Rosalind's complaining, she'd overheard her humming "The Holly and the Ivy" in the shower on more than one occasion. Rosalind hadn't suddenly become a fan of Christmas, that was far too much to ask for, but she had found some enjoyment in a few of the aspects of Christmas.

Ellie had enjoyed watching Rosalind's reaction to different Christmas songs over the years and added the ones that Rosalind appeared to enjoy, or at least tolerate, to a special list.

Every year, the list grew.

Ellie pressed a button and the playlist began. She turned and looked out of the window and sighed happily. Flakes of snow were starting to fall, and the chances of a white Christmas were high. She was travelling with the two loves of her life to see her family at her favourite time of year. Life couldn't be any more perfect.

They arrived a little earlier than scheduled, having missed most of the traffic due to Rosalind's decision to leave a day earlier than usual. She'd claimed it was solely to miss the traffic, but the truth was that she enjoyed the Torquay Christmas break, and extending it by an extra day was something she was more than happy to do.

As soon as they came to a stop in the car park, Ellie jumped out of the car and ran into the waiting arms of her father, Nick.

Rosalind smiled as she watched him easily lift Ellie off the ground and give her a little spin. She turned around and put a gentle hand on Ava's knee to wake her up.

Her eyes fluttered open.

"We're here," Rosalind said. "Get your things packed away and then hug your grandfather."

Ava grinned happily and quickly gathered her things. It had felt strange to label Ellie's parents as Ava's grandparents at first, but that faded within the first year of their relationship. Now Nick was casually referred to as Grandpa by Ava, and it was clear to all that he adored his new teenage granddaughter.

Rosalind got out of the car and was swept up in a hug by Nick.

"Ros! Good to see you!" he announced. "And congratulations!"

She'd been surprised by the warm welcome she had received that first visit five years ago. She'd felt sure that Ellie's parents would be concerned about this older woman corrupting their daughter. But both Nick and Helen had been very friendly on that first visit, and that had grown each time they met up. Now Rosalind felt at home and part of the family, something she hadn't realised she'd been missing in her life before.

"Thank you. Nice to be here," Rosalind said.

Helen rushed down the steps of the hotel towards Ellie. "Let me see, let me see!"

Ellie blushed and held up her hand for her mother to inspect the ring Rosalind had given her a couple of days ago. It had been the fifth anniversary of the Caldwell & Atkinson Christmas party that had brought them together. It seemed to Rosalind like a good anniversary to get down on one knee and ask Ellie to stay with her forever.

Nick elbowed her gently. "Took your time."

"I didn't want to rush things," Rosalind said, enjoying watching Ellie and Helen cooing over the ring.

"She moved in three months after you two started dating," Nick pointed out.

Rosalind had to admit, he had her there. Thankfully, she didn't need to come up with a reply as Ava got out of the car and jogged over to join them.

"Ava, how can you possibly have grown since I last saw you?" Nick asked. He pulled Ava into a hug, and Rosalind noted they were nearly the same height now.

"We put her on the rack every night," Rosalind said.

"They do—they are so mean," Ava agreed.

"Ros, that ring is stunning!" Helen said, opening her arms wide.

Rosalind stepped into the hug. "She told me I couldn't spend more than fifty pounds on it. Obviously I ignored her."

"When's the wedding?" Helen asked.

"We're still planning," Ellie said.

"Never mind when," Nick said. "*Where* is the wedding going to be held? Do you know anyone with a hotel? Some events space? A list of reliable suppliers?"

Helen smacked him in the chest. "Nick, don't! It's Ellie and Ros's big day. Let them choose where they want to get married."

Nick put one arm over Helen's shoulders and ushered Ava under his other arm. "I'm just saying, it all makes sense. Doesn't it, Ava?"

The three of them walked into the hotel, Ava agreeing that it would be the best choice. Rosalind strongly suspected that was because Ava had gotten used to summer weekends at the hotel to work on her tan by the pool. It was her home away from home.

Ellie looped her arm through hers and leaned her head on Rosalind's upper arm.

"Thank you for driving us," Ellie said.

"Thank you for the massage you'll be giving me later."

Ellie hated driving for long periods of time so handed the duty over to Rosalind with the promise of a full-body massage upon arrival. Rosalind loved long car journeys and therefore knew she was on to a win-win situation.

"Do you want to have the wedding here?" Rosalind asked.

"God, no." Ellie shuddered.

Rosalind laughed. "Whyever not?"

"Because my dad will be the bridezilla that you and I could never hope to be. He'll make enemies for miles. Florists and caterers will be left quaking in his wake in search of the very best for his daughter."

Rosalind nodded her agreement. "I hadn't considered that. Maybe we should go to Lapland and I'll find a Santa to marry us."

It had been an off the cuff joke, but Ellie's eyes lit up with excitement. "Really?"

Rosalind panicked and was wondering how to backtrack on the offer when Ellie burst out laughing.

"Oh, wow, you should have seen your face." Ellie struggled to breathe because she was laughing so hard. "That was sheer terror, right there. I can just see it now. I'll be on Santa's knee, and you'll be sliding a ring on my finger."

Rosalind sighed as Ellie continued to laugh so hard that she had started to cry.

"Little elves as bridesmaids," Ellie added. "No confetti, just snow."

"Are you finished?" Rosalind asked.

Ellie wiped her eyes and nodded. "I am."

Rosalind placed a soft kiss on her lips. "I'd do it, you know. If you really wanted that."

Ellie's expression sobered immediately. "I know. I appreciate that. But no more events in spaces they really ought not be in."

"Agreed. We can talk about it later. We have all the time in the world."

"We do," Ellie agreed. "I love you so much."

"I love you, too." Rosalind kissed her fiancée again. "Merry Christmas, darling."

About the Author

Amanda Radley had no desire to be a writer but accidentally turned into an award-winning, best-selling author. Residing in the UK with her wife and pets, she loves to travel. She gave up her marketing career in order to make stuff up for a living instead. She claims the similarities are startling.

Books Available From Bold Strokes Books

A Fairer Tomorrow by Kathleen Knowles. For Maddie Weeks and Gerry Stern, the Second World War brought them together, but the end of the war might rip them apart. (978-1-63555-874-6)

Changing Majors by Ana Hartnett Reichardt. Beyond a love, beyond a coming-out, Bailey Sullivan discovers what lies beyond the shame and self-doubt imposed on her by traditional Southern ideals. (978-1-63679-081-7)

Highland Whirl by Anna Larner. Opposites attract in the Scottish Highlands, when feisty Alice Campbell falls for city girl about town Roxanne Barns. (978-1-63555-892-0)

Holiday Hearts by Diana Day-Admire and Lyn Cole. Opposites attract during Christmastime chaos in Kansas City. (978-1-63679-128-9)

Humbug by Amanda Radley. With the corporate Christmas party in jeopardy, CEO Rosalind Caldwell hires Christmas Girl Ellie Pearce as her personal assistant. The only problem is, Ellie isn't a PA, has never planned a party, and develops a ridiculous crush on her totally intimidating new boss. (978-1-63555-965-1)

On the Rocks by Georgia Beers. Schoolteacher Vanessa Martini makes no apologies for her dating checklist, and newly single mom Grace Chapman ticks all Vanessa's Do Not Date boxes. Of course, they're never going to fall in love. (978-1-63555-989-7)

Song of Serenity by Brey Willows. Arguing with the Muse of music and justice is complicated, falling in love with her even more so. (978-1-63679-015-2)

Wisdom by Jesse J. Thoma. When Sophia and Reggie are chosen for the governor's new community design team and tasked with tackling substance abuse and mental health issues, battle lines are drawn even as sparks fly. (978-1-63555-886-9)

The Christmas Proposal by Lisa Moreau. Stranded together in a Christmas village on a snowy mountain, Grace and Bridget face their past and question their dreams for the future. (978-1-63555-648-3)

The Infinite Summer by Morgan Lee Miller. While spending the summer with her dad in a small beach town, Remi Brenner falls for Harper Hebert and accidentally finds herself tangled up in an intense restaurant rivalry between her famous stepmom and her first love. (978-1-63555-969-9)

A Convenient Arrangement by Aurora Rey and Jaime Clevenger. Cuffing season has come for lesbians, and for Jess Archer and Cody Dawson, their convenient arrangement becomes anything but. (978-1-63555-818-0)

An Alaskan Wedding by Nance Sparks. The last thing either Andrea or Riley expects is to bump into the one who broke her heart fifteen years ago, but when they meet at the welcome party, their feelings come rushing back. (978-1-63679-053-4)

Beulah Lodge by Cathy Dunnell. It's 1874, and newly betrothed Ruth Mallowes is set on marriage and life as a missionary…until she falls in love with the housemaid at Beulah Lodge. (978-1-63679-007-7)

Gia's Gems by Toni Logan. When Lindsey Speyer discovers that popular travel columnist Gia Williams is a complete fake and threatens to expose her, blackmail has never been so sexy. (978-1-63555-917-0)

Holiday Wishes & Mistletoe Kisses by M. Ullrich. Four holidays, four couples, four chances to make their wishes come true. (978-1-63555-760-2)

Love By Proxy by Dena Blake. Tess has a secret crush on her best friend, Sophie, so the last thing she wants is to help Sophie fall in love with someone else, but how can she stand in the way of her happiness? (978-1-63555-973-6)

Marry Me by Melissa Brayden. Allison Hale attempts to plan the wedding of the century to a man who could save her family's business, if only she wasn't falling for her wedding planner, Megan Kinkaid. (978-1-63555-932-3)

Pathway to Love by Radclyffe. Courtney Valentine is looking for a woman exactly like Ben—smart, sexy, and not in the market for anything serious. All she has to do is convince Ben that sex-without-strings is the perfect pathway to pleasure. (978-1-63679-110-4)

BOLDSTROKESBOOKS.COM

Looking for your next great read?

Visit BOLDSTROKESBOOKS.COM
to browse our entire catalog of paperbacks, ebooks,
and audiobooks.

Want the first word on what's new?
Visit our website for event info,
author interviews, and blogs.

Subscribe to our free newsletter for sneak peeks,
new releases, plus first notice of promos
and daily bargains.

SIGN UP AT
BOLDSTROKESBOOKS.COM/signup

Bold Strokes Books is an award-winning publisher committed to quality and diversity in LGBTQ fiction.